# SILENT NIGHTS

## CHRISTMAS MYSTERIES

Edited and Introduced by
Martin Edwards

First published in 2015 by
The British Library
96 Euston Road
London NW1 2DB

Introduction and notes copyright © 2015 Martin Edwards

Cataloguing in Publication Data
A catalogue record for this book is available from the British Library

ISBN 978 0 7123 5610 7

Typeset by IDSUK (DataConnection) Ltd
Printed and bound by
CPI Group (UK) Ltd, Croydon, CR0 4YY

# CONTENTS

# INTRODUCTION

Christmas may be when we dream of peace on earth, and entertain feelings of goodwill to all men (and women), but there are limits. It is a mysterious, as well as magical, time of year. Strange things can happen, and this helps to explain the hallowed tradition of telling ghost stories around the fireside as the year draws to a close. Christmas tales of crime and detection have a similar appeal. When television becomes tiresome, and party games pall, the prospect of curling up in the warm with a good mystery is enticing – and much better for the digestion than yet another helping of plum pudding.

Crime writers are just as susceptible as readers to the countless attractions of Christmas. Over the years, distinguished practitioners ranging from Agatha Christie to Mary Higgins Clark have given one or more of their stories a Yuletide setting. There is nothing new about this. Influenced by his friend Charles Dickens, Wilkie Collins wrote an early novella, *Mr Wray's Cash-Box* (also known as *The Stolen Mask*), which had a rather sentimental Christmas theme. Later, Arthur Conan Doyle set one of his first Sherlock Holmes short stories at Christmas; superior to Collins' effort, it remains a pleasure to read, and despite its familiarity, its inclusion here is deserved. By contrast, "The Raffles Relics", a story about "the amateur cracksman" A.J. Raffles written by Conan Doyle's brother-in-law, E.W. Hornung, lacks a particularly strong seasonal flavour, and is much less well known. This illustrates the point that the most memorable Christmas mysteries blend a lively storyline with an atmospheric evocation of the festive season. Getting the mixture right is much harder than it looks.

The British Library's series of Crime Classics concentrates on stories associated with "the Golden Age of murder", during which the formation of the Detection Club marked a valiant attempt to raise the standards of crime writing. Membership of the Club was by election, and confined to those authors whose work was regarded by their peers as exemplary. Edgar Wallace was among those not deemed eligible to join, because of his focus on writing thrillers rather than carefully plotted whodunnits. In terms of literary merit, his work was often slapdash, but neither Wallace nor his stories were ever lacking in energy or exuberance, and he is represented here by a tale written with his characteristic verve.

G.K. Chesterton was the first President of the Detection Club (the honour was offered to Conan Doyle, but he was too frail to accept), and owed this distinction mainly to his creation of Father Brown, a priest and gifted amateur detective. Father Brown has gained a new following in recent years thanks to his reincarnation on television in the person of Mark Williams; the screenplays bear little resemblance to the original stories, but the popularity of the show has helped to revive interest in Chesterton's crime fiction. "The Flying Stars", written when Chesterton was at the peak of his powers, is one of the best-loved stories featuring Father Brown.

Agatha Christie, a founder member of the Detection Club, adored Christmas, but her finest Yuletide whodunnit was a novel, rather than a short story. *Hercule Poirot's Christmas* is a classic country house murder mystery with a "least likely person" culprit revealed by the brilliant little Belgian. Christie's friend and Detection Club colleague Dorothy L. Sayers created in Lord Peter Wimsey another of fiction's "great detectives", and a Christmastime investigation featuring Wimsey, also set in a country house, appears here. Sayers admired the writing of J. Jefferson Farjeon, two of whose mystery novels have been reprinted recently by the British Library; an early example of his detective fiction is included in this volume.

H.C. Bailey, now almost forgotten, but in his day regarded as one of the finest practitioners of the form, was unusual among the group of detective writers who emerged after the First World War in that most of his best work was done in the short story form. Pungent and powerfully written, Reggie Fortune's recorded cases suffer from a dated literary style, but remain worth reading. Bailey too was a founder member of the Detection Club. Two more writers of quality represented here, Margery Allingham and Nicholas Blake (the pen-name of Cecil Day-Lewis), joined the Club's ranks during the Thirties. Allingham's Albert Campion was brought to the TV screens in 1989, with Peter Davison playing Campion. In contrast, Blake's regular detective, Nigel Strangeways, has never quite managed a television series of his own, although one Strangeways story, *The Beast Must Die*, was adapted for the legendary BBC series *Detective* in 1968. Edmund Crispin, elected to the Detection Club in 1947, created another likeable sleuth in the Oxford don Gervase Fen. The Fen story which appears here is taken from *Beware of the Trains*, a late – and highly enjoyable – example of a short story collection featuring a detective firmly in the Golden Age tradition.

Of the remaining contributors to this volume, Marjorie Bowen and Joseph Shearing were both pen-names used by the same woman. Like Bowen/Shearing, Leo Bruce (another alias) was a popular writer of considerable distinction. "Beef for Christmas" is, however, a rare story which has never, as far as I know, appeared in an anthology before. The same is, I believe, true of "Parlour Tricks". The author, Ralph Plummer, was a man of mystery in more ways than one, and it has proved impossible to find out anything about him. A little sleuthing has, however, unearthed biographical information about the little-known Raymund Allen, as well as background detail concerning the gifted but reclusive and publicity-hating Ethel Lina White.

This book, like other short story collections in the British Library's Crime Classics series, aims to introduce a new generation

# THE BLUE CARBUNCLE

## Arthur Conan Doyle

Arthur Conan Doyle (1859–1930) achieved literary immortality through his creation of Sherlock Holmes. The first two long stories about the great consulting detective, *A Study in Scarlet* and *The Sign of Four*, did not make a big splash, but once Conan Doyle began to contribute short stories featuring Sherlock's cases to the *Strand Magazine*, readers fell in love with the brilliant eccentric. Today, he remains as popular as ever.

"The Adventure of the Blue Carbuncle" was first published in January 1892, long before Conan Doyle's enthusiasm for writing about Holmes began to wane. The deductions that Holmes makes from the seedy and disreputable old felt hat are bravura flourishes, while in keeping with the spirit of Christmas, he is not presented in this story as merely a cold and ruthless reasoning machine. "I suppose I am commuting a felony," he says at the end, "but it is just possible that I am saving a soul."

\*  \*  \*  \*  \*

I had called upon my friend Sherlock Holmes upon the second morning after Christmas, with the intention of wishing him the compliments of the season. He was lounging upon the sofa in a purple dressing-gown, a pipe-rack within his reach upon the right, and a pile of crumpled morning papers, evidently newly studied, near at hand. Beside the couch was a wooden chair, and on the angle of the back hung a very seedy and disreputable hard felt hat, much the worse for wear, and cracked in several places. A lens and a forceps lying upon the seat of the chair suggested that the hat had been suspended in this manner for the purpose of examination.

"You are engaged," said I; "perhaps I interrupt you."

"Not at all. I am glad to have a friend with whom I can discuss my results. The matter is a perfectly trivial one" (he jerked his thumb in the direction of the old hat), "but there are points in connection with it which are not entirely devoid of interest, and even of instruction."

I seated myself in his armchair, and warmed my hands before his crackling fire, for a sharp frost had set in, and the windows were thick with the ice crystals. "I suppose," I remarked, "that, homely as it looks, this thing has some deadly story linked on to it—that it is the clue which will guide you in the solution of some mystery, and the punishment of some crime."

"No, no. No crime," said Sherlock Holmes, laughing. "Only one of those whimsical little incidents which will happen when you have four million human beings all jostling each other within the space of a few square miles. Amid the action and reaction of so dense a swarm of humanity, every possible combination of events may be expected to take place, and many a little problem will be presented which may be striking and bizarre without being criminal. We have already had experience of such."

"So much so," I remarked, "that, of the last six cases which I have added to my notes, three have been entirely free of any legal crime."

"Precisely. You allude to my attempt to recover the Irene Adler papers, to the singular case of Miss Mary Sutherland, and to the adventure of the man with the twisted lip. Well, I have no doubt that this small matter will fall into the same innocent category. You know Peterson, the commissionaire?"

"Yes."

"It is to him that this trophy belongs."

"It is his hat."

"No, no; he found it. Its owner is unknown. I beg that you will look upon it, not as a battered billycock, but as an intellectual problem. And, first as to how it came here. It arrived upon Christmas morning, in company with a good fat goose, which is, I have no doubt, roasting at this moment in front of Peterson's fire. The facts are these. About four o'clock on Christmas morning, Peterson, who, as you know, is a very honest fellow, was returning from some small jollification, and was making his way homewards down Tottenham Court Road. In front of him he saw, in the gaslight, a tallish man, walking with a slight stagger, and carrying a white goose slung over his shoulder. As he reached the corner of Goodge Street a row broke out between this stranger and a little knot of roughs. One of the latter knocked off the man's hat, on which he raised his stick to defend himself, and, swinging it over his head, smashed the shop window behind him. Peterson had rushed forward to protect the stranger from his assailants, but the man, shocked at having broken the window and seeing an official-looking person in uniform rushing towards him, dropped his goose, took to his heels, and vanished amid the labyrinth of small streets which lie at the back of Tottenham Court Road. The roughs had also fled at the appearance of Peterson, so that he was left in possession of the field of battle, and also of the spoils of victory in the shape of this battered hat and a most unimpeachable Christmas goose."

"Which surely he restored to their owner?"

"My dear fellow, there lies the problem. It is true that 'For Mrs Henry Baker' was printed upon a small card which was tied to the bird's left leg, and it is also true that the initials 'H.B.' are legible upon the lining of this hat; but, as there are some thousands of Bakers, and some hundreds of Henry Bakers in this city of ours, it is not easy to restore lost property to any one of them."

"What, then, did Peterson do?"

"He brought round both hat and goose to me on Christmas morning, knowing that even the smallest problems are of interest to me. The goose we retained until this morning, when there were signs that, in spite of the slight frost, it would be well that it should be eaten without unnecessary delay. Its finder has carried it off therefore to fulfil the ultimate destiny of a goose, while I continue to retain the hat of the unknown gentleman who lost his Christmas dinner."

"Did he not advertise?"

"No."

"Then, what clue could you have as to his identity?"

"Only as much as we can deduce."

"From his hat?"

"Precisely."

"But you are joking. What can you gather from this old battered felt?"

"Here is my lens. You know my methods. What can you gather yourself as to the individuality of the man who has worn this article?"

I took the tattered object in my hands, and turned it over rather ruefully. It was a very ordinary black hat of the usual round shape, hard and much the worse for wear. The lining had been of red silk, but was a good deal discoloured. There was no maker's name; but, as Holmes had remarked, the initials "H.B." were scrawled upon one side. It was pierced in the brim for a hat-securer, but the elastic was missing. For the rest, it was cracked, exceedingly dusty, and spotted in several places, although there seemed to have been some attempt to hide the discoloured patches by smearing them with ink.

"I can see nothing," said I, handing it back to my friend.

"On the contrary, Watson, you can see everything. You fail, however, to reason from what you see. You are too timid in drawing your inferences."

"Then, pray tell me what it is that you can infer from this hat?"

He picked it up, and gazed at it in the peculiar introspective fashion which was characteristic of him. "It is perhaps less suggestive than it might have been," he remarked, "and yet there are a few inferences which are very distinct, and a few others which represent at least a strong balance of probability. That the man was highly intellectual is of course obvious upon the face of it, and also that he was fairly well-to-do within the last three years, although he has now fallen upon evil days. He had foresight, but has less now than formerly, pointing to a moral retrogression, which, when taken with the decline of his fortunes, seems to indicate some evil influence, probably drink, at work upon him. This may account also for the obvious fact that his wife has ceased to love him."

"My dear Holmes!"

"He has, however, retained some degree of self-respect," he continued, disregarding my remonstrance. "He is a man who leads a sedentary life, goes out little, is out of training entirely, is middle-aged, has grizzled hair which he has had cut within the last few days, and which he anoints with lime-cream. These are the more patent facts which are to be deduced from his hat. Also, by the way, that it is extremely improbable that he has gas laid on in his house."

"You are certainly joking, Holmes."

"Not in the least. Is it possible that even now when I give you these results you are unable to see how they are attained?"

"I have no doubt that I am very stupid; but I must confess that I am unable to follow you. For example, how did you deduce that this man was intellectual?"

For answer Holmes clapped the hat upon his head. It came right over the forehead and settled upon the bridge of his nose. "It is a question of cubic capacity," said he: "a man with so large a brain must have something in it."

"The decline of his fortunes, then?"

"This hat is three years old. These flat brims curled at the edge came in then. It is a hat of the very best quality. Look at the band of ribbed silk, and the excellent lining. If this man could afford to buy so expensive a hat three years ago, and has had no hat since, then he has assuredly gone down in the world."

"Well, that is clear enough, certainly. But how about the foresight and the moral retrogression?"

Sherlock Holmes laughed. "Here is the foresight," said he, putting his finger upon the little disc and loop of the hat-securer. "They are never sold upon hats. If this man ordered one, it is a sign of a certain amount of foresight, since he went out of his way to take this precaution against the wind. But since we see that he has broken the elastic, and has not troubled to replace it, it is obvious that he has less foresight now than formerly, which is a distinct proof of a weakening nature. On the other hand, he has endeavoured to conceal some of these stains upon the felt by daubing them with ink, which is a sign that he has not entirely lost his self-respect."

"Your reasoning is certainly plausible."

"The further points, that he is middle-aged, that his hair is grizzled, that it has been recently cut, and that he uses lime-cream, are all to be gathered from a close examination of the lower part of the lining. The lens discloses a large number of hair ends, clean cut by the scissors of the barber. They all appear to be adhesive, and there is a distinct odour of lime-cream. This dust, you will observe, is not the gritty, grey dust of the street, but the fluffy brown dust of the house, showing that it has been hung up indoors most of the time; while the marks of moisture upon the inside are proof positive that the wearer perspired very freely, and could, therefore, hardly be in the best of training."

"But his wife—you said that she had ceased to love him."

"This hat has not been brushed for weeks. When I see you, my dear Watson, with a week's accumulation of dust upon your hat, and when your wife allows you to go out in such a state, I shall fear that you also have been unfortunate enough to lose your wife's affection."

"But he might be a bachelor."

"Nay, he was bringing home the goose as a peace-offering to his wife. Remember the card upon the bird's leg."

"You have an answer to everything. But how on earth do you deduce that the gas is not laid on in the house?"

"One tallow stain, or even two, might come by chance; but, when I see no less than five, I think that there can be little doubt that the individual must be brought into frequent contact with burning tallow—walks upstairs at night probably with his hat in one hand and a guttering candle in the other. Anyhow, he never got tallow stains from a gas jet. Are you satisfied?"

"Well, it is very ingenious," said I, laughing; "but since, as you said just now, there has been no crime committed, and no harm done save the loss of a goose, all this seems to be rather a waste of energy."

Sherlock Holmes had opened his mouth to reply, when the door flew open, and Peterson the commissionaire rushed into the compartment with flushed cheeks and the face of a man who is dazed with astonishment.

"The goose, Mr Holmes! The goose, sir!" he gasped.

"Eh! What of it, then? Has it returned to life, and flapped off through the kitchen window?" Holmes twisted himself round upon the sofa to get a fairer view of the man's excited face.

"See here, sir! See what my wife found in its crop!" He held out his hand, and displayed upon the centre of the palm a brilliantly scintillating blue stone, rather smaller than a bean in size, but of such purity and radiance that it twinkled like an electric point in the dark hollow of his hand.

Sherlock Holmes sat up with a whistle. "By Jove, Peterson," said he, "this is a treasure-trove indeed! I suppose you know what you have got?"

"A diamond, sir! A precious stone! It cuts into glass as though it were putty."

"It's more than a precious stone. It's *the* precious stone."

"Not the Countess of Morcar's blue carbuncle?" I ejaculated.

"Precisely so. I ought to know its size and shape, seeing that I have read the advertisement about it in *The Times* every day lately. It is absolutely unique, and its value can only be conjectured, but the reward offered of a thousand pounds is certainly not within a twentieth part of the market price."

"A thousand pounds! Great Lord of mercy!" The commissionaire plumped down into a chair, and stared from one to the other of us.

"That is the reward, and I have reason to know that there are sentimental considerations in the background which would induce the Countess to part with half of her fortune if she could but recover the gem."

"It was lost, if I remember aright, at the Hotel Cosmopolitan," I remarked.

"Precisely so, on the twenty-second of December, just five days ago. John Horner, a plumber, was accused of having abstracted it from the lady's jewel-case. The evidence against him was so strong that the case has been referred to the Assizes. I have some account of the matter here, I believe." He rummaged amid his newspapers, glancing over the dates, until at last he smoothed one out, doubled it over, and read the following paragraph:

"Hotel Cosmopolitan Jewel Robbery. John Horner, 26, plumber, was brought up upon the charge of having upon the 22nd inst., abstracted from the jewel-case of the Countess of Morcar the valuable gem known as the blue carbuncle. James Ryder, upper-attendant at the hotel, gave his evidence to the effect that he had shown Horner up to the dressing-room of the Countess of Morcar upon the day of the robbery in order that he might solder the second bar of the grate, which was loose. He had remained with Horner some little time but had finally been called away. On returning he found that Horner had disappeared, that the bureau had been forced open, and that the small morocco casket in which, as it afterwards transpired, the Countess was accustomed to keep her jewel, was lying empty upon the dressing-table. Ryder instantly gave the alarm, and Horner was arrested the same evening; but the stone could not be found either upon his person or in his rooms. Catherine Cusack, maid to the Countess, deposed to having heard Ryder's cry of dismay on discovering the robbery, and to having rushed into the room, where she found matters were as described by the last witness. Inspector Bradstreet, B Division, gave evidence as to the arrest of Horner, who struggled frantically, and protested his innocence in the strongest terms. Evidence of a previous conviction for robbery having been given against the prisoner, the magistrate refused to deal summarily with the offence, but referred it to the Assizes. Horner, who had shown signs of intense emotion during the proceedings, fainted away at the conclusion, and was carried out of court."

"Hum! So much for the police-court," said Holmes thoughtfully, tossing aside his paper. "The question for us now to solve is the sequence of events leading from a rifled jewel-case at one end to the crop of a goose in Tottenham Court Road at the other. You see, Watson, our little deductions have suddenly assumed a much more important and less innocent aspect. Here is the stone; the stone came from the goose, and the goose came from Mr Henry Baker, the gentleman with the bad hat and all the other characteristics with which I have bored you. So now we must set ourselves very seriously to finding this gentleman, and ascertaining what part he has played in this little mystery. To do this, we must try the simplest means first, and these lie undoubtedly in an advertisement in all the evening papers. If this fail, I shall have recourse to other methods."

"What will you say?"

"Give me a pencil, and that slip of paper. Now, then: 'Found at the corner of Goodge Street, a goose and a black felt hat. Mr Henry Baker can have the same by applying at 6.30 this evening at 221B Baker Street.' That is clear and concise."

"Very. But will he see it?"

"Well, he is sure to keep an eye on the papers, since, to a poor man, the loss was a heavy one. He was clearly so scared by his mischance in breaking the window, and by the approach of Peterson, that he thought of nothing but flight; but since then he must have bitterly regretted the impulse which caused him to drop his bird. Then, again, the introduction of his name will cause him to see it, for every one who knows him will direct his attention to it. Here you are, Peterson, run down to the advertising agency, and have this put in the evening papers."

"In which, sir?"

"Oh, in the *Globe*, *Star*, *Pall Mall*, *St James's Gazette*, *Evening News*, *Standard*, *Echo*, and any others that occur to you."

"Very well, sir. And this stone?"

"Ah, yes, I shall keep the stone. Thank you, And, I say, Peterson, just buy a goose on your way back, and leave it here with me, for we must have one to give to this gentleman in place of the one which your family is now devouring."

When the commissionaire had gone, Holmes took up the stone and held it against the light. "It's a bonny thing," said he. "Just see how it glints and sparkles. Of course it is a nucleus and focus of crime. Every good stone is. They are the devil's pet baits. In the larger and older jewels every facet may stand for a bloody deed.

This stone is not yet twenty years old. It was found in the banks of the Amoy River in Southern China, and is remarkable in having every characteristic of the carbuncle, save that it is blue in shade, instead of ruby red. In spite of its youth, it has already a sinister history. There have been two murders, a vitriol-throwing, a suicide, and several robberies brought about for the sake of this forty-grain weight of crystallized charcoal. Who would think that so pretty a toy would be a purveyor to the gallows and the prison? I'll lock it up in my strong-box now, and drop a line to the Countess to say that we have it."

"Do you think this man Horner is innocent?"

"I cannot tell."

"Well, then, do you imagine that this other one, Henry Baker, had anything to do with the matter?"

"It is, I think, much more likely that Henry Baker is an absolutely innocent man, who had no idea that the bird which he was carrying was of considerably more value than if it were made of solid gold. That, however, I shall determine by a very simple test, if we have an answer to our advertisement."

"And you can do nothing until then?"

"Nothing."

"In that case I shall continue my professional round. But I shall come back in the evening at the hour you have mentioned, for I should like to see the solution of so tangled a business."

"Very glad to see you. I dine at seven. There is a woodcock, I believe. By the way, in view of recent occurrences, perhaps I ought to ask Mrs Hudson to examine its crop."

I had been delayed at a case, and it was a little after half-past six when I found myself in Baker Street once more. As I approached the house I saw a tall man in a Scotch bonnet, with a coat which was buttoned up to his chin, waiting outside in the bright semi-circle which was thrown from the fanlight. Just as I arrived, the door was opened, and we were shown up together to Holmes' room.

"Mr Henry Baker, I believe," said he, rising from his armchair, and greeting his visitor with the easy air of geniality which he could so readily assume. "Pray take this chair by the fire, Mr Baker. It is a cold night, and I observe that your circulation is more adapted for summer than for winter. Ah, Watson, you have just come at the right time. Is that your hat, Mr Baker?"

"Yes, sir, that is undoubtedly my hat."

He was a large man, with rounded shoulders, a massive head, and a broad, intelligent face, sloping down to a pointed beard of grizzled brown. A touch of red in nose and cheeks, with a slight tremor of his extended hand, recalled Holmes' surmise as to his habits. His rusty black frock-coat was buttoned right up in front, with the collar turned up, and his lank wrists protruded from his sleeves without a sign of cuff or shirt. He spoke in a low staccato fashion, choosing his words with care, and gave the impression generally of a man of learning and letters who had had ill-usage at the hands of fortune.

"We have retained these things for some days," said Holmes, "because we expected to see an advertisement from you giving your address. I am at a loss to know now why you did not advertise."

Our visitor gave a rather shamefaced laugh. "Shillings have not been so plentiful with me as they once were," he remarked. "I had no doubt that the gang of roughs who assaulted me had carried off both my hat and the bird. I did not care to spend more money in a hopeless attempt at recovering them."

"Very naturally. By the way, about the bird—we were compelled to eat it."

"To eat it!" Our visitor half rose from his chair in his excitement.

"Yes; it would have been no use to anyone had we not done so. But I presume that this other goose upon the sideboard, which is about the same weight and perfectly fresh, will answer your purpose equally well?"

"Oh, certainly, certainly!" answered Mr Baker, with a sigh of relief.

"Of course, we still have the feathers, legs, crop, and so on of your own bird, if you so wish——"

The man burst into a hearty laugh. "They might be useful to me as relics of my adventure," said he, "but beyond that I can hardly see what use the *disjecta membra* of my late acquaintance are going to be to me. No, sir, I think that, with your permission, I will confine my attentions to the excellent bird which I perceive upon the sideboard."

Sherlock Holmes glanced sharply across at me with a slight shrug of his shoulders.

"There is your hat, then, and there your bird," said he. "By the way, would it bore you to tell me where you got the other one from? I am somewhat of a fowl fancier, and I have seldom seen a better-grown goose."

"Certainly, sir," said Baker, who had risen and tucked his newly gained property under his arm. "There are a few of us who frequent the Alpha Inn near the Museum—we are to be found in the Museum itself during the day, you understand. This year our good host, Windigate by name, instituted a goose-club, by which, on consideration of some few pence every week, we were to receive a bird at Christmas. My pence were duly paid, and the rest is familiar to you. I am much indebted to you, sir, for a Scotch bonnet is fitted neither to my years nor my gravity." With a comical pomposity of manner he bowed solemnly to both of us, and strode off upon his way.

"So much for Mr Henry Baker," said Holmes, when he had closed the door behind him. "It is quite certain that he knows nothing whatever about the matter. Are you hungry, Watson?"

"Not particularly."

"Then I suggest that we turn our dinner into a supper, and follow up this clue while it is still hot."

"By all means."

It was a bitter night, so we drew on our ulsters and wrapped cravats about our throats. Outside, the stars were shining coldly in a cloudless sky, and the breath of the passers-by blew out into smoke like so many pistol shots. Our footfalls rang out crisply and loudly as we swung through the doctors' quarter, Wimpole Street, Harley Street, and so through Wigmore Street into Oxford Street. In a quarter of an hour we were in Bloomsbury at the Alpha Inn, which is a small public-house at the corner of one of the streets which runs down into Holborn. Holmes pushed open the door of the private bar, and ordered two glasses of beer from the ruddy-faced, white-aproned landlord.

"Your beer should be excellent if it is as good as your geese," he said.

"My geese!" The man seemed surprised.

"Yes. I was speaking only half an hour ago to Mr Henry Baker, who was a member of your goose-club."

"Ah! yes, I see. But you see, sir, them's not *our* geese."

"Indeed! Whose, then?"

"Well, I get the two dozen from a salesman in Covent Garden."

"Indeed! I know some of them. Which was it?"

"Breckinridge is his name."

"Ah! I don't know him. Well, here's your good health, landlord, and prosperity to your house. Good night."

"Now for Mr Breckinridge," he continued, buttoning up his coat, as we came out into the frosty air. "Remember, Watson, that though we have so homely a thing as a goose at one end of this chain, we have at the other a man who will certainly get seven years' penal servitude, unless we can establish his innocence. It is possible that our inquiry may but confirm his guilt; but, in any case, we have a line of investigation which has been missed by the police, and which a singular chance has placed in our hands. Let us follow it out to the bitter end. Faces to the south, then, and quick march!"

We passed across Holborn, down Endell Street, and so through a zigzag of slums to Covent Garden Market. One of the largest stalls bore the name of Breckinridge upon it, and the proprietor, a horsy-looking man, with a sharp face and trim side-whiskers, was helping a boy to put up the shutters.

"Good evening. It's a cold night," said Holmes.

The salesman nodded, and shot a questioning glance at my companion.

"Sold out of geese, I see," continued Holmes, pointing at the bare slabs of marble.

"Let you have five hundred tomorrow morning."

"That's no good."

"Well, there are some on the stall with the gas flare."

"Ah, but I was recommended to you."

"Who by?"

"The landlord of the 'Alpha.'"

"Ah, yes; I sent him a couple of dozen."

"Fine birds they were, too. Now where did you get them from?"

To my surprise the question provoked a burst of anger from the salesman.

"Now then, mister," said he, with his head cocked and his arms akimbo, "what are you driving at? Let's have it straight, now."

"It is straight enough. I should like to know who sold you the geese which you supplied to the 'Alpha.'"

'Well, then, I shan't tell you. So now!'

"Oh, it's a matter of no importance; but I don't know why you should be so warm over such a trifle."

"Warm! You'd be as warm, maybe, if you were as pestered as I am. When I pay good money for a good article there should be an end of the business; but it's 'Where are the geese?' and 'Who did you sell the geese to?' and 'What will you take for the geese?' One would think they were the only geese in the world, to hear the fuss that is made over them."

"Well, I have no connexion with any other people who have been making inquiries," said Holmes carelessly. "If you won't tell us the bet is off, that is all. But I'm always ready to back my opinion on a matter of fowls, and I have a fiver on it that the bird I ate is country bred."

"Well, then, you've lost your fiver, for it's town bred," snapped the salesman.

"It's nothing of the kind."

"I say it is."

"I don't believe you."

"D'you think you know more about fowls than I, who have handled them ever since I was a nipper? I tell you, all those birds that went to the 'Alpha' were town bred."

"You'll never persuade me to believe that."

"Will you bet, then?"

"It's merely taking your money, for I know that I am right. But I'll have a sovereign on with you, just to teach you not to be obstinate."

The salesman chuckled grimly. 'Bring me the books, Bill,' said he.

The small boy brought round a small thin volume and a great greasy-backed one, laying them out together beneath the hanging lamp.

"Now then, Mr Cocksure," said the salesman, "I thought that I was out of geese, but before I finish you'll find that there is still one left in my shop. You see this little book?"

"Well?"

"That's the list of the folk from whom I buy. D'you see? Well, then, here on this page are the country folk, and the numbers after their names are where their accounts are in the big ledger. Now, then! You see this other page in red ink? Well, that is a list of my town suppliers. Now, look at that third name. Just read it out to me."

"Mrs Oakshott, 117 Brixton Road—249," read Holmes.

"Quite so. Now turn that up in the ledger."

Holmes turned to the page indicated. "Here you are, 'Mrs Oakshott, 117 Brixton Road, egg and poultry supplier'."

"Now, then, what's the last entry?"

"'December 22. Twenty-four geese at 7s 6d'."

"Quite so. There you are. And underneath?"

"'Sold to Mr Windigate of the 'Alpha' at 12s'."

"What have you to say now?"

Sherlock Holmes looked deeply chagrined. He drew a sovereign from his pocket and threw it down upon the slab, turning away with the air of a man whose disgust is too deep for words. A few yards off he stopped under a lamp-post, and laughed in the hearty, noiseless fashion which was peculiar to him.

"When you see a man with whiskers of that cut and the 'Pink 'Un' protruding out of his pocket, you can always draw him by a bet," said he. "I dare say that if I had put a hundred pounds down in front of him that man would not have given me such complete information as was drawn from him by the idea that he was doing me on a wager. Well, Watson, we are, I fancy, nearing the end of our quest, and the only point which remains to be determined is whether we should go on to this Mrs Oakshott tonight, or whether we should reserve it for tomorrow. It is clear from what that surly fellow said that there are others besides ourselves who are anxious about the matter, and I should——"

His remarks were suddenly cut short by a loud hubbub which broke out from the stall which we had just left. Turning round we saw a little rat-faced fellow standing in the centre of the circle of yellow light which was thrown by the swinging lamp, while Breckinridge the salesman, framed in the door of his stall, was shaking his fists fiercely at the cringing figure.

"I've had enough of you and your geese," he shouted. "I wish you were all at the devil together. If you come pestering me any more with your silly talk I'll set the dog at you. You bring Mrs Oakshott here and I'll answer her, but what have you to do with it? Did I buy the geese off you?"

"No; but one of them was mine all the same," whined the little man.

"Well, then, ask Mrs Oakshott for it."

"She told me to ask you."

"Well, you can ask the King of Proosia, for all I care. I've had enough of it. Get out of this!" He rushed fiercely forward, and the inquirer flitted away into the darkness.

"Ha, this may save us a vist to Brixton Road," whispered Holmes. "Come with me, and we will see what is to be made of this fellow." Striding through the scattered knots of people who lounged round the flaring stalls, my companion speedily overtook the little man and touched him upon the shoulder. He sprang round, and I could see in the gaslight that every vestige of colour had been driven from his face.

"Who are you, then? What do you want?" he asked in a quavering voice.

"You will excuse me," said Holmes blandly, "but I could not help overhearing the questions which you put to the salesman just now. I think that I could be of assistance to you."

"You? Who are you? How could you know anything of the matter?"

"My name is Sherlock Holmes. It is my business to know what other people don't know."

"But you can know nothing of this?"

"Excuse me, I know everything of it. You are endeavouring to trace some geese which were sold by Mrs Oakshott, of Brixton Road, to a salesman named Breckinridge, by him in turn to Mr Windigate, of the 'Alpha', and by him to his club, of which Mr Henry Baker is a member."

"Oh, sir, you are the very man whom I have longed to meet," cried the little fellow, with outstretched hands and quivering fingers. "I can hardly explain to you how interested I am in this matter."

Sherlock Holmes hailed a four-wheeler which was passing. "In that case we had better discuss it in a cosy room rather than in this wind-swept market-place," said he. "But pray tell me, before we go further, who it is that I have the pleasure of assisting."

The man hesitated for an instant. "My name is John Robinson," he answered, with a sidelong glance.

"No, no; the real name," said Holmes sweetly. "It is always awkward doing business with an *alias*."

A flush sprang to the white cheeks of the stranger. "Well, then," said he, "my real name is James Ryder."

"Precisely so. Head attendant at the Hotel Cosmopolitan. Pray step into the cab, and I shall soon be able to tell you everything which you would wish to know."

The little man stood glancing from one to the other of us with half-frightened, half-hopeful eyes, as one who is not sure whether he is on the verge of a windfall or of a catastrophe. Then he stepped into the cab, and in half an hour we were back in the sitting-room at Baker Street. Nothing had been said during our drive, but the high, thin breathings of our new companion, and the claspings and unclaspings of his hands, spoke of the nervous tension within him.

"Here we are!" said Holmes cheerily, as we filed into the room. "The fire looks very seasonable in this weather. You look cold, Mr Ryder. Pray take the basket chair. I will just put on my slippers before we settle this little matter of yours. Now, then! You want to know what became of those geese?"

"Yes, sir."

"Or rather, I fancy, of that goose. It was one bird, I imagine, in which you were interested—white, with a black bar across the tail."

Ryder quivered with emotion. "Oh, sir," he cried, "can you tell me where it went to?"

"It came here."

"Here?"

"Yes, and a most remarkable bird it proved. I don't wonder that you should take an interest in it. It laid an egg after it was dead—the bonniest, brightest little blue egg that ever was seen. I have it here in my museum."

Our visitor staggered to his feet, and clutched the mantelpiece with his right hand. Holmes unlocked his strong-box, and held up the blue carbuncle, which shone out like a star, with a cold, brilliant, many-pointed radiance. Ryder stood glaring with a drawn face, uncertain whether to claim or to disown it.

"The game's up, Ryder," said Holmes quietly. "Hold up, man, or you'll be into the fire. Give him an arm back into his chair, Watson.

He's not got blood enough to go in for felony with impunity. Give him a dash of brandy. So! Now he looks a little more human. What a shrimp it is, to be sure!"

For a moment he had staggered and nearly fallen, but the brandy brought a tinge of colour into his cheeks, and he sat staring with frightened eyes at his accuser.

"I have almost every link in my hands, and all the proofs which I could possibly need, so there is little which you need tell me. Still, that little may as well be cleared up to make the case complete. You had heard, Ryder, of this blue stone of the Countess of Morcar's?"

"It was Catherine Cusack who told me of it," said he, in a crackling voice.

"I see. Her ladyship's waiting-maid. Well, the temptation of sudden wealth so easily acquired was too much for you, as it has been for better men before you; but you were not very scrupulous in the means you used. It seems to me, Ryder, that there is the making of a very pretty villain in you. You knew that this man Horner, the plumber, had been concerned in some such matter before, and that suspicion would rest the more readily upon him. What did you do, then? You made some small job in my lady's room—you and your confederate Cusack—and you managed that he should be the man sent for. Then, when he had left, you rifled the jewel-case, raised the alarm, and had this unfortunate man arrested. You then——"

Ryder threw himself down suddenly upon the rug, and clutched at my companion's knees. "For God's sake, have mercy!" he shrieked. "Think of my father! Of my mother! It would break their hearts. I never went wrong before! I never will again. I swear it. I'll swear it on a Bible. Oh, don't bring it into court! For Christ's sake, don't!"

"Get back into your chair!" said Holmes sternly. "It is very well to cringe and crawl now, but you thought little enough of this poor Horner in the dock for a crime of which he knew nothing."

"I will fly, Mr Holmes. I will leave the country, sir. Then the charge against him will break down."

"Hum! We will talk about that. And now let us hear a true account of the next act. How came the stone into the goose, and how came the goose into the open market? Tell us the truth, for there lies your only hope of safety."

Ryder passed his tongue over his parched lips. "I will tell you it just as it happened, sir," said he. "When Horner had been arrested, it seemed to me that it would be best for me to get away with the stone at once, for I did not know at what moment the police might not take it into their heads to search me and my room. There was no place about the hotel where it would be safe. I went out, as if on some commission, and I made for my sister's house. She had married a man named Oakshott, and lived in Brixton Road, where she fattened fowls for the market. All the way there every man I met seemed to me to be a policeman or a detective, and for all that it was a cold night, the sweat was pouring down my face before I came to the Brixton Road. My sister asked me what was the matter, and why I was so pale; but I told her that I had been upset by the jewel robbery at the hotel. Then I went into the back-yard, and smoked a pipe, and wondered what it would be best to do.

"I had a friend once called Maudsley, who went to the bad, and has just been serving his time in Pentonville. One day he had met me, and fell into talk about the ways of thieves and how they could get rid of what they stole. I knew that he would be true to me, for I knew one or two things about him, so I made up my mind to go right on to Kilburn, where he lived, and take him into my confidence. He would show me how to turn the stone into money. But how to get to him in safety? I thought of the agonies I had gone through in coming from the hotel. I might at any moment be seized and searched, and there would be the stone in my waistcoat pocket.

I was leaning against the wall at the time, and looking at the geese which were waddling about round my feet, and suddenly an idea came into my head which showed me how I could beat the best detective that ever lived.

"My sister had told me some weeks before that I might have the pick of her geese for a Christmas present, and I knew that she was always as good as her word. I would take my goose now, and in it I would carry my stone to Kilburn. There was a little shed in the yard, and behind this I drove one of the birds, a fine big one, white, with a barred tail. I caught it and, prising its bill open, I thrust the stone down its throat as far as my finger could reach. The bird gave a gulp, and I felt the stone pass along its gullet and down into its crop. But the creature flapped and struggled, and out came my sister to know what was the matter. As I turned to speak to her the brute broke loose, and fluttered off among the others.

"'Whatever were you doing with that bird, Jem?' says she.

"'Well,' said I, 'you said you'd give me one for Christmas, and I was feeling which was the fattest.'

"'Oh,' says she, 'we've set yours aside for you. Jem's bird, we call it. It's the big, white one over yonder. There's twenty-six of them, which makes one for you, and one for us, and two dozen for the market.'

"'Thank you, Maggie,' says I; 'but if it is all the same to you I'd rather have that one I was handling just now.'

"'The other is a good three pound heavier,' she said, 'and we fattened it expressly for you.'

"'Never mind. I'll have the other, and I'll take it now,' said I.

"'Oh, just as you like,' said she, a little huffed. 'Which is it you want, then?'

"'That white one, with the barred tail, right in the middle of the flock.'

" 'Oh, very well. Kill it and take it with you.'

"Well, I did what she said, Mr Holmes, and I carried the bird all the way to Kilburn. I told my pal what I had done, for he was a man that it was easy to tell a thing like that to. He laughed until he choked, and we got a knife and opened the goose. My heart turned to water, for there was no sign of the stone, and I knew that some terrible mistake had occurred. I left the bird, rushed back to my sister's, and hurried into the back-yard. There was not a bird to be seen there.

" 'Where are they all, Maggie?' I cried.

" 'Gone to the dealer's.'

" 'Which dealer's?'

" 'Breckinridge, of Covent Garden.'

" 'But was there another with a barred tail?' I asked, 'the same as the one I chose?'

" 'Yes, Jem, there were two barred-tailed ones, and I could never tell them apart.'

"Well, then, of course, I saw it all, and I ran off as hard as my feet would carry me to this man Breckinridge; but he had sold the lot at once, and not one word would he tell me as to where they had gone. You heard him yourselves tonight. Well, he has always answered me like that. My sister thinks that I am going mad. Sometimes I think that I am myself. And now—and now I am myself a branded thief, without ever having touched the wealth for which I sold my character. God help me! God help me!" He burst into convulsive sobbing, with his face buried in his hands.

There was a long silence, broken only by his heavy breathing, and by the measured tapping of Sherlock Holmes' finger-tips upon the edge of the table. Then my friend rose, and threw open the door.

"Get out!" said he.

"What, sir! Oh, Heaven bless you!"

"No more words. Get out!"

And no more words were needed. There was a rush, a clatter upon the stairs, the bang of a door, and the crisp rattle of running footfalls from the street.

"After all, Watson," said Holmes, reaching up his hand for his clay pipe, "I am not retained by the police to supply their deficiencies. If Horner were in danger it would be another thing, but this fellow will not appear against him, and the case must collapse. I suppose that I am commuting a felony, but it is just possible that I am saving a soul. This fellow will not go wrong again. He is too terribly frightened. Send him to gaol now, and you make him a gaolbird for life. Besides, it is the season of forgiveness. Chance has put in our way a most singular and whimsical problem, and its solution is its own reward. If you will have the goodness to touch the bell, Doctor, we will begin another investigation, in which also a bird will be the chief feature."

# PARLOUR TRICKS

## Ralph Plummer

Ralph Plummer is a long-forgotten writer, and "Parlour Tricks" an exceptionally obscure short story. It appeared in print (for, to the best of my knowledge, the first and only time) in the *Passing Show Christmas Holiday Annual* of 1930. I know nothing of Plummer's life, but am indebted to the late Bob Adey, an expert in "locked room" and impossible crime mysteries, and owner of one of the most impressive collections of detective fiction in the world, for referring me to this story, and kindly supplying me with a copy. I share Bob's view that it deserves to be rescued from oblivion, and I only wish that I had been able to find out more about its author.

\*  \*  \*  \*  \*

Peter Mullinger sipped at his drink, chuckled in a rumbling bass at his joke, and smiled encouragingly across the cheery smoke-room of the Grand Private Hotel at young Glover.

Eric Glover had just concluded several simple conjuring tricks for the entertainment of a bevy of old ladies, a stern-looking man with side-whiskers, and a retired colonel who divided his time between staring fiercely into space, twisting his moustache, and emptying glasses of port.

"Christmas in a small hotel can be a dull affair," commented Mr Mullinger, lighting a cigar and looking about the old-fashioned room with a genial eye. "Unless you get the spirit of the thing, that is. I have spent Christmases in similar places to this. Just the same old-fashioned hotels with wide fireplaces, shining brasses and polished oak. For dull days, folks, commend me to an old-world environment with dull people in it. Christmas of itself, despite all this talk of rosy-faced children and merry hours, is a solemn time.

"It is a good job we have a go-ahead youngster among us like Mr Glover. Never knew such a young man for getting things going."

There was a chorus of assent, and the old ladies beamed archly at the young gentleman himself.

"Such jokes I never heard before," asserted a dowager with green eyes and multiple chins, "and he tells them so well. I wonder why we are none of us to leave the hotel until given permission?"

"Bit of a mystery," commented young Glover. "Oh, well, who cares? It's Christmas, and snowing like billy-ho outside."

"Let it snow," growled the old colonel, reaching for another port and staring at the logs in the grate.

"I was going to," agreed Glover. "Did any of you hear about the station-master's dog who always chased up the track in pursuit of every express that dashed through the station?"

"Do tell us," urged a stout lady of forty, trying to look up at him through distressingly short eyelashes.

Glover plunged into his five-hundredth humorous story since his arrival at the little hotel two days previously. As he progressed, old Mr Mullinger chuckled again.

"Inexhaustible," he murmured, nodding at Mr Warboys, a permanent resident of the Grand. "Tricks, stories, games—he seems to know them all."

"Wonderful young man," said Mr Warboys, setting his bottom teeth against his top in order that speech may be facilitated.

"A great asset here at a time like Christmas. Been the life and soul of the place. What are they keeping us indoors for? The manager requested that no one leaves the hotel until given permission."

"Some Christmas surprise," put in a thin lady, ceasing to eat nuts and raisins for the first time since dinner, and nodding brightly as she patted her hair. "I've heard of such things before. Sometimes they have someone to call dressed as Santa Claus, and every guest gets a gift."

"When?" said a small, sandy man with a tartan tie, emerging from his nap.

"Quite an idea," agreed Mr Mullinger.

"Confined to barracks, by Gad," snapped the colonel fiercely, and reached for the decanter.

There came a discreet hurricane of fluttering applause from the table across the room. Young Glover had just completed another conjuring trick.

"What's the noise about?" demanded the old colonel, preening his moustache, and vaguely trying to light a match with a cigarette.

"Astoundin'," remarked a stout commercial traveller. "Dipped a piece of white paper right into a glass of ink? an' when he pulled the paper out again? it was all black but the ink in the glass had changed to pure water. Makes Maskylion look silly he does; makes Maskylion look silly. Dipped a piece of white paper——"

"Quite simple," said young Glover modestly. "You see it was only a glass of clean water with some black silk inside the glass, sticking lightly against the side. When I stuck the paper in the water I drew it out with the black silk on it."

There was enthusiastic applause.

"Talking about conjuring," said Mr Mullinger lightly, "I once heard a chap say that it was possible for him to leave a glass full of water on a table in the room, that he would go out, and when he walked into the room again within a few minutes, the glass would be empty."

"Confederate in the room," said the stout dowager excitedly.

"No, he said not," said Mr Mullinger. "No one else in the room was to touch the glass at all. All bunk, of course. Quite impossible. I would bet a sovereign it couldn't be done. Don't know whether the chap was trying to impress us with psychic stuff or whatever you call it, but——"

"I could do it!"

Mr Mullinger stared at Eric Glover's eager face with surprise.

"You would leave a glass full of water inside this room, go out, and when you walked in again the glass would be empty. Impossible!"

"You spoke about a pound bet," said Mr Glover playfully. "I'll call you!"

Mr Mullinger stared in silence. Chairs scraped near in an interested circle.

"There is a glass here," said the ancient Mr Warboys, snapping his upper set more tightly into position.

"I shall want that," snapped the old colonel, irritably removing the other's fingers from the stem. What about that glass young Glover has been using? Use that, dammit!"

"I'd like to see that glass," muttered Mr Mullinger. He got up, examined the glass carefully and flicked it ringingly with his fingernail.

"No false bottom there," grinned Glover.

"Let's know where we stand," grunted the older man. "Do you know what you have undertaken to do?"

Glover nodded.

"I will go out of this room, leaving that glass full of water. No one else is to touch it; it shall stand on the table in full view of everybody. When I walk in again—which I shall do within five minutes of walking out—the glass will still be on the table BUT EMPTY."

"Impossible," declared Mr Mullinger.

Glover smiled quietly. He filled the glass from a decanter of water and set it on the table, where it stood palely agleam against the dark polish of the oak.

"I know a good way of keeping milk from going sour," put in the commercial traveller suddenly.

"What way?" demanded a sour-looking woman, looking up from a woollen pullover she was committing for a nephew.

"Leave it in the cow," said the commercial traveller, laughing uproariously and turning it into a cough as no one took any notice.

When Glover reached the door, leaving everybody seated and waiting expectantly, he turned and spoke:

"When I walk in again, that glass will be empty."

The door closed behind him.

"Watch that glass," counselled Mr Warboys, staring at the table with tense eyes. "Watch it!"

They watched it. There fell a dead silence.

The door opened within the minute. Grinning wickedly, Mr Glover made his appearance and progressed to the table on his hands and knees.

He coolly lifted the glass, drank its contents with a solemn "Good health, everybody," and set the glass back as he had found it.

Amid some laughs and partial surprise, he crawled out of the room again. Brows puckered in thought until the commercial traveller burst in with enlightenment.

"That's what it is," he boomed. "He didn't *walk* in that time! HE CRAWLED IN! Now, when he walks in the glass will be empty, won't it?"

Smilingly, Glover returned, walked calmly up to the table, and raised the glass.

Mullinger nodded with a little shrug.

"I owe you a pound," he admitted. "Will you give me an opportunity to win it back? A thought-reading trick, it is called. It isn't really, but I'd like to bet you a pound that I can be taken out of this room, blindfolded, brought back, twisted round several times if you like, and then led by the hand round the room.

"Before we start making the round of the room, though, you will name some object which has been hidden whilst I have been out being blindfolded. I will undertake to call a halt when I am directly opposite the place where the object is hidden. Come, you are game?"

"That's new on me," nodded Glover.

"But how do I know you won't choose a confederate to signal to you while you are being guided by him? No offence, of course; simply look at the thing from a fool-proof standpoint."

"Easy," agreed Mr Mullinger, counter sly. "You can guide me yourself, Glover."

Blindfolded very thoroughly, Mr Mullinger was led back into the smoking room. There was general laughter as Glover rotated him several times, and little Mullinger swayed dizzily upon his feet.

"If he has the slightest idea of the lay-out of the room now," grinned Glover, "I'll eat my boots, rubber heels and all!"

He took Mr Mullinger's hand and led him slowly along the sides of the room. Interestedly, the others stared as the pair approached the dish of wax fruit secreted within the gramophone cabinet. There was a general gasp of wonder as the pair reached the instrument and Mr Mullinger called a halt.

"Here," he chuckled, removed the bandage from his eyes and took in his surroundings. His eye lit on the gramophone before which they had paused. In a moment he opened the doors of the cabinet, looked in and spotted the imitation fruit.

"Yes," he suggested.

"You couldn't see?" demanded Mr Warboys.

"Let us do it again," said Mr Mullinger. "We'll start again from the door. Bandage my eyes very tightly, Glover. That is the idea, my boy. Lead me to the door. Good. Now, turn me several times."

Glover did as instructed. He took the older man's hand and steadied him as he reeled dizzily.

"Now," Mr Mullinger spoke very steadily, "we will walk slowly round the walls again. I don't know where it is, but I shall undertake to call 'halt' opposite eighty-five pounds and some securities."

There was an electric silence.

The man in the tartan tie emerged again from a doze.

"Eighty-five pounds and some securities. Where?"

"I don't know," confessed Mr Mullinger quietly. "But if Mr Glover will take my hand and lead me round the room. I shall stop by them! Something weird about this? Come on, Glover!"

Eric Glover forced a smile which found no support in his eyes. A little muscle in his neck showed momentarily.

The pair progressed slowly along the first wall. There was a pause as they turned. It was Mr Mullinger who began the second wall with slow, deliberate, shuffling steps.

"Halt!" he called suddenly, and stopped at a point halfway across the width of the second wall.

Glover's gasp was lost in the triumph of the word. Mullinger tore off the bandage, stared at the floor, at the wall.

\*   \*   \*   \*   \*

There was no furniture at that point. But Mr Mullinger raised his eyes and smiled gently at a picture, massive, ancient, which graced the wall directly opposite where he stood.

"Of course," he chuckled. "Quite simple, really. I had expected somewhere more subtle. A hidden panel or something like that. Well, well!"

There was a mild chaos as the others crowded around. Mr Mullinger had taken down the picture carefully. He released the twist-catches holding the wooden back in position, and forced out the sheet of shrivelled boarding. There was a fluttering of papers to the floor.

"Eighty-five pounds, I imagine," said Mr Mullinger smoothly. "And securities to the value of another three hundred. *The contents of the hotel safe robbed in the early hours of Christmas Eve morning.*"

"Extraordinary," whispered Glover.

"Nothing extraordinary, really," drawled Mr Mullinger. "You were good enough to explain your trick, so I'll do the same. When you led me round the room. Glover, after the hiding of the wax fruit in the gramophone cabinet, you gave me the tip when I reached the spot with you holding my hand. Psychological reason, of course. You squeezed my hand slightly. Quite unconsciously, you squeezed it, though.

"The knowledge that we were at the very point where the object was hidden caused a keying up of your nervous system. Suspense, really. Your balance, as it were—will he stop or won't he?—was affected. The suspense of the moment causes a contraction of your fingers holding mine. You see, it had to be someone leading me who *knew* when we would reach the object. THAT WAS WHY I CHOSE YOU AGAIN WHEN SETTING OUT TO DISCOVER WHERE THE PROCEEDS FROM THE SAFE HAD BEEN HIDDEN!"

Glover started violently.

"By heaven, do you dare to suggest that I knew ... that I——?"

"You and none other," nodded Mr Mullinger. "You knew where the notes and securities had been hidden—naturally, seeing that *you hid them there till opportunity offered to get them away from the hotel.*"

"It is a lie," grated Glover. He laughed harshly. "You can prove nothing, either."

"No?" Mr Mullinger never took his hand from his pocket. He stared dispassionately at the pale face of the other. "The emptying of the glass trick over which you—again most obligingly—tumbled, was one I have done myself for the amusement of parties. I guessed you would know it, hence my affording you the opportunity.

"You see, Glover, fingerprints are easy to obtain. People leave them everywhere in normal actions. But knee-prints are more difficult to obtain. People don't leave knee-prints about; it was difficult to establish comparison with the knee-prints the thief left on the polished floor about the safe!"

Glover swore suddenly; his hand went swiftly behind him.

"It isn't there," said Mr Mullinger, gently. "I have it here, look! I abstracted it quite unostentatiously when you crawled on all fours to the table to empty the glass."

Glover stared ashen-faced at his own automatic, pointed steadily in the grasp of Mr Mullinger.

"You see," pursued Mr Mullinger evenly, "I suspected you quite early. And from the fact that you haunted this room practically all day on Christmas-eve, and again today—subconscious desire to be near the booty, my dear Glover, and know it is safe—it was fairly good proof that the proceeds were hidden here somewhere.

"Your knees have provided some excellent prints on the polished floor here. Identical with those left by the safe. And the distances between the impressions are identical, too, my young friend."

"A blasted detective!" snarled Glover.

Mullinger smiled and nodded.

"I was," he admitted. "Retired from the Force. Retiring, Glover—but not BACKWARD! Colonel, can you forsake the port long enough to ring up the police and summon the manager in here? Thank you."

# A HAPPY SOLUTION

## Raymund Allen

Raymund Allen (1863–1943) was a Welsh-born, Cambridge-educated barrister who spent much of his legal career working as District Probate Registrar in Llandaff. An obituary in *The Times* described him as "a stimulating companion, a witty talker with a strong love of argument, and an excellent *raconteur* who had a strong fund of legal stories with a South Wales setting". His wife, Alice Pattinson, was a well-known bookbinder.

Allen wrote on legal subjects such as the Workers' Compensation Act, but his passion was for chess, and he contributed short stories about the game to the *Strand Magazine* for over twenty years. "The Black Knight", which appeared in 1892, was a story of the uncanny, while "A Happy Solution", published in 1916, combined chess with detection to such good effect that twelve years later, Dorothy L. Sayers included it in her ground-breaking anthology *Great Short Stories of Detection, Mystery and Horror*. Allen was also the author of *Irregular Forces: A Story of Chess and War* (1915) and yet another chess story, "Allah Knows Best".

\*     \*     \*     \*     \*

The portmanteau, which to Kenneth Dale's strong arm had been little more than a feather-weight on leaving the station, seemed to have grown heavier by magic in the course of the half-mile that brought him to Lord Churt's country house. He put the portmanteau down in the porch with a sense of relief to his cramped arm, and rang the bell.

He had to wait for a few minutes, and then Lord Churt opened the door in person. His round, rubicund face, that would hardly have required any make-up to present an excellent "Mr Pickwick", beamed a welcome. "Come in, my dear boy, come in. I'm delighted to see you. I wish you a merry Christmas."

It was Christmas Eve, and his manner was bubbling over with the kindliness appropriate to the season. He seized the portmanteau and carried it into the hall.

"I am my own footman and parlour-maid and everything else for the moment. Packed all the servants off to a Christmas entertainment at the village school and locked the doors after 'em. My wife's gone, too, and Aunt Blaxter."

"And Norah?" Kenneth inquired.

"Ah! Norah!" Churt answered, with a friendly clap on Kenneth's shoulder. "Norah's the only person that really matters, of course she is, and quite right too. Norah stayed in to send off a lot of Christmas cards, and I fancy she is still in her room, but she must have disposed of the cards, because they are in the letter-bag. She would have been on the look-out for you, no doubt, but your letter said you were not coming."

"Yes, I know. I thought I couldn't get away, but today my chief's heart was softened, and he said he would manage to do without me till the day after tomorrow. So I made a rush for the two-fifteen, and just caught it."

"And here you are as a happy surprise for your poor, disappointed Norah—and for us all," he added, genially.

"I hope you approve of my fiancée," Kenneth remarked, with a smile that expressed confidence as to the answer.

"My dear Kenneth," Churt replied, "I can say with sincerity that I think her both beautiful and charming. We were very glad to ask her here, and her singing is a great pleasure to us." He hesitated for a moment before continuing. "You must forgive us cautious old people if we think the engagement just a little bit precipitate.

As Aunt Blaxter was saying today, you can't really know her very well on such a short acquaintance, and you know nothing at all of her people."

Kenneth mentally cursed Aunt Blaxter for a vinegar-blooded old killjoy, but did not express any part of the sentiment aloud.

"We must have another talk about your great affair later," Churt went on. "Now come along to the library. I am just finishing a game of chess with Sir James Winslade, and then we'll go and find where Miss Norah is hiding."

He stopped at a table in the passage that led from the hall to the library, and took a bunch of keys out of his pocket. "She was sending you a letter, so there can be no harm in our rescuing it out of the bag." He unlocked the private letter-bag and turned out a pile of letters on to the table, muttering an occasional comment as he put them back, one by one, in the bag, in his search for the letter he was looking for. "Aunt Emma—ah, I ought to have written to her too; must write for her birthday instead. Mrs Dunn—same thing there, I'm afraid. Red Cross—hope that won't get lost; grand work, the Red Cross. Ah, here we are: 'Kenneth Dale, Esq., 31, Valpy Street, London, S.W.'" He tumbled the rest of the letters back into the bag and re-locked it. "Put it in your pocket and come along, or Winslade will think I am never coming back."

He was delayed a few moments longer, however, to admit the servants on their return from the village, and he handed the bag to one of them to be taken to the post-office.

In the library Sir James Winslade was seated at the chess-board, and Churt's private secretary, Gornay, a tall, slender figure, with a pale complexion and dark, clever eyes, was watching the game.

The secretary greeted Kenneth rather frigidly, and turned to to Churt. "Have the letters gone to post yet?"

"Yes; did you want to send any?"

"Only a card that I might have written," Gornay answered, "but it isn't of any consequence"; and he sat down again beside the chess-players.

Churt had the black pieces, black nominally only, for actually they were the little red pieces of a travelling board. He appeared to have got into difficulties, and, greatly to the satisfaction of Kenneth, who was impatient to go in quest of Norah, the game came to an end after a few more moves.

"I don't see any way out of this," Churt remarked, after a final, perplexed survey of the position. "You come at me, next move, with queen or knight, and, either way, I am done for. It is your game. I resign."

"A lucky win for you, Sir James," Gornay observed.

"Why lucky?" Winslade asked. "You told us we had both violated every sound principle of development in the opening but could Black have done any better for the last few moves?"

"He can win the game as the pieces now stand," Gornay answered.

He proved the statement by making a few moves on the board, and then replaced the pieces as they had been left.

"Well, it's your game fair and square, all the same," Churt remarked good-humouredly. "I should never have found the right reply for myself."

Gornay continued to study the board with attention, and his face assumed an expression of keenness, as though he had discovered some fresh point to interest him in the position. At the moment Kenneth merely chafed at the delay. It was an hour or so later only that the secretary's comments on the game assumed for him a vital importance that made him recall them with particularity.

"If the play was rather eccentric sometimes, I must say it was bold and dashing enough on both sides," Gornay commented. "For instance, when Lord Churt gave up his knight for nothing, and

WHITE.

BLACK.

Black to play and win

when you gave him the choice of taking your queen with either of two pawns at your queen's knight's sixth." He turned to Churt. "Possibly you might have done better to take the queen with the bishop's pawn instead of with the rook's."

"I daresay, I daresay," Churt replied. "I should have probably got into a mess, whatever I played. But come along, now, all of you, and see if we can find some tea."

Kenneth contrived, before entering the drawing-room, to intercept Norah for an exchange of greetings in private, and her face was still radiant with the delight of the unexpected meeting as they entered the room.

After tea Sir James carried off the secretary to keep him company in the smoking-room, and Churt turned to Norah. "You must sing one of the Christmas carols you promised us, and then you young folk may go off to the library to talk over your own private affairs. I know you must both be longing to get away from us old fogies."

"Thank you, Lord Churt, for 'old fogies', on behalf of your wife and myself," Aunt Blaxter commented, with a mild sarcasm that somehow failed of its intended playful effect. But Norah had sat down at once to the piano, and her voice rang out in a joyous carol before he could frame a suitable reply.

A second carol was asked for, that the others might join in, and in the course of it Kenneth's hand came upon the letter in his pocket. He was opening the envelope as Norah rose from the piano. Her eye caught her own handwriting and she blushed very red. "Be careful, Ken. Don't let anything fall out!" she cried in alarm.

Thus warned, he drew the letter out delicately, being careful to leave in the envelope a little curl of brown hair, a lover's token that she would have been shy to see exposed to the eyes of the others. But, in his care for this, a thin bit of paper fluttered from the fold of the letter to the carpet, and all eyes instinctively followed it. It was a Bank of England note for a thousand pounds.

Kenneth looked at Norah in wonder, but got no enlightenment. Then at Lord Churt, as the bare possibility occurred to his mind that, in a Christmas freak of characteristic generosity, he might have somehow contrived to get it enclosed with her letter. But Churt's dumbfounded expression was not the acting of any genial comedy. His hands trembled as he put on his glasses to compare an entry in his pocket-book with the number on the note. He was the first to break the amazed silence. "This is a most extraordinary thing. This is the identical bank-note that I put into the Red Cross envelope this afternoon as my Christmas gift, the very same that I got for the purpose of sending anonymously, and that you ladies were interested to inspect at breakfast time."

Each looked at the others for an explanation, till all eyes settled on Norah, as the person who might be expected to give one.

Churt looked vexed and troubled, Aunt Blaxter severely suspicious, as she saw that the girl remained silent, with a face that was losing its colour. "As the note was found in a letter sent by Norah, she would be the natural person to explain how it got there," she remarked.

"I haven't the remotest notion how it got there," Norah replied. "I can only say that I did not put it there, and that I never saw it again since breakfast time, until it dropped out of my letter a few moments ago."

"Very strange," Aunt Blaxter remarked, drily. Kenneth turned upon her hotly. "You don't suggest that Norah stole the note, I imagine!"

"My dear people," Churt intervened, soothingly, "do let us keep our heads cool, and not have any unpleasant scene."

Kenneth still glared. "If Norah had put the note into this envelope, she would have referred to it in her letter. I suppose you will accept my word that she doesn't."

"Read out the postcript, Ken," Norah requested. "Miss Blaxter may like to suggest that it refers to the note." The girl looked at her with a face that was now blazing with anger, and Kenneth read out: "P.S. Don't let anybody see what I am sending you!" It had not occurred to him that it could be taken as anything but a jesting reference to the lock of hair, the note of exclamation at the end giving the effect of "As though I should ever dream you would", or some equivalent. The matter was growing too serious for any shamefacedness, and he produced the lock of hair in explanation. It was cruel luck, he reflected, that the unfortunate postcript should be capable of misconstruction. He had counted on Norah's making a triumphant conquest of the Churt household, and it was exceedingly galling to find her, instead, exposed to an odious suspicion. Aunt Blaxter's demeanour was all the more maddening that he could think of no means to prove its unreasonableness. He looked gratefully at Lady Churt, as her gentle voice gave the discussion a fresh turn. "How long has Mr Gornay been with us?" she asked her husband.

Churt looked shocked. "My dear, we musn't make any rash insinuations in a matter of this kind. What possible motive could Gornay have for putting the note into Norah's letter, if he meant to steal it? Besides, my evidence clears him."

"Would you mind telling us what you did with the note after you showed it at the breakfast table this morning?" Kenneth asked.

"I'll tell you exactly," Churt answered. "When it had made the round of the breakfast table, I put it back in my pocket-book and kept it in my pocket till this afternoon. It was while we were playing chess that I remembered that the bag would be going to post earlier than usual, and I put the note in the Red Cross envelope with the printed address and stuck it down and put it into the bag. I came straight back to the library, and I remember being surprised at the move I found Winslade had played, because he was offering me his queen for nothing. Just at that moment it occurred to my mind that Norah had probably already put her letters into the bag, and that, if so, I might as well lock it at once, for fear of forgetting to do so later. I looked at the chessboard for a few minutes, standing up, and then went and found that Norah's letters were in the bag, and I locked it, and came back and took Winslade's queen."

"But I don't quite see what all that has to do with Mr Gornay, or how it clears him." Lady Churt remarked.

"Why, my dear, whoever took the note out of one envelope, and put it into the other must have done so in the few minutes between my two visits to the bag. It was the only time that the letter was in the bag without its being locked. And during that time Gornay was watching the chess, so it can't have been him."

"Was he in the library all the time you were playing?" Kenneth asked.

"I can't say that," Churt replied. "I don't think he was. I didn't notice particularly. But I am positive that he did not enter or leave the room while I was standing looking at Winslade's move, and he must have been there when Winslade offered his queen and when I took it, because he was commenting on those very moves after the game was finished, and suggesting that I might have done better to take with the other pawn. You heard him yourself."

"Yes," Kenneth answered. "I follow that. But there is such a thing as picking a lock, you know."

"The makers guarantee that it can't be done to this one," Churt answered, "and the key has always been in my possession, so he couldn't have had a duplicate made, even if there had been any time."

Norah interposed in a voice that trembled with indignation. "In short, Lord Churt, you think the evidence conclusive against the only other person, except Sir James Winslade, who was in the house. I have only my word to give against it."

"It is worth all the evidence in the world," Kenneth cried, and she thanked her champion with a bright glance.

"Lady Churt is quite right," Kenneth went on. "I'd stake my life it was that sneaking Gornay. Have him in here now, and see if his face doesn't show his guilt when I call him a thief."

"Not for the world!" Churt exclaimed, aghast. "We should have a most painful scene. This is no case for rash precipitancy." He assumed the air of judicial solemnity with which, from the local bench, he would fine a rascal five shillings who ought to have gone down for six months. "I entirely refuse to entertain any suspicion of anybody under this roof, guests, servants, or anyone else. It will probably turn out that some odd little accident has occurred, that will seem simple enough when it is explained. On the other hand, it is just conceivable that some evil-disposed person from outside should have got into the house, though I confess I can't understand the motive of their action if they did. In any case, I feel it my duty, for the credit of my household, to have the matter cleared up by the proper authority."

"What do you mean by the proper authority?" Lady Churt asked. "I didn't think the local police were very clever that time when poor Kelpie got stolen."

The Aberdeen terrier at her feet looked up at the sound of his name, and Churt continued: "I shall telephone to Scotland Yard. If Shapland is there, I am sure he would come down at once in his car. He could be here in less than two hours. Until he, or somebody else, arrives I beg that none of you say a word about this affair to anyone who is not now present in this room."

"Quite the most proper course," Aunt Blaxter observed. "It is only right that guilt should be brought home to the proper person, *whoever* that person may be."

With a tact of which Kenneth had hardly thought him capable, Churt turned to Norah. "I have no doubt Shapland will clear up the mystery for us satisfactorily. Meantime, my dear girl, you and I find ourselves in the same boat, for there is only my word for it that I ever put the note into the Red Cross envelope at all."

The kindness of his manner brought the tears to her eyes, and Kenneth took her away to the library.

"Fancy their thinking I was a thief—a thief, Ken—a common mean *thief*!"

"Nonsense, my darling girl," he said. "Nobody could believe any such rubbish."

"That odious Aunt Blaxter does, at any rate. She as good as said so." She sat down in a chair, and began to grow calmer, while he paced about the room, angry but thoughtful.

"I was glad I had you to stick up for me, Ken, and Lord Churt is an old dear."

"He's a silly old dear, all the same," he answered. "He has more money than he knows what to do with, but fancy fluttering a thousand-pound note through the Christmas post, to get lost among all the robins and good wishes!"

They were interrupted at this point by the entry of Gornay.

"I am not going to stay," he said, in answer to their not very welcoming expressions. "I have only come to ask a quite small favour. I am having a great argument with Sir James about character-reading from handwriting, and I want specimens from people we both know. Any little scrap will do."

Kenneth took up a sheet of note-paper from a writing table and wrote, "All is not gold that glitters", and Norah added below, "Birds of a feather flock together". It seemed the quickest way to get rid of him.

Gornay looked at the sheet with a not quite satisfied air. "I would *rather* have had something not written specially. Nobody ever writes quite naturally when they know that it is for this sort of purpose. You haven't got an old envelope, or something like that?"

Neither could supply what he wanted, and he went off, looking a little disappointed.

"I wonder whether that was really what he wanted the writing for," Kenneth remarked, suspiciously. "He's a quick-witted knave. Look how sharp he was to see the right move in that game of chess. It wasn't very obvious."

The chess-board was lying open on the table, where Churt had left it before tea. He glanced at it, casually at first, and then with growing interest. He took up one of the pieces to examine it, then replaced it, to do the same with others, his manner showing all the time an increasing excitement.

"What is it, Ken?" Norah asked.

"Just a glimmer of something." He dropped into a chair. "I want to think—to think harder than ever in my life."

He leant forward, with his head resting on his hands, and she waited in silence till, after some minutes, he looked up.

"Yes, I begin to see light—more than a glimmer. He's a subtle customer, is Mr Gornay, oh, very subtle!" He smiled, partly with the pleasure of finding one thread of a tangled web, partly with admiration for the cleverness that had woven it. "Would you like to know what he was really after when he came in here just now?"

"Very much," she answered. "But do you mean that he never had any argument with Sir James?"

"Oh, I daresay he had the argument all right—got it up for the occasion; but what he really wanted was this." He took out of his pocket the envelope in which the bank-note had been discovered. "The character-reading rot was not a bad shot at getting hold of it, and probably his only chance. But no, friend Gornay, you are not going to have that envelope—not for the thousand pounds you placed in it!"

"Do explain, Ken," Norah begged.

"I will presently," he answered, "but I want to piece the whole jigsaw together. There is still the other difficulty."

He dropped his eyes to the hearthrug again, and began to do his thinking aloud for her benefit. "Churt's reasoning is that Gornay must have been in here, watching the game, at the only time when the letters could have been tampered with, because he knew afterwards the move that was played just at the beginning of that time, and the move that was played just at the end. But why might not Winslade have told him about those two moves while Churt was letting me in at the front door? That would solve the riddle. I should have thought Winslade would have been too punctilious to talk about the game while his opponent was out of the room, but I'll go and ask him. I needn't tell him the reason why I want to know."

He came back almost immediately. "No, there was no conversation about the game while Churt was out of the room. Very well. Try the thing the other way round. Assume—as I think I can prove—that Gornay *did* tamper with the letters, the question is how could he tell that those two moves had been played?"

He took up the chess-board again and looked at it so intently and so long that, at last, Norah grew impatient.

"My dear boy, what *can* you be doing, poring all this time over the chess?"

"I have a curious sort of chess problem to solve before the Sherlock Holmes man turns up from Scotland Yard. Follow this a moment. If there was any way by which Gornay could find out that the two important moves had been played, without being present at the time and without being told, then Churt's argument goes for nothing, doesn't it?"

"Clearly; but what other way was there? Did he look in through the window?"

"I think we shall find it was something much cleverer than that. I think I shall be able to show that he could infer that those two moves had been played, without any other help, from the position of the pieces as they stood at the end of the game; as they stand on the board now." He again bent down over the board. "White plays queen to queen's knight's sixth, not taking anything, and Black takes the queen with the rook's pawn; those are the two moves."

For nearly another half-hour Norah waited in loyal silence, watching the alternations of his face as it brightened with the light of comprehension and clouded again with fresh perplexity.

At last he shut up the board and put it down, looking profoundly puzzled.

"Can it not be proved that the queen must have been taken at that particular square?" Norah inquired.

"No," he answered. "It might equally have been a rook. I can't make the matter out. So many of the jigsaw bits fit in that I know I must be right, and yet there is just one little bit that I can't find. By Jove!" he added, suddenly starting up, "I wonder if Churt could supply it?"

He was just going off to find out when a servant entered the room with a message that Lord Churt requested their presence in his study.

The conclave assembled in the study consisted of the same persons who, in the drawing-room, had witnessed the discovery of the bank-note, with the addition of Shapland, the detective from Scotland Yard. Lord Churt presided, sitting at the table, and Shapland sat by his side, with a face that might have seemed almost unintelligent in its lack of expression but for the roving eyes, that scrutinized in turn the other faces present.

Norah and Kenneth took the two chairs that were left vacant, and, as soon as the door was shut, Kenneth asked Churt a question.

"When you played your game of chess with Sir James Winslade this afternoon, did he give you the odds of the queen's rook?"

Everyone, except Norah and the sphinx-like detective, whose face gave no clue to his thoughts, looked surprised at the triviality of the question.

"I should hardly have thought this was a fitting occasion to discuss such a frivolous matter as a game of chess," Aunt Blaxter remarked sourly.

"I confess I don't understand the relevance of your question," Churt answered. "As a matter of fact, he did give me those odds."

"Thank God!" Kenneth exclaimed, with an earnestness that provoked a momentary sign of interest from Shapland.

"I should like to hear what Mr Dale has to say about this matter," he remarked. "Lord Churt has put me in possession of the circumstances."

"I have an accusation to make against Lord Churt's private secretary, Mr Gornay. Perhaps he had better be present to hear it."

"Quite unnecessary, quite unnecessary," Churt interposed. "We will not have any unpleasant scenes if we can help it."

"Very well," Kenneth continued. "I only thought it might be fairer. I accuse Gornay of stealing the thousand-pound bank-note out of the envelope addressed to the Red Cross and putting it into a letter addressed to me. *I accuse him of using colourless ink, of a kind that would become visible after a few hours, to cross out my address and substitute another*, the address of a confederate, no doubt."

"You must be aware, Mr Dale," Shapland observed, "that you are making a very serious allegation in the presence of witnesses. I presume you have some evidence to support it?"

Kenneth opened the chess-board. "Look at the stains on those chess pieces. They were not there when the game was finished. They were there, not so distinctly as now, about an hour ago. Precisely those pieces, and only those, are stained that Gornay touched in showing that Lord Churt might have won the game. If they are not stains of invisible ink, why should they grow more distinct? If they are invisible ink, how did it get there, unless from Gornay's guilty fingers?"

He took out of his pocket the envelope of Norah's letter, and a glance at it brought a look of triumph to his face. He handed it to Shapland. "The ink is beginning to show there, too. It seems to act more slowly on the paper than on the polish of the chessmen."

"It is a difference of exposure to the air," Shapland corrected. "The envelope has been in your pocket. If we leave it there on the table, we shall see presently whether your deduction is sound. Meanwhile, if Mr Gornay was the guilty person, how can you account for his presence in the library at the only time when a crime could have been committed?"

"By denying it," Kenneth answered. "What proof have we that he was there at that particular time?"

"How else could he know the moves that were played at that time?" Shapland asked.

Kenneth pointed again to the chess-board. "From the position of the pieces at the end of the game. Here it is. I can prove, from the position of those pieces alone, *provided the game was played at the odds of queen's rook*, that White must, in the course of the game, have played his queen to queen's knight's sixth, not making a capture, and that Black must have taken it with the rook's pawn. If I can draw those inferences from the position, so could Gornay. We know how quickly he can think out a combination from the way in which he showed that Lord Churt could have won the game, when it looked so hopeless that he resigned."

The detective, fortunately, had an elementary knowledge of chess sufficient to enable him to follow Kenneth's demonstration.

"I don't suggest," Kenneth added, when the accuracy of the demonstration was admitted, "that he planned this alibi beforehand. It was a happy afterthought, that occurred to his quick mind when he saw that the position at the end of the game made it possible. What he relied on was the invisible ink trick, and that would have succeeded by itself, if I hadn't happened to turn up unexpectedly in time to intercept my letter from Norah."

While Kenneth was giving this last bit of explanation, Shapland had taken up the envelope again. As he had foretold, exposure to the air had brought out the invisible writing so that, although still faint, it was already legible. Only the middle line of the address, the number and name of the street, had been struck out with a single stroke, and another number and name substituted. The detective handed it to Churt. "Do you recognize the second handwriting, my lord?"

Churt put on his glasses and examined it. "I can't say that I do," he answered, "but it is not that of Mr Gornay." He took another envelope out of his pocket-book, addressed to himself in his secretary's hand, and pointed out the dissimilarity of the two writings. Norah cast an anxious look at Kenneth, and Aunt Blaxter one of her sourest at the girl. The detective showed no surprise.

"None the less, my lord, I think it might forward our investigation if you would have Mr Gornay summoned to this room. I don't think you need be afraid that there will be any scene," he added, and, for an instant, the faintest of smiles flitted across his lips.

Churt rang the bell and told the servant to ask his secretary to come to him.

"Mr Gornay left an hour ago, my lord. He was called away suddenly and doesn't expect to see his grandmother alive."

"Poor old soul! On Christmas Eve, too!" Churt muttered, sympathetically, and this time Shapland allowed himself the indulgence of a rather broader smile.

"I guessed as much," he observed, "when I recognized the handwriting in which the envelope had been redirected, or I should have taken the precaution of going to fetch the gentleman, whom you know as Mr Gornay, myself. He is a gentleman who is known to us at the Yard by more than one name, as well as by more than one handwriting, and now that we have so fortunately discovered his present whereabouts I can promise you that he will soon be laid by the heels.

Perhaps Lord Churt will be kind enough to have my car ordered and to allow me to use his telephone."

"But you'll stay to dinner?" Churt asked. "It will be ready in a few minutes, and we shall none of us have time to dress."

"I am much obliged, my lord, but Mr Dale has done my work for me here in a way that any member of the Yard might be proud of, and now I must follow the tracks while they are fresh. It may not prove necessary to trouble you any further about this matter, but I think you are likely to see an important development in the great Ashfield forgery case reported in the newspapers before very long."

"Well," Churt observed, "I think we may all congratulate ourselves on having got this matter cleared up without any unpleasant scenes. Now we shall be able to enjoy our Christmas. I call it a happy solution, a very happy solution."

His face beamed with relief and good humour as he once more produced his pocket-book. "Norah, my dear, you must accept an old man's apology for causing you a very unpleasant afternoon; and you must accept this as well. No, I shall not take a refusal, and it will be much safer to send a *cheque* to the Red Cross."

[The solution of the end-game given in this story, and the proof that a white queen must have been taken by the pawn at Q Kt 3, is given on page 283.]

# THE FLYING STARS

## G.K. Chesterton

Gilbert Keith Chesterton (1874–1936) was described by his "friendly enemy", George Bernard Shaw, with whom he often crossed swords, as "a man of colossal genius". His interests were extraordinarily wide-ranging, and he was a prolific writer, not least in his own paper, *G.K.'s Weekly*. At a Requiem Mass for Chesterton in Westminster Cathedral, Father Ronald Knox (himself a noted detective novelist) said, "All of this generation has grown up under Chesterton's influence so completely that we do not even know when we are thinking Chesterton."

Father Brown was Chesterton's most enduring fictional creation, and typically, "The Flying Stars" offers a literary parable, which sees the little priest urging Flambeau to abandon his life of crime. Chesterton was – unlike many of his contemporaries – a ferocious opponent of eugenics, but not all his views and attitudes have stood the test of time. His admirers continue to defend him against the charge that he was anti-Semitic, but there is a short passage at the start of this story which illustrates why the accusation is sometimes made.

\* \* \* \* \*

"THE most beautiful crime I ever committed," Flambeau would say in his highly moral old age, "was also, by a singular coincidence, my last. It was committed at Christmas. As an artist I had always attempted to provide crimes suitable to the special season or land-scapes in which I found myself, choosing this or that terrace or garden for a catastrophe, as if for a statuary group. Thus squires should be swindled in long rooms panelled with oak; while Jews, on the other hand, should rather find themselves unexpectedly penniless among the lights and screens of the Cafe Riche. Thus, in England, if I wished to relieve a dean of his riches (which is not so easy as you might suppose), I wished to frame him, if I make myself clear, in the green lawns and grey towers of some cathedral town. Similarly, in France, when I had got money out of a rich and wicked peasant (which is almost impossible), it gratified me to get his indignant head relieved against a grey line of clipped poplars, and those solemn plains of Gaul over which broods the mighty spirit of Millet.

"Well, my last crime was a Christmas crime, a cheery, cosy, English middle-class crime; a crime of Charles Dickens. I did it in a good old middle-class house near Putney, a house with a crescent of carriage drive, a house with a stable by the side of it, a house with the name on the two outer gates, a house with a monkey tree. Enough, you know the species. I really think my imitation of Dickens' style was dexterous and literary. It seems almost a pity I repented the same evening."

Flambeau would then proceed to tell the story from the inside; and even from the inside it was odd. Seen from the outside it was perfectly incomprehensible, and it is from the outside that the stranger must study it. From this standpoint the drama may be said to have begun when the front doors of the house with the stable opened on the garden with the monkey tree, and a young girl came out with bread to feed the birds on the afternoon of Boxing Day. She had a pretty face, with brave brown eyes; but her figure was beyond conjecture, for she was so wrapped up in brown furs that it was hard to say which was hair and which was fur. But for the attractive face she might have been a small toddling bear.

The winter afternoon was reddening towards evening, and already a ruby light was rolled over the bloomless beds, filling them, as it were, with the ghosts of the dead roses. On one side of the house stood the stable, on the other an alley or cloister of laurels led to the larger garden behind. The young lady, having scattered bread for the birds (for the fourth or fifth time that day, because the dog ate it), passed unobtrusively down the lane of laurels and into a glimmering plantation of evergreens behind. Here she gave an exclamation of wonder, real or ritual, and looking up at the high garden wall above her, beheld it fantastically bestridden by a somewhat fantastic figure.

"Oh, don't jump, Mr Crook," she called out in some alarm; "it's much too high."

The individual riding the party wall like an aerial horse was a tall, angular young man, with dark hair sticking up like a hairbrush, intelligent and even distinguished lineaments, but a sallow and almost alien complexion. This showed the more plainly because he wore an aggressive red tie, the only part of his costume of which he seemed to take any care. Perhaps it was a symbol. He took no notice of the girl's alarmed adjuration, but leapt like a grasshopper to the ground beside her, where he might very well have broken his legs.

"I think I was meant to be a burglar," he said placidly, "and I have no doubt I should have been if I hadn't happened to be born in that nice house next door. I can't see any harm in it, anyhow."

"How can you say such things?" she remonstrated.

"Well," said the young man, "if you're born on the wrong side of the wall, I can't see that it's wrong to climb over it."

"I never know what you will say or do next," she said.

"I don't often know myself," replied Mr Crook; "but then I am on the right side of the wall now."

"And which is the right side of the wall?" asked the young lady, smiling.

"Whichever side you are on," said the young man named Crook.

As they went together through the laurels towards the front garden a motor horn sounded thrice, coming nearer and nearer, and a car of splendid speed, great elegance, and a pale green colour swept up to the front doors like a bird and stood throbbing.

"Hullo, hullo!" said the young man with the red tie, "here's somebody born on the right side, anyhow. I didn't know, Miss Adams, that your Santa Claus was so modern as this."

"Oh, that's my godfather, Sir Leopold Fischer. He always comes on Boxing Day."

Then, after an innocent pause, which unconsciously betrayed some lack of enthusiasm, Ruby Adams added:

"He is very kind."

John Crook, journalist, had heard of that eminent City magnate; and it was not his fault if the City magnate had not heard of him; for in certain articles in *The Clarion* or *The New Age* Sir Leopold had been dealt with austerely. But he said nothing and grimly watched the unloading of the motor-car, which was rather a long process. A large, neat chauffeur in green got out from the front, and a small, neat manservant in grey got out from the back, and between them they deposited Sir Leopold on the doorstep and began to unpack him, like some very carefully protected parcel. Rugs enough to stock a bazaar, furs of all the beasts of the forest, and scarves of all the colours of the rainbow were unwrapped one by one, till they revealed something resembling the human form; the form of a friendly, but foreign-looking old gentleman, with a grey goat-like beard and a beaming smile, who rubbed his big fur gloves together.

Long before this revelation was complete the two big doors of the porch had opened in the middle, and Colonel Adams (father of the furry young lady) had come out himself to invite his eminent guest inside. He was a tall, sunburnt, and very silent man, who wore a red smoking-cap like a fez, making him look like one of the English

Sirdars or Pashas in Egypt. With him was his brother-in-law, lately
come from Canada, a big and rather boisterous young gentleman-
farmer, with a yellow beard, by name James Blount. With him also
was the more insignificant figure of the priest from the neighbouring
Roman Church; for the colonel's late wife had been a Catholic, and
the children, as is common in such cases, had been trained to follow
her. Everything seemed undistinguished about the priest, even down
to his name, which was Brown; yet the colonel had always found
something companionable about him, and frequently asked him to
such family gatherings.

In the large entrance hall of the house there was ample room
even for Sir Leopold and the removal of his wraps. Porch and
vestibule, indeed, were unduly large in proportion to the house,
and formed, as it were, a big room with the front door at one end,
and the bottom of the staircase at the other. In front of the large
hall fire, over which hung the colonel's sword, the process was
completed and the company, including the saturnine Crook, presented to Sir Leopold Fischer. That venerable financier, however,
still seemed struggling with portions of his well-lined attire, and
at length produced from a very interior tail-coat pocket, a black
oval case which he radiantly explained to be his Christmas present for his god-daughter. With an unaffected vain-glory that had
something disarming about it he held out the case before them all;
it flew open at a touch and half-blinded them. It was just as if a
crystal fountain had spurted in their eyes. In a nest of orange velvet
lay like three eggs, three white and vivid diamonds that seemed
to set the very air on fire all round them. Fischer stood beaming
benevolently and drinking deep of the astonishment and ecstasy of
the girl, the grim admiration and gruff thanks of the colonel, the
wonder of the whole group.

"I'll put 'em back now, my dear," said Fischer, returning the case to the tails of his coat. "I had to be careful of 'em coming down. They're the three great African diamonds called 'The Flying Stars', because they've been stolen so often. All the big criminals are on the track; but even the rough men about in the streets and hotels could hardly have kept their hands off them. I might have lost them on the road here. It was quite possible."

"Quite natural, I should say," growled the man in the red tie. "I shouldn't blame 'em if they had taken 'em. When they ask for bread, and you don't even give them a stone, I think they might take the stone for themselves."

"I won't have you talking like that," cried the girl, who was in a curious glow. "You've only talked like that since you became a horrid what's-his-name. You know what I mean. What do you call a man who wants to embrace the chimney-sweep?"

"A saint," said Father Brown.

"I think," said Sir Leopold, with a supercilious smile, "that Ruby means a Socialist."

"A Radical does not mean a man who lives on radishes," remarked Crook, with some impatience; "and a Conservative does not mean a man who preserves jam. Neither, I assure you, does a Socialist mean a man who desires a social evening with the chimney-sweep. A Socialist means a man who wants all the chimneys swept and all the chimney-sweeps paid for it."

"But who won't allow you," put in the priest in a low voice, "to own your own soot."

Crook looked at him with an eye of interest and even respect. "Does one want to own soot?" he asked.

"One might," answered Brown, with speculation in his eye. "I've heard that gardeners use it. And I once made six children happy at Christmas when the conjuror didn't come, entirely with soot—applied externally."

"Oh, splendid," cried Ruby. "Oh, I wish you'd do it to this company."

The boisterous Canadian, Mr Blount, was lifting his loud voice in applause, and the astonished financier his (in some considerable deprecation), when a knock sounded at the double front doors. The priest opened them, and they showed again the front garden of evergreens, monkey-tree and all, now gathering gloom against a gorgeous violet sunset. The scene thus framed was so coloured and quaint, like a back scene in a play, that they forgot for a moment the insignificant figure standing in the door. He was dusty-looking and in a frayed coat, evidently a common messenger. "Any of you gentlemen Mr Blount?" he asked, and held forward a letter doubtfully. Mr Blount started, and stopped in his shout of assent. Ripping up the envelope with evident astonishment he read it; his face clouded a little, and then cleared, and he turned to his brother-in-law and host.

"I'm sick at being such a nuisance, colonel," he said, with the cheery colonial convention; "but would it upset you if an old acquaintance called on me here tonight on business? In point of fact it's Florian, that famous French acrobat and comic actor; I knew him years ago out West (he was a French-Canadian by birth), and he seems to have business for me, though I hardly guess what."

"Of course, of course," replied the colonel carelessly. "My dear chap, any friend of yours. No doubt he will prove an acquisition."

"He'll black his face, if that's what you mean," cried Blount, laughing. "I don't doubt he'd black everyone else's eyes. I don't care; I'm not refined. I like the jolly old pantomime where a man sits on his top hat."

"Not on mine, please," said Sir Leopold Fischer, with dignity.

"Well, well," observed Crook, airily, "don't let's quarrel. There are lower jokes than sitting on a top hat."

Dislike of the red-tied youth, born of his predatory opinions and evident intimacy with the pretty godchild, led Fischer to say, in his most sarcastic, magisterial manner: "No doubt you have found something much lower than sitting on a top hat. What is it, pray?"

"Letting a top hat sit on you, for instance," said the Socialist.

"Now, now, now," cried the Canadian farmer with his barbarian benevolence, "don't let's spoil a jolly evening. What I say is, let's do something for the company tonight. Not blacking faces or sitting on hats, if you don't like those—but something of the sort. Why couldn't we have a proper old English pantomime—clown, columbine, and so on. I saw one when I left England at twelve years old, and it's blazed in my brain like a bonfire ever since. I came back to the old country only last year, and I find the thing's extinct. Nothing but a lot of snivelling fairy plays. I want a hot poker and a policeman made into sausages, and they give me princesses moralizing by moonlight, Blue Birds, or something. Blue Beard's more in my line, and him I liked best when he turned into the pantaloon."

"I'm all for making a policeman into sausages," said John Crook. "It's a better definition of Socialism than some recently given. But surely the get-up would be too big a business."

"Not a scrap," cried Blount, quite carried away. "A harlequinade's the quickest thing we can do, for two reasons. First, one can gag to any degree; and, second, all the objects are household things—tables and towel-horses and washing baskets, and things like that."

"That's true," admitted Crook, nodding eagerly and walking about. "But I'm afraid I can't have my policeman's uniform? Haven't killed a policeman lately."

Blount frowned thoughtfully a space, and then smote his thigh. "Yes, we can!" he cried. "I've got Florian's address here, and he knows every costumier in London. I'll 'phone him to bring a police dress when he comes." And he went bounding away to the telephone.

"Oh, it's glorious, godfather," cried Ruby, almost dancing. "I'll be columbine and you shall be pantaloon."

The millionaire held himself stiff with a sort of heathen solemnity. "I think, my dear," he said, "you must get someone else for pantaloon."

"I will be pantaloon, if you like," said Colonel Adams, taking his cigar out of his mouth, and speaking for the first and last time.

"You ought to have a statue," cried the Canadian, as he came back, radiant, from the telephone. "There, we are all fitted. Mr Crook shall be clown; he's a journalist and knows all the oldest jokes. I can be harlequin, that only wants long legs and jumping about. My friend Florian 'phones he's bringing the police costume; he's changing on the way. We can act it in this very hall, the audience sitting on those broad stairs opposite, one row above another. These front doors can be the back scene, either open or shut. Shut, you see an English interior. Open, a moonlit garden. It all goes by magic." And snatching a chance piece of billiard chalk from his pocket, he ran it across the hall floor, halfway between the front door and the staircase, to mark the line of the footlights.

How even such a banquet of bosh was got ready in the time remained a riddle. But they went at it with that mixture of recklessness and industry that lives when youth is in a house; and youth was in that house that night, though not all may have isolated the two faces and hearts from which it flamed. As always happens, the invention grew wilder and wilder through the very tameness of the *bourgeois* conventions from which it had to create. The columbine looked charming in an outstanding skirt that strangely resembled the large lamp-shade in the drawing-room. The clown and pantaloon made themselves white with flour from the cook, and red with rouge from some other domestic, who remained (like all true Christian benefactors) anonymous. The harlequin, already clad in silver paper out of cigar boxes, was, with difficulty, prevented from smashing the old Victorian lustre chandeliers, that he might cover himself with resplendent crystals. In fact he would certainly have done so, had not Ruby unearthed some old pantomime paste jewels she had worn at a fancy dress party as the Queen of Diamonds. Indeed, her uncle, James Blount, was getting almost out of hand in his excitement; he was like a schoolboy. He put a paper donkey's head unexpectedly on Father Brown, who bore it patiently, and even found some private manner of moving his ears. He even essayed to put the paper donkey's tail to the coat-tails of Sir Leopold Fischer. This, however, was frowned down. "Uncle is too absurd," cried Ruby to Crook, round whose shoulders she had seriously placed a string of sausages. "Why is he so wild?"

"He is harlequin to your columbine," said Crook. "I am only the clown who makes the old jokes."

"I wish you were the harlequin," she said, and left the string of sausages swinging.

Father Brown, though he knew every detail done behind the scenes, and had even evoked applause by his transformation of a pillow into a pantomime baby, went round to the front and sat among the audience with all the solemn expectation of a child at his first matinée. The spectators were few, relations, one or two local friends, and the servants; Sir Leopold sat in the front seat, his full and still fur-collared figure largely obscuring the view of the little cleric behind him; but it has never been settled by artistic authorities whether the cleric lost much. The pantomime was utterly chaotic, yet not contemptible; there ran through it a rage of improvisation which came chiefly from Crook the clown. Commonly he was a clever man, and he was inspired tonight with a wild omniscience, a folly wiser than the world, that which comes to a young man who has seen for an instant a particular expression on a particular face. He was supposed to be the clown, but he was really almost everything else, the author (so far as there was an author), the prompter, the scene-painter, the scene-shifter, and, above all, the orchestra. At abrupt intervals in the outrageous performance he would hurl himself in full costume at the piano and bang out some popular music equally absurd and appropriate.

The climax of this, as of all else, was the moment when the two front doors at the back of the scene flew open, showing the lovely moonlit garden, but showing more prominently the famous professional guest; the great Florian, dressed up as a policeman. The clown at the piano played the constabulary chorus in the "Pirates of Penzance", but it was drowned in the deafening applause, for every gesture of the great comic actor was an admirable though restrained version of the carriage and manner of the police. The harlequin leapt upon him and hit him over the helmet; the pianist playing "Where did you get that hat?" he faced about in admirably simulated astonishment, and then the leaping harlequin hit him again (the pianist suggesting a few bars of "Then we had another one"). Then the harlequin rushed right into the arms of the policeman and fell on top of him, amid a roar of applause. Then it was that the strange actor gave that celebrated imitation of a dead man, of which the fame still lingers round Putney. It was almost impossible to believe that a living person could appear so limp.

The athletic harlequin swung him about like a sack or twisted or tossed him like an Indian club; all the time to the most maddeningly ludicrous tunes from the piano. When the harlequin heaved the comic constable heavily off the floor the clown played "I arise from dreams of thee". When he shuffled him across his back, "With my bundle on my shoulder", and when the harlequin finally let fall the policeman with a most convincing thud, the lunatic at the instrument struck into a jingling measure with some words which are still believed to have been, "I sent a letter to my love and on the way I dropped it".

At about this limit of mental anarchy Father Brown's view was obscured altogether; for the City magnate in front of him rose to his full height and thrust his hands savagely into all his pockets. Then he sat down nervously, still fumbling, and then stood up again. For an instant it seemed seriously likely that he would stride across the footlights; then he turned a glare at the clown playing the piano; and then he burst in silence out of the room.

The priest had only watched for a few more minutes the absurd but not inelegant dance of the amateur harlequin over his splendidly unconscious foe. With real though rude art, the harlequin danced slowly backwards out of the door into the garden, which was full of moonlight and stillness. The vamped dress of silver paper and paste, which had been too glaring in the footlights, looked more and more magical and silvery as it danced away under a brilliant moon. The audience was closing in with a cataract of applause, when Brown felt his arm abruptly touched, and he was asked in a whisper to come into the colonel's study.

He followed his summoner with increasing doubt, which was not dispelled by a solemn comicality in the scene of the study. There sat Colonel Adams, still unaffectedly dressed as a pantaloon, with the knobbed whalebone nodding above his brow, but with his poor old eyes sad enough to have sobered a Saturnalia. Sir Leopold Fischer was leaning against the mantelpiece and heaving with all the importance of panic.

"This is a very painful matter, Father Brown," said Adams. "The truth is, those diamonds we all saw this afternoon seem to have vanished from my friend's tail-coat pocket. And as you——"

"As I," supplemented Father Brown, with a broad grin, "was sitting just behind him——"

"Nothing of the sort shall be suggested," said Colonel Adams, with a firm look at Fischer, which rather implied that some such thing *had* been suggested. "I only ask you to give me the assistance that any gentleman might give."

"Which is turning out his pockets," said Father Brown, and proceeded to do so, displaying seven and sixpence, a return ticket, a small silver crucifix, a small breviary, and a stick of chocolate.

The colonel looked at him long, and then said, "Do you know, I should like to see the inside of your head more than the inside of your pockets. My daughter is one of your people, I know; well, she has lately——" and he stopped.

"She has lately," cried out old Fischer, "opened her father's house to a cut-throat Socialist, who says openly he would steal anything from a richer man. This is the end of it. Here is the richer man—and none the richer."

"If you want the inside of my head you can have it," said Brown rather wearily. "What it's worth you can say afterwards. But the first thing I find in that disused pocket is this; that men who mean to steal diamonds don't talk Socialism. They are more likely," he added demurely, "to denounce it."

Both the others shifted sharply and the priest went on:

"You see, we know these people, more or less. That Socialist would no more steal a diamond than a pyramid. We ought to look at once to the one man we don't know. The fellow acting the policeman—Florian. Where is he exactly at this minute, I wonder."

The pantaloon sprang erect and strode out of the room. An interlude ensued, during which the millionaire stared at the priest, and the priest at his breviary; then the pantaloon returned and said, with *staccato* gravity, "The policeman is still lying on the stage. The curtain has gone up and down six times; he is still lying there."

Father Brown dropped his book and stood staring with a look of blank mental ruin. Very slowly a light began to creep back in his grey eyes, and then he made the scarcely obvious answer.

"Please forgive me, colonel, but when did your wife die?"

"My wife!" replied the staring soldier, "she died this year two months. Her brother James arrived just a week too late to see her."

The little priest bounded like a rabbit shot. "Come on!" he cried in quite unusual excitement. "Come on! We've got to go and look at that policeman!"

They rushed on to the now curtained stage, breaking rudely past the columbine and clown (who seemed whispering quite contentedly), and Father Brown bent over the prostrate comic policeman.

"Chloroform," he said as he rose; "I only guessed it just now."

There was a startled stillness, and then the colonel said slowly, "Please say seriously what all this means."

Father Brown suddenly shouted with laughter, then stopped, and only struggled with it for instants during the rest of his speech. "Gentlemen," he gasped, "there's not much time to talk. I must run after the criminal. But this great French actor who played the policeman—this clever corpse the harlequin waltzed with and dandled and threw about—he was——" His voice again failed him, and he turned his back to run.

"He was?" called Fischer inquiringly.

"A real policeman," said Father Brown, and ran away into the dark.

There were hollows and bowers at the extreme end of that leafy garden, in which the laurels and other immortal shrubs showed against sapphire sky and silver moon, even in that midwinter, warm colours as of the south. The green gaiety of the waving laurels, the rich purple indigo of the night, the moon like a monstrous crystal, make an almost irresponsibly romantic picture; and among the top branches of the garden trees a strange figure is climbing, who looks not so much romantic as impossible. He sparkles from head to heel, as if clad in ten million moons; the real moon catches him at every movement and sets a new inch of him on fire. But he swings, flashing and successful, from the short tree in this garden to the tall, rambling tree in the other, and only stops there because a shade has slid under the smaller tree and has unmistakably called up to him.

"Well, Flambeau," says the voice, "you really look like a Flying Star; but that always means a Falling Star at last."

The silver, sparkling figure above seems to lean forward in the laurels and, confident of escape, listens to the little figure below.

"You never did anything better, Flambeau. It was clever to come from Canada (with a Paris ticket, I suppose) just a week after Mrs Adams died, when no one was in a mood to ask questions. It was cleverer to have marked down the Flying Stars and the very day of Fischer's coming. But there's no cleverness, but mere genius, in what followed. Stealing the stones, I suppose, was nothing to you. You could have done it by sleight of hand in a hundred other ways besides that pretence of putting a paper donkey's tail to Fischer's coat. But in the rest you eclipsed yourself."

The silvery figure among the green leaves seems to linger as if hypnotized, though his escape is easy behind him; he is staring at the man below.

"Oh, yes," says the man below, "I know all about it. I know you not only forced the pantomime, but put it to a double use. You were going to steal the stones quietly; news came by an accomplice that you were already suspected, and a capable police officer was coming to rout you up that very night. A common thief would have been thankful for the warning and fled; but you are a poet. You already had the clever notion of hiding the jewels in a blaze of false stage jewellery. Now, you saw that if the dress were a harlequin's the appearance of a policeman would be quite in keeping. The worthy officer started from Putney police station to find you, and walked into the queerest trap ever set in this world. When the front door opened he walked straight on to the stage of a Christmas pantomime, where he could be kicked, clubbed, stunned, and drugged by the dancing harlequin, amid roars of laughter from all the most respectable people in Putney. Oh, you will never do anything better. And now, by the way, you might give me back those diamonds."

The green branch on which the glittering figure swung, rustled as if in astonishment; but the voice went on:

"I want you to give them back, Flambeau, and I want you to give up this life. There is still youth and honour and humour in you; don't fancy they will last in that trade. Men may keep a sort of level of good, but no man has ever been able to keep on one level of evil. That road goes down and down. The kind man drinks and turns cruel; the frank man kills and lies about it. Many a man I've known started like you to be an honest outlaw, a merry robber of the rich, and ended stamped into slime. Maurice Blum started out as an anarchist of principle, a father of the poor; he ended a greasy spy and tale-bearer that both sides used and despised. Harry Burke started his free money movement sincerely enough; now he's sponging on a half-starved sister for endless brandies and sodas. Lord Amber went into wild society in a sort of chivalry; now he's paying black-mail to the lowest vultures in London. Captain Barillon was the great gentleman-apache before your time; he died in a madhouse, screaming with fear of the "narks" and receivers that had betrayed him and hunted him down. I know the woods look very free behind you, Flambeau; I know that in a flash you could melt into them like a monkey. But some day you will be an old grey monkey, Flambeau. You will sit up in your free forest cold at heart and close to death, and the tree-tops will be very bare."

Everything continued still, as if the small man below held the other in the tree in some long invisible leash; and he went on:

"Your downward steps have begun. You used to boast of doing nothing mean, but you are doing something mean tonight. You are leaving suspicion on an honest boy with a good deal against him already; you are separating him from the woman he loves and who loves him. But you will do meaner things than that before you die."

Three flashing diamonds fell from the tree to the turf. The small man stooped to pick them up, and when he looked up again the green cage of the tree was emptied of its silver bird.

The restoration of the gems (accidentally picked up by Father Brown, of all people) ended the evening in uproarious triumph; and Sir Leopold, in his height of good humour, even told the priest that though he himself had broader views, he could respect those whose creed required them to be cloistered and ignorant of this world.

# STUFFING

## Edgar Wallace

Richard Horatio Edgar Wallace (1875–1932), the adopted son of a porter in Billingsgate Fish Market, was earning money by selling newspapers at Ludgate Circus at the age of eleven; this marked the start of a lifelong connection with the Press. After a spell in the army, he worked as a reporter in England and South Africa, and regarded it as a distinction that he was the first journalist ever to be dismissed by the *Daily Mail*.

A prolific novelist and playwright with a flair for enterprise and self-advertisement, Wallace was the leading thriller writer of his era. He made a fortune, and spent it freely, not least at the racetrack. He became chairman of British Lion Film Corporation, and stood unsuccessfully as a Liberal candidate for Parliament. Offered a script-writing contract in Hollywood, he moved to the United States, but there succumbed to double pneumonia. He was only fifty-six, but few people have packed quite so much into a single life.

\* \* \* \* \*

There are several people concerned in this story whom it is impossible within a limited space to describe. If you are on friendly terms with the great men of Scotland Yard you may inspect the photographs and fingerprints of two—Harry the Valet and Joe the Runner.

Lord Carfane's picture you can see at intervals in the best of the illustrated weeklies. He was once plain Ferdie Gooberry, before he became a contractor and supplied the army with odds and ends and himself with a fortune and a barony.

In no newspaper, illustrated or otherwise, do the names of John and Angela Willett appear. Their marriage at a small registrar's office had excited no public comment, although he was a BA of Cambridge and she was the grand-niece of Peter Elmer, the shipping magnate, who had acknowledged his relationship by dictating to her a very polite letter wishing her every happiness.

They lived in one furnished room in Pimlico, this good-looking couple, and they had the use of the kitchen. He was confident that he would one day be a great engineer. She also believed in miracles.

Three days before Christmas they sat down calmly to consider the problem of the great annual festival and how it might best be spent. Jack Willett scratched his cheek and did a lightning calculation.

"Really, we ought not to spend an unnecessary penny," he said dolefully. "We may be a week in Montreal before I start work, and we shall need a little money for the voyage."

They were leaving on Boxing Day for Canada; their berths had been taken. In Montreal a job was awaiting Jack in the office of an old college friend: and although twenty-five dollars' per did not exactly represent luxury, it was a start.

Angela looked at him thoughtfully.

"I am quite sure Uncle Peter is going to do something awfully nice for us," she said stoutly.

Jack's hollow laugh was not encouraging.

There was a tap at the door, and the unpleasant but smiling face of Joe the Runner appeared. He occupied an attic bedroom, and was a source of worry to his landlady. Once he had been in the newspaper business, running evening editions, and the name stuck to him. He had long ceased to be associated with the Press, save as a subject for its crime reporters, but this the Willetts did not know.

"Just thought I'd pop in and see you before I went, miss," he said. "I'm going off into the country to do a bit of work for a gentleman. About that dollar, miss, that you lent me last week."

Angela looked uncomfortable.

"Oh, please don't mention it," she said hastily.

"I haven't forgotten it," said Joe, nodding solemnly. "The minute I come back, I'll bring it to you." And with a large and sinister grin he vanished.

"I lent him the money because he couldn't pay his rent," said Angela penitently, but her husband waved her extravagance away.

"Let's talk about Christmas dinner. What about sausages...!"

"If Uncle Peter——" she began.

"Let's talk about sausages," said Jack gently.

Foodstuffs were also the topic of conversation between Lord Carfane and Prince Riminoff as they sat at lunch at the Ritz-Carlton. Lord Carfane emphasized his remarks with a very long cigar.

"I always keep up the old English custom of distributing food to the poor," he said. "Every family on my estate on Christmas Eve has a turkey from my farm. All my workers," he corrected himself carefully, "except old Timmins. Old Timmins has been very rude to me, and I have had to sack him. All the tenants assemble in the great hall ... But you'll see that for yourself, Prince."

Prince Riminoff nodded gravely and tugged at his short beard. That beard had taken Harry the Valet five months to grow, and it was so creditable a production that he had passed Chief Inspector Malling in the vestibule of the Ritz-Carlton and had not been recognized.

Very skilfully he switched the conversation into more profitable channels.

"I do hope, my dear Lord Carfane, that you have not betrayed my identity to your guests?"

Ferdie smiled.

"I am not quite a fool," he said, and meant it.

"A great deal of the jewellery that I am disposing of, and of which you have seen specimens, is not mine. I think I have made that clear. I am acting for several of my unfortunate compatriots, and frankly it would be embarrassing for me if it leaked out that I was the vendor."

Ferdie nodded. He suspected that a great deal of the property which he was to acquire had been secured by underhand means. He more than suspected that, for all his princely origin, his companion was not too honest.

"That is why I have asked that the money you pay should be in American currency. By the way, have you made that provision?" Lord Carfane nodded. "And, of course, I shall not ask you to pay a single dollar until you are satisfied that the property is worth what I ask. It is in fact worth three times as much."

Lord Carfane was nothing if not frank.

"Now, I'm going to tell you, my dear chap," he said, "there will only be one person at Carfane Hall who will know anything whatever about this little transaction of ours. He's an expert jeweller. He is an authority, and he will examine every piece and price it before I part with a single bob!"

His Highness heartily, but gravely, approved of this act of precaution.

Lord Carfane had met his companion a few weeks before in a highly respectable night club, the introduction having been effected through the medium of a very beautiful lady who had accidentally spilt a glass of champagne over his lordship's dress trousers. She was so lovely a personage that Lord Carfane did no more than smile graciously, and a few minutes later was introduced to her sedate and imposing presence.

Harry the Valet invariably secured his introductions by this method. Usually he worked with Molly Kien, and paid her a hundred pounds for every introduction.

He spoke no more of jewels smuggled from Russia and offered at ridiculous prices, but talked sorrowfully of the misfortunes of his country; spoke easily of his estates in the Crimea and his mines in the Urals, now, alas! in Bolshevik hands. Lord Carfane was immensely entertained.

On the following evening, Harry drove down in Lord Carfane's limousine to Berkshire, and was introduced to the glories of Carfane Hall; to the great banqueting chamber with its high-raftered roof; to the white-tiled larder where petrified turkeys hung in rows, each grisly corpse decorated with a gay rosette …

"My tenants come in on Christmas Eve," explained Lord Carfane, "and my butler presents each one with a turkey and a small bag of groceries—"

"An old feudal custom?" suggested the Prince gravely.

Lord Carfane agreed with equal gravity.

The Prince had brought with him a large, heavily locked and strapped handbag, which had been deposited in the safe, which was the most conspicuous feature of Ferdie's library. The expert jeweller was arriving on the morrow, and his lordship looked forward, with a sense of pleasurable anticipation, to a day which would yield him 400 per cent profit on a considerable outlay.

"Yes," said Ferdie at dinner that night, "I prefer a combination safe. One can lose keys, but not if they're here"—he tapped his narrow forehead and smiled.

Harry the Valet agreed. One of his greatest charms was his complete agreement with anything anybody said or did or thought.

Whilst he dwelt in luxury in the halls of the great, his unhappy confederate had a more painful task. Joe the Runner had collected from a garage a small, light trolley. It was not beautiful to look upon, but it was fast, and under its covered tilt, beneath sacks and amidst baskets, a man making a swift getaway might lie concealed and be carried to London without exciting attention.

Joe made a leisurely way into Berkshire and came to the rendez-vous at the precise minute he had been ordered. It was a narrow lane at the termination of a footpath leading across the Carfane estate to the house. It was a cold, blue-fingered, red nosed job, and for three hours he sat and shivered. And then, coming across the field in the blue dusk, he saw an old man staggering, carrying a rush basket in one hand and an indescribable something in the other. He was evidently in a hurry, this ancient. From time to time he looked back over his shoulder as though he expected pursuit. Breathlessly, he mounted the stile and fell over rather than surmounted it.

Stumbling to his feet, he saw Joe sitting at the wheel of the van, and gaped at him toothlessly, his eyes wide with horror. Joe the Runner recognized the signs.

"What have you been doin'?" he demanded sternly.

For a few minutes the breathless old man could not speak; blinked fearfully at his interrogator; and then:

"He's fired me," he croaked. "Wouldn't give me no turkey or nothin, so I went up to the 'All and pinched one."

"Oh!" said Joe judiciously.

It was not an unpleasant sensation, sitting in judgement on a fellow creature.

"There was such a bother and a fuss and shouting going on … what with the safe bein' found broke open, and that foreign man being caught, that nobody seed me," whimpered the elderly Mr Timmins.

"Eh?" said Joe. "What's that—safe broken open?"

The old man nodded.

"I heered 'em when I was hiding in the pantry. His lordship found that the safe had been opened an' money took. He sent for the constable, and they've got the prince locked up in a room, with the undergardener and the butler on guard outside the door——"

He looked down at the frozen turkey in his red, numbed hand; and his lips twitched pathetically.

"His lordship promised me a turkey and his lordship said I shouldn't have——"

Joe Runner was a quick thinker. "Jump up in the truck," he commanded roughly. "Where do you live?"

"About three miles from here," began Mr Timmins.

Joe leaned over, and pulled him up, parcel, bag and turkey.

"Get through into the back, and keep quiet."

He leapt down, cranked up the engine with some difficulty, and sent the little trolley lumbering on to the main road. When he passed three officers in a police car speeding towards Carfane Hall his heart was in his mouth, but he was not challenged. Presently, at the urgent desire of the old man, he stopped at the end of a row of cottages.

"Gawd bless you, mister!" whimpered Mr Timmins. "I'll never do a thing like this again——"

"Hi!" said Joe sternly. "What do I get out of this?"

And then, as the recollection of a debt came to him:

"Leave the turkey—and hop!"

Mr Timmins hopped.

It was nine o'clock on Christmas morning, and Angela Willett had just finished her packing.

Outside the skies were dark and cheerless, snow and rain were falling together, so that this tiny furnished room had almost a palatial atmosphere in comparison with the drear world outside.

"I suppose it's too early to cook the sausages—by the way, our train leaves at ten tonight, so we needn't invent ways of spending the evening—come in."

It was Joe the Runner, rather wet but smiling. He carried under his arm something wrapped in an old newspaper.

"Excuse me, miss," he said, as he removed the covering, "but a gent I met in the street asked me to give you this."

"A turkey!" gasped Angela. "How wonderful … who was it?"

"I don't know, miss—an old gentleman," said Joe vaguely. "He said 'Be sure an' give it to the young lady herself—wishin' her a happy Christmas'."

They gazed on the carcase in awe and ecstasy. As the front door slammed, announcing Joe's hasty departure:

"An old gentleman," said Angela slowly. "Uncle Peter!"

"Uncle grandmother!" smiled John. "I believe he stole it!"

"How uncharitable you are!" she reproached him. "It's the sort of thing Uncle Peter would do. He always had that Haroun al Raschid complex—I wrote and told him we were leaving for Canada tonight. I'm sure it was he."

Half-convinced, John Willett prodded at the bird. It seemed a little tough.

"Anyway, it's turkey," he said, "And, darling, I adore turkey stuffed with chestnuts. I wonder if there are any shops open——"

There was a large cavity at one end of the bird, and as he lifted the turkey up by the neck, the better to examine it, something dropped to the table with a flop. It was a tight roll of paper. He shook the bird again and a second fell from its unoffending body.

"Good God!" gasped John.

With trembling hands he cut the string that bound the roll——

"It's money!" she whispered.

John nodded.

"Hundred dollar bills … five hundred of them at least!" he said hollowly.

Their eyes met.

"Uncle Peter!" she breathed. "The darling!"

Mr Peter Elmer, the eminent shipowner, received the following day a telegram which was entirely meaningless:

Thank you a thousand times for your thought and generosity. You have given us a wonderful start and we shall be worthy of your splendid kindness.

It was signed "Angela". Mr Peter Elmer scratched his head.

And at that moment Inspector Malling was interrogating Harry the Valet in the little police station at Carfane.

"Now come across, Harry," he said kindly. "We know you got the money out of the safe. Where did you plant it? You couldn't have taken it far, because the butler saw you leaving the room. Just tell us where the money is, and I'll make it all right for you when you come up in front of the old man."

"I don't know what you're talking about," said Harry the Valet, game to the last.

# THE UNKNOWN MURDERER

## H.C. BAILEY

Henry Christopher Bailey (1878–1961) began his literary career writing historical novels with a romantic flavour, and later worked for many years as a journalist with the *Daily Telegraph*. In 1920, he published *Call Mr Fortune*, a book of short stories. They introduced Reggie Fortune, a doctor associated with the Home Office, whose cherubic appearance concealed a ruthless streak. Soon Fortune was regarded as one of British fiction's most notable detectives, although he did not appear in a full-length novel until more than a decade after his first appearance in print.

Agatha Christie was among Bailey's many admirers. She name-checked him in *The Body in the Library*, and had Tommy and Tuppence Beresford parody Reggie Fortune in "The Ambassador's Boots", included in her book *Partners in Crime*. Bailey's reputation went into a steep decline after the Second World War, in part because his style of writing began to seem very dated. But he was a distinctive writer who dared to be different, and his best stories remain memorable.

\*     \*     \*     \*     \*

Once upon a time a number of men in a club discussed how Mr Reginald Fortune came to be the expert adviser of the Home Office upon crime. The doctors admitted that though he is a competent surgeon, pathologist and what not, he never showed international form. There was a Fellow of the Royal Society who urged that Fortune knew more about natural science than most schoolboys, politicians and civil servants. An artist said he had been told Fortune understood business, and his banker believed Fortune was a judge of old furniture. But they all agreed that he is a jolly good fellow. Which means, being interpreted, he can be all things to all men.

Mr Fortune himself is convinced that he was meant by Providence to be a general practitioner: to attend to my lumbago and your daughter's measles. He has been heard to complain of the chance that has made him, knowing something of everything, nothing completely, into a specialist. His only qualification, he will tell you, is that he doesn't get muddled.

There you have it, then. He is singularly sensitive to people. "Very odd how he knows men," said Superintendent Bell reverently. "As if he had an extra sense to tell him of people's souls, like smells or colours." And he has a clear head. He is never confused about what is important and what isn't, and he has never been known to hesitate in doing what is necessary.

Consider his dealing with the affair of the unknown murderer.

There was not much interesting crime that Christmas. The singular case of Sir Humphrey Bigod, who was found dead in a chalkpit on the eve of his marriage, therefore obtained a lot of space in the papers, which kept it up, even after the coroner's jury had declared for death by misadventure, with irrelevant inventions and bloodthirsty hints of murder and tales of clues. This did not disturb the peace of the scientific adviser to the Criminal Investigation Department, who knew that the lad was killed by a fall and that there was no means of knowing any more. Mr Fortune was much occupied in being happy, for after long endeavour he had engaged Joan Amber to marry him. The lady has said the endeavour was hers, but I am not now telling that story. Just after Christmas she took him to the children's party at the Home of Help.

It is an old-fashioned orphanage, a huge barrack of a building, but homely and kind. Time out of mind people of all sorts, with old titles and new, with money and with brains, have been the friends of its children. When Miss Amber brought Reggie Fortune under the flags and the strings of paper roses into its hall, which was as noisy as the parrot house, he gasped slightly. "Be brave, child," she said. "This is quiet to what it will be after tea. And cool. You will be much hotter. You don't know how hot you'll be."

"Woman, you have deceived me," said Mr Fortune bitterly. "I thought philanthropists were respectable."

"Yes, dear. Don't be frightened. You're only a philanthropist for the afternoon."

"I ask you. Is that Crab Warnham?"

"Of course it's Captain Warnham." Miss Amber smiled beautifully at a gaunt man with a face like an old jockey. He flushed as he leered back. "Do you know his wife? She's rather precious."

"Poor woman. He doesn't look comfortable here, does he? The last time I saw Crab Warnham was in a place that's several kinds of hell in Berlin. He was quite at home there."

"Forget it," said Miss Amber gently. "You will when you meet his wife. And their boy's a darling."

"His boy?" Reggie was startled.

"Oh, no. She was a widow. He worships her and the child."

Reggie said nothing. It appeared to him that Captain Warnham, for a man who worshipped his wife, had a hungry eye on women. And the next moment Captain Warnham was called to attention. A small woman, still pretty though earnest, talked to him like a mother or a commanding officer. He was embarrassed, and when she had done with him he fled.

The small woman, who was austerely but daintily clad in black with some white at the neck, continued to flit among the company, finding everyone a job of work. "She says to one, Go, and he goeth, and to another, Come, and he cometh. And who is she, Joan?"

"Lady Chantry," said Miss Amber. "She's Providence here, you know."

And Lady Chantry was upon them. Reggie found himself looking down into a pair of uncommonly bright eyes and wondering what it felt like to be as strenuous as the little woman who was congratulating him on Joan, thanking him for being there and arranging his afternoon for him all in one breath. He had never heard anyone talk so fast. In a condition of stupor he saw Joan reft from him to tell the story of Cinderella to magic lantern pictures in one dormitory, while he was led to another to help in a scratch concert. And as the door closed on him he heard the swift clear voice of Lady Chantry exhorting staff and visitors to play round games.

He suffered. People who had no voices sang showy songs, people who had too much voice sang ragtime to those solemn, respectful children. In pity for the children and himself he set up as a conjurer, and the dormitory was growing merry when a shriek cut into his patter. "That's only my bones creaking," he went on quickly, for the children were frightened; "they always do that when I put the knife in at the ear and take it out of my hind leg. So. But it doesn't hurt. As the motor-car said when it ran over the policeman's feet. All done by kindness. Come here, Jenny Wren. You mustn't use your nose as a money-box." A small person submitted to have pennies taken out of her face.

The door opened and a pallid nurse said faintly: "The doctor. Are you the doctor?"

"Of course," said Reggie. "One moment, people. Mr Punch has fallen over the baby. It always hurts him. In the hump. Are we downhearted? No. Pack up your troubles in the old kit bag——" He went out to a joyful roar of that lyric. "What's the trouble?" The nurse was shaking.

"In there, sir—she's up there."

Reggie went up the stairs in quick time. The door of a little sitting-room stood open. Inside it people were staring at a woman who sat at her desk. Her dress was dark and wet. Her head lolled forward. A deep gash ran across her throat.

"Yes. There's too many of us here," he said, and waved the spectators away. One lingered, an old woman, large and imposing, and announced that she was the matron. Reggie shut the door and came back to the body in the chair. He held the limp hands a moment, he lifted the head and looked close into the flaccid face. "When was she found? When I heard that scream? Yes." He examined the floor. "Quite so." He turned to the matron. "Well, well. Who is she?"

"It's our resident medical officer, Dr Emily Hall. But Dr Fortune, can't you do anything?"

"She's gone," said Reggie.

"But this is terrible, doctor. What does it mean?"

"Well, I don't know what it means. Her throat was cut by a highly efficient knife, probably from behind. She lingered a little while quite helpless, and died. Not so very long ago. Who screamed?"

"The nurse who found her. One of our own girls, Dr Fortune, Edith Baker. She was always a favourite of poor Dr Hall's. She has been kept on here at Dr Hall's wish to train as a nurse. She was devoted to Dr Hall. One of these girlish passions."

"And she came into the room and found—this—and screamed?"

"So she tells me," said the matron.

"Well, well," Reggie sighed. "Poor kiddies! And now you must send for the police."

"I have given instructions, Dr Fortune," said the matron with dignity.

"And I think you ought to keep Edith Baker from talking about it." Reggie opened the door.

"Edith will not talk," said the matron coldly. "She is a very reserved creature."

"Poor thing. But I'm afraid some of our visitors will. And they had better not, you know." At last he got rid of the lady and turned the key in the lock and stood looking at it. "Yes, quite natural, but very convenient," said he, and turned away from it and contemplated a big easy chair. The loose cushion on the seat showed that somebody had been sitting in it, a fact not in itself remarkable. But there was a tiny smear of blood on the arm still wet. He picked up the cushion. On the under side was a larger smear of blood. Mr Fortune's brow contracted. "The unknown murderer cuts her throat—comes over here—makes a mess on the chair—turns the cushion over—and sits down—to watch the woman die. This is rather diabolical." He began to wander round the room. It offered him no other signs but some drops of blood on the hearthrug and the hearth. He knelt down and peered into the fire, and with the tongs drew from it a thin piece of metal. It was a surgical knife. He looked at the dead woman. "From your hospital equipment, Dr Hall. And Edith Baker is a nurse. And Edith Baker had 'a girlish passion' for you. I wonder."

Some one was trying the door. He unlocked it, to find an inspector of police. "I am Reginald Fortune," he explained. "Here's your case."

"I've heard of you, sir," said the inspector reverently. "Bad business, isn't it? I'm sure it's very lucky you were here."

"I wonder," Reggie murmured.

"Could it be suicide, sir?"

Reggie shook his head. "I wish it could. Not a nice murder. Not at all a nice murder. By the way, there's the knife. I picked it out of the fire."

"Doctor's tool, isn't it, sir? Have you got any theory about it?" Reggie shook his head. "There's the girl who gave the alarm: she's a nurse in the hospital, I'm told."

"I don't know the girl," said Reggie. "You'd better see what you make of the room. I shall be downstairs."

In the big hall the decorations and the Christmas tree with its ungiven presents glowed to emptiness and silence. Joan Amber came forward to meet him. He did not speak to her. He continued to stare at the ungiven presents on the Christmas tree. "What do you want to do?" she said at last.

"This is the end of a perfect day," said Mr Fortune. "Poor kiddies."

"The matron packed them all off to their dormitories."

Mr Fortune laughed. "Just as well to rub it in, isn't it?"

Miss Amber did not answer him for a moment. "Do you know, you look rather terrible?" she said, and indeed his normally plump, fresh-coloured, cheery face had a certain ferocity.

"I feel like a fool, Joan. Where is everybody?"

"She sent everybody away too."

"She would. Great organizer. No brain. My only aunt! A woman's murdered and every stranger who was in the place is hustled off before the police get to work. This isn't a crime, it's a nightmare."

"Well, of course they were anxious to go."

"They would be."

"Reggie, who are you thinking of?"

"I can't think. There are no facts. Where's this matron now?"

The inspector came upon them as they were going to her room. "I've finished upstairs, sir. Not much for me, is there? Plenty downstairs, though. I reckon I'll hear some queer stories before I've done. These homes are always full of gossip. People living too close together, wonderful what bad blood it makes. I——" He broke off and stared at Reggie. From the matron's room came the sound of sobbing. He opened the door without a knock.

The matron sat at her writing-table, coldly judicial. A girl in nurse's uniform was crying on the bosom of Lady Chantry, who caressed her and murmured in her ear.

"Sorry to interrupt, ma'am," the inspector said, staring hard.

"You don't interrupt. This girl is Edith Baker, who seems to have been the last person who saw Dr Hall alive and was certainly the first person who saw her dead."

"And who was very, very fond of her," Lady Chantry said gently. "Weren't you, dear?"

"I'll have to take her statement," said the inspector. But the girl was torn with sobbing.

"Come, dear, come." Lady Chantry strove with her. "The Inspector only wants you to say how you left her and how you found her."

"Edith, you must control yourself." The matron lifted her voice.

"I hate you," the girl cried, and tore herself away and rushed out of the room.

"She'll have to speak, you know, ma'am," the inspector said.

"I am very sorry to say she has always had a passionate temperament," said the matron.

"Poor child!" Lady Chantry rose. "She was so fond of the doctor, you see. I'll go to her, matron, and see what I can do."

"Does anyone here know what the girl was up to this afternoon, ma'am?" said the inspector.

"I will try to find out for you," said the matron, and rang her bell.

"Well, well," said Reggie Fortune. "Every little helps. You might find out what all the other people were doing this afternoon."

The matron stared at him. "Surely you're not thinking of the visitors, Mr Fortune?"

"I'm thinking of your children," said Reggie, and she was the more amazed. "Not a nice murder, you know, not at all a nice murder."

And then he took Miss Amber home. She found him taciturn, which is his habit when he is angry. But she had never seen him angry before. She is a wise woman. When he was leaving her:

"Do you know what it is about you, sir?" she said. "You're always just right."

When the Hon. Sidney Lomas came to his room in Scotland Yard the next morning, Reggie Fortune was waiting for him. "My dear fellow!" he protested. "What is this? You're not really up, are you? It's not eleven. You're an hallucination."

"Zeal, all zeal, Lomas. The orphanage murder is my trouble."

"Have you come to give yourself up? I suspected you from the first, Fortune. Where is it?" He took a copy of the "Daily Wire" from the rack. "Yes. 'Dr Reginald Fortune, the eminent surgeon, was attending the function and was able to give the police a first-hand account of the crime. Dr Fortune states that the weapon used was a surgical knife.' My dear fellow, the case looks black indeed."

Reggie was not amused. "Yes. I also was present. And several others," he said. "Do you know anything about any of us?"

Lomas put up his eyeglass. "There's a certain bitterness about you, Fortune. This is unusual. What's the matter?"

"I don't like this murder," said Reggie. "It spoilt the children's party."

"That would be a by-product," Lomas agreed. "You're getting very domestic in your emotions. Oh, I like it, my dear fellow. But it makes you a little irrelevant."

"Domestic be damned. I'm highly relevant. It spoilt the children's party. Why did it happen at the children's party? Lots of other nice days to kill the resident medical officer."

"You're suggesting it was one of the visitors?"

"No, no. It isn't the only day visitors visit. I'm suggesting life is real, life is earnest—and rather diabolical sometimes."

"I'll call for the reports," Lomas said, and did so. "Good Gad! Reams! Barton's put in some heavy work."

"I thought he would," said Reggie, and went to read over Lomas' shoulder.

At the end Lomas lay back and looked up at him. "Well? Barton's put his money on this young nurse, Edith Baker."

"Yes. That's the matron's tip. I saw the matron. One of the world's organizers, Lomas. A place for everything and everything in its place. And if you don't fit, God help you. Edith Baker didn't fit. Edith Baker has emotions. Therefore she does murders. Q.E.D."

"Well, the matron ought to know the girl."

"She ought," Reggie agreed. "And our case is, gentlemen, that the matron who ought to know girls says Edith Baker isn't a nice young person. Lomas dear, why do policemen always believe what they're told? What the matron don't like isn't evidence."

"There is some evidence. The girl had one of these hysterical affections for the dead woman, passionately devoted and passionately jealous and so forth. The girl had access to the hospital instruments. All her time in the afternoon can't be accounted for, and she was the first to know of the murder."

"It's not good enough, Lomas. Why did she give the alarm?"

Lomas shrugged. "A murderer does now and then. Cunning or fright."

"And why did she wait for the children's party to do the murder?"

"Something may have happened there to rouse her jealousy."

"Something with one of the visitors?" Reggie suggested. "I wonder." And then he laughed. "A party of the visitors went round the hospital, Lomas. They had access to the surgical instruments."

"And were suddenly seized with a desire for homicide? They also went to the gymnasium and the kitchen. Did any of them start boiling potatoes? My dear Fortune, you are not as plausible as usual."

"It isn't plausible," Reggie said. "I know that. It's too dam' wicked."

"Abnormal," Lomas nodded. "Of course the essence of the thing is that it's abnormal. Every once in a while we have these murders in an orphanage or school or some place where women and children are herded together. Nine times out of ten they are cases of hysteria. Your young friend Miss Baker seems to be a highly hysterical subject."

"You know more than I do."

"Why, that's in the evidence. And you saw her yourself half crazy with emotion after the murder."

"Good Lord!" said Reggie. "Lomas, old thing, you do run on. Pantin' time toils after you in vain. That girl wasn't crazy. She was the most natural of us all. You send a girl in her teens into the room where the woman she is keen on is sitting with her throat cut. She won't talk to you like a little lady. The evidence! Why do you believe what people tell you about people? They're always lying—by accident if not on purpose. This matron don't like the girl because she worshipped the lady doctor. Therefore the girl is called abnormal and jealous. Did you never hear of a girl in her teens worshipping a teacher? It's common form. Did you never hear of another teacher being vicious about it? That's just as common."

"Do you mean the matron was jealous of them both?"

Reggie shrugged. "It hits you in the eye."

"Good Gad!" said Lomas. "Do you suspect the matron?"

"I suspect the devil," said Reggie gravely. "Lomas, my child, whoever did that murder cut the woman's throat and then sat down in her easy chair and watched her die. I call that devilish." And he told of the bloodstains and the turned cushions.

"Good Gad," said Lomas once more, "there's some hate in that."

"Not a nice murder. Also it stopped the children's party."

"You harp on that." Lomas looked at him curiously. "Are you thinking of the visitors?"

"I wonder," Reggie murmured. "I wonder."

"Here's the list," Lomas said, and Reggie came slowly to look. "Sir George and Lady Bean, Lady Chantry, Mrs Carroway"—he ran his pencil down—"all well-known, blameless busybodies, full of good works. Nothing doing."

"Crab Warnham," said Reggie.

"Oh, Warnham: his wife took him, I suppose. She's a saint, and he eats out of her hand, they say. Well, he was a loose fish, of course, but murder! I don't see Warnham at that."

"He has an eye for a woman."

"Still? I dare say. But good Gad, he can't have known this lady doctor. Was she pretty?" Reggie nodded. "Well, we might look for a link between them. Not likely, is it?"

"We're catching at straws," said Reggie sombrely.

Lomas pushed the papers away. "Confound it, it's another case without evidence. I suppose it can't be suicide like that Bigod affair?"

Reggie, who was lighting a cigar, looked up and let the match burn his fingers. "Not suicide. No," he said. "Was Bigod's?"

"Well, it was a deuced queer death by misadventure."

"As you say." Reggie nodded and wandered dreamily out.

This seems to have been the first time that anyone thought of comparing the Bigod case to the orphanage murder. When the inquest on the lady doctor was held the police had no more evidence to produce than you have heard, and the jury returned a verdict of murder by some person or persons unknown. Newspapers strove to enliven the dull calm of the holiday season by declaiming against the inefficiency of a police force which allowed murderers to remain anonymous, and hashed up the Bigod case again to prove that the fall of Sir Humphrey Bigod into his chalkpit, though called accidental, was just as mysterious as the cut throat of Dr Hall. And the Hon. Sidney Lomas cursed the man who invented printing.

These assaults certainly did not disturb Reggie Fortune, who has never cared what people say of him. With the help of Joan Amber he found a quiet remote place for the unhappy girl suspected of the murder (Lady Chantry was prettily angry with Miss Amber about that, protesting that she wanted to look after Edith herself), and said he was only in the case as a philanthropist. After which he gave all his time to preparing his house and Miss Amber for married life. But the lady found him dreamy.

It was in fact while he was showing her how the new colours in the drawing-room looked under the new lighting that Dr Eden called him up. Dr Eden has a general practice in Kensington. Dr Eden wanted to consult him about a case: most urgent: 3 King William's Walk.

"May I take the car?" said Reggie to Joan. "He sounds rattled. You can go on home afterwards. It's not far from you either. I wonder who lives at 3 King William's Walk."

"But it's Mrs Warnham!" she cried.

"Oh, my aunt!" said Reggie Fortune; and said no more.

And Joan Amber did not call him out of his thoughts. She was as grave as he. Only when he was getting out of the car, "Be good to her, dear," she said gently. He kissed the hand on his arm.

The door was opened by a woman in evening-dress. "It is Mr Fortune, isn't it? Please come in. It's so kind of you to come." She turned to the maid in the background. "Tell Dr Eden, Maggie. It's my little boy—and we are so anxious."

"I'm very sorry, Mrs Warnham." Reggie took her hand and found it cold. The face he remembered for its gentle calm was sternly set. "What is the trouble?"

"Gerald went to a party this afternoon. He came home gloriously happy and went to bed. He didn't go to sleep at once, he was rather excited, but he was quite well. Then he woke up crying with pain and was very sick. I sent for Dr Eden. It isn't like Gerald to cry, Mr Fortune. And——"

A hoarse voice said "Catherine, you oughtn't to be out there in the cold." Reggie saw the gaunt face of Captain Warnham looking round a door at them.

"What does it matter?" she cried. "Dr Eden doesn't want me to be with him, Mr Fortune. He is still in pain. And I don't think Dr Eden knows."

Dr Eden came down in time to hear that. A large young man, he stood over them looking very awkward and uncomfortable.

"I'm sure Dr Eden has done everything that can be done," said Reggie gently. "I'll go up, please." And they left the mother to her husband, that flushed, gaunt face peering round the corner as they kept step on the stairs.

"The child's seven years old," said Eden. "There's no history of any gastric trouble. Rather a good digestion. And then this—out of the blue!"

Reggie went into a nursery where a small boy lay huddled and restless with all the apparatus of sickness by his bed. He raised a pale face on which beads of sweat stood.

"Hallo, Gerald," Reggie said quietly. "Mother sent me up to make you all right again." He took the child's hand and felt for the pulse. "I'm Mr Fortune, your fortune, good fortune." The child tried to smile and Reggie's hands moved over the uneasy body and all the while he murmured softly nonsense talk. ...

The child did not want him to go, but at last he went off with Eden into a corner of the room. "Quite right to send for me," he said gravely, and Eden put his hand to his head. "I know. I know. It's horrible when it's a child. One of the irritant poisons. Probably arsenic. Have you given an emetic?"

"He's been very sick. And he's so weak."

"I know. Have you got anything with you?"

"I sent home. But I didn't care to——"

"I'll do it. Sulphate of zinc. You go and send for a nurse. And find some safe milk. I wouldn't use the household stuff."

"My God, Fortune! Surely it was at the party?"

"Not the household stuff," Reggie repeated, and he went back to the child…

It was many hours afterwards that he came softly downstairs. In the hall husband and wife met him. It seemed to him that it was the man who had been crying. "Are you going away?" Mrs Warnham said.

"There's no more pain. He is asleep."

Her eyes darkened. "You mean he's—dead?" the man gasped.

"I hope he'll live longer than any of us, Captain Warnham. But no one must disturb him. The nurse will be watching, you know. And I'm sure we all want to sleep sound—don't we?" He was gone. But he stayed a moment on the doorstep. He heard emotions within.

On the next afternoon Dr Eden came into his laboratory at St Saviour's. "One moment. One moment." Reggie was bent over a notebook. "When I go to hell they'll set me doing sums." He frowned at his figures. "The third time is lucky. That's plausible if it isn't right. Well, how's our large patient?"

"He's doing well. Quite easy and cheerful."

Reggie stood up. "I think we might say, Thank God."

"Yes, rather. I thought he was gone last night, Fortune. He would have been without you. It was wonderful how he bucked up in your hands. You ought to have been a children's specialist."

"My dear chap! Oh, my dear chap! I'm the kind of fellow who would always ought to have been something else. And so I'm doing sums in a laboratory which God knows I'm not fit for."

"Have you found out what it was?"

"Oh, arsenic, of course. Quite a fair dose he must have had. It's queer how they always will use arsenic."

Eden stared at him. "What are we to do?" he said in a low voice. "Fortune, I suppose it couldn't have been accidental?"

"What is a child likely to eat in which he would find grains of accidental arsenic?"

"Yes, but then——I mean, who could want to kill that child?"

"That is the unknown quantity in the equation. But people do want to murder children, quite nice children."

Eden grew pale. "What do you mean? You know he's not Warnham's child. Warnham's his step-father."

"Yes. Yes. Have you ever seen the two together?"

Eden hesitated. "He—well he didn't seem to take to Warnham. But I'd have sworn Warnham was fond of him."

"And that's all quite natural, isn't it? Well, well. I hope he's in."

"What do you mean to do?"

"Tell Mrs Warnham—with her husband listening."

Dr Eden followed him out like a man going to be hanged.

Mrs Warnham indeed met them in her hall. "Mr Fortune"—she took his hand, she had won back her old calm, but her eyes grew dark as she looked at him—"Gerald has been asking for you. And I want to speak to you."

"I shall be glad to talk over the case with you and Captain Warnham," said Reggie gravely. "I'll see the small boy first, if you don't mind." And the small boy kept his Mr Fortune a long time.

Mrs Warnham had her husband with her when the doctors came down. "I say, Fortune," Captain Warnham started up, "awfully good of you to take so much trouble. I mean to say"—he cleared his throat—"I feel it, you know. How is the little beggar?"

"There's no reason why he shouldn't do well," Reggie said slowly. "But it's a strange case, Captain Warnham. Yes, a strange case. You may take it, there is no doubt the child was poisoned."

"Poisoned!" Warnham cried out in that queer hoarse voice.

"You mean it was something Gerald shouldn't have eaten?" Mrs Warnham said gently.

"It was arsenic, Captain Warnham. Not much more than an hour before the time he felt ill, perhaps less, he had swallowed enough arsenic to kill him."

"I say, are you certain of all that? I mean to say, no doubt about anything?" Warnham was flushed. "Arsenic—and the time—and the dose? It's pretty thick, you know."

"There is no doubt. I have found arsenic. I can estimate the dose. And arsenic acts within that time."

"But I can't believe it," Mrs Warnham said. "It would be too horribly cruel. Mr Fortune, couldn't it have been accident? Something in his food?"

"It was certainly in his food or drink. But not accident, Mrs Warnham. That is not possible."

"I say, let's have it all out, Fortune," Warnham growled. "Do you suspect anyone?"

"That's rather for you, isn't it?" said Reggie.

"Who could want to poison Gerald?" Mrs Warnham cried.

"He says some one did," Warnham growled.

"When do you suppose he took the stuff, Fortune? At the party or after he came home?"

"What did he have when he came home?"

Warnham looked at his wife. "Only a little milk. He wouldn't eat anything," she said. "And I tasted his milk, I remember. It was quite nice."

"That points to the party," Eden said.

"But I can't believe it. Who could want to poison Gerald?"

"I've seen some of the people who were there," Eden frowned. "I don't believe there's another child ill. Only this one of the whole party."

"Yes. Yes. A strange case," said Reggie. "Was there anyone there with a grudge against you, Mrs Warnham?"

"I don't think there's anyone with a grudge against me in the world."

"I don't believe there is, Catherine," her husband looked at her. "But damn it, Fortune found the stuff in the child. I say, Fortune, what do you advise?"

"You're sure of your own household? There's nobody here jealous of the child?"

Mrs Warnham looked her distress. "I couldn't, I couldn't doubt anybody. There isn't any reason. You know, it doesn't seem real."

"And there it is," Warnham growled.

"Yes. Well, I shouldn't talk about it, you know. When he's up again take him right away, somewhere quiet. You'll live with him yourself, of course. That's all safe. And I—well, I shan't forget the case. Good-bye."

"Oh, Mr Fortune——" she started up and caught his hands.

"Yes, yes, good-bye," said Reggie, and got away. But as Warnham let them out he felt Warnham's lean hand grip into his arm.

"A little homely comfort would be grateful," Reggie murmured. "Come and have tea at the Academies, Eden. They keep a pleasing muffin." He sank down in his car at Eden's side with a happy sigh.

But Eden's brow was troubled. "Do you think the child will be safe now, Fortune?" he said.

"Oh, I think so. If it was Warnham or Mrs Warnham who poisoned him——"

"Good Lord! You don't think that?"

"They are frightened," said Reggie placidly. "I frightened 'em quite a lot. And if it was somebody else—the child is going away and Mrs Warnham will be eating and drinking everything he eats and drinks. The small Gerald will be all right. There remains only the little problem, who was it?"

"It's a diabolical affair. Who could want to kill that child?"

"Diabolical is the word," Reggie agreed. "And a little simple food is what we need," and they went into the club and through a long tea he talked to Eden of rock gardens and Chinese nursery rhymes.

But when Eden, somewhat dazed by his appetite and the variety of his conversation, was gone, he made for that corner of the club where Lomas sat drinking tea made in the Russian manner. He pointed a finger at the clear weak fluid. " 'It was sad and bad and mad' and it was not even sweet," he complained. "Take care, Lomas. Think what's happened to Russia. You would never be happy as a Bolshevik."

"I understand that the detective police force is the one institution which has survived in Russia."

"Put down that repulsive concoction and come and take the air."

Lomas stared at him in horror. "Where's your young lady? I thought you were walking out. You're a faithless fellow, Fortune. Go and walk like a little gentleman." But there was that in Reggie's eye which made him get up with a groan. "You're the most ruthless man I know."

The car moved away from the club and Reggie shrank under his rug as the January east wind met them. "I hope you are cold," said Lomas. "What is it now?"

"It was nearly another anonymous murder," and Reggie told him the story.

"Diabolical," said Lomas.

"Yes, I believe in the devil," Reggie nodded.

"Who stood to gain by the child's death? It's clear enough. There's only Warnham. Mrs Warnham was left a rich woman when her first husband died, old Staveleigh. Every one knew that was why Warnham was after her. But the bulk of the fortune would go to the child. So he took the necessary action. Good Gad! We all knew Crab Warnham didn't stick at a trifle. But this——! Cold-blooded scoundrel. Can you make a case of it?"

"I like you, Lomas. You're so natural," Reggie said. "That's all quite clear. And it's all wrong. This case isn't natural, you see. It hath a devil."

"Do you mean to say it wasn't Warnham?"

"It wasn't Warnham. I tried to frighten him. He was frightened. But not for himself. Because the child has an enemy and he doesn't know who it is."

"Oh, my dear fellow! He's not a murderer because you like his face."

"Who could like his face? No. The poison was given at the party where Warnham wasn't."

"But why? What possible motive? Some homicidal lunatic goes to a Kensington children's party and picks out this one child to poison. Not very credible, is it?"

"No, it's diabolical. I didn't say a lunatic. When you tell me what lunacy is, we'll discuss whether the poisoner was sane. But the diabolical is getting a little too common, Lomas. There was Bigod: young, healthy, well off, just engaged to a jolly girl. He falls into a chalkpit and the jury says it was misadventure. There was the lady doctor: young, clean-living, not a ghost of a past, everybody liking her. She is murdered and a girl who was very fond of her nearly goes mad over it. Now there's the small Gerald: a dear kid, his mother worships him, his step-father's mighty keen on him, everybody likes him. Somebody tries to poison him and nearly brings it off."

"What are you arguing, Fortune? It's odd the cases should follow one another. It's deuced awkward we can't clean them up. But what then? They're not really related. The people are unconnected. There's a different method of murder—if the Bigod case was murder. The only common feature is that the man who attempted murder is not known."

"You think so? Well, well. What I want to know is, was there any one at Mrs Lawley's party in Kensington who was also at the Home of Help party and also staying somewhere near the chalkpit when Bigod fell into it. Put your men on to that."

"Good Gad!" said Lomas. "But the cases are not comparable—not in the same class. Different method—different kind of victim. What motive could any creature have for picking out just these three to kill?"

Reggie looked at him. "Not nice murders, are they?" he said. "I could guess—and I dare say we'll only guess in the end."

That night he was taking Miss Amber, poor girl, to a state dinner of his relations. They had ten minutes together before the horrors of the ceremony began and she was benign to him about the recovery of the small Gerald. "It was dear of you to ring up and tell me. I love Gerry. Poor Mrs Warnham! I just had to go round to her and she was sweet. But she has been frightened. You're rather a wonderful person, sir. I didn't know you were a children's doctor—as well as a million other things. What was the matter? Mrs Warnham didn't tell us. It must——"

"Who are 'us,' Joan?"

"Why, Lady Chantry was with her. She didn't tell us what it really was. After we came away Lady Chantry asked me if I knew."

"But I'm afraid you don't," Reggie said. "Joan, I don't want you to talk about the small Gerry? Do you mind?"

"My dear, of course not." Her eyes grew bigger. "But Reggie—the boy's going to be all right?"

"Yes. Yes. You're rather a dear, you know."

And at the dinner-table which then received them his family found him of an unwonted solemnity. It was agreed, with surprise and reluctance, that his engagement had improved him: that there might be some merit in Miss Amber after all.

A week went by. He had been separated from Miss Amber for one long afternoon to give evidence in the case of the illegitimate Pekinese when she rang him up on the telephone. Lady Chantry, she said, had asked her to choose a day and bring Mr Fortune to dine. Lady Chantry did so want to know him.

"Does she, though?" said Mr Fortune.

"She was so nice about it," said the telephone. "And she really is a good sort, Reggie. She's always doing something kind."

"Joan," said Mr Fortune, "you're not to go into her house."

"Reggie!" said the telephone.

"That's that," said Mr Fortune. "I'll speak to Lady Chantry."

Lady Chantry was at home. She sat in her austere pleasant drawing-room, toasting a foot at the fire, a small foot which brought out a pretty leg. Of course she was in black with some white about her neck, but the loose gown had grace. She smiled at him and tossed back her hair. Not a thread of white showed in its crisp brown and it occurred to Reggie that he had never seen a woman of her age carry off bobbed hair so well. What was her age? Her eyes were as bright as a bird's and her clear pallor was unfurrowed.

"So good of you, Mr Fortune——"

"Miss Amber has just told me——"

They spoke together. She got the lead then. "It was kind of her to let you know at once. But she's always kind, isn't she? I did so want you to come, and make friends with me before you're married, and it will be very soon now, won't it? Oh, but do let me give you some tea."

"No tea, thank you."

"Won't you? Well, please ring the bell. I don't know how men can exist without tea. But most of them don't now, do they? You're almost unique, you know. I suppose it's the penalty of greatness."

"I came round to say that Miss Amber won't be able to dine with you, Lady Chantry."

It was a moment before she answered. "But that is too bad. She told me she was sure you could find a day."

"She can't come," said Reggie sharply.

"The man has spoken," she laughed. "Oh, of course, she mustn't go behind that." He was given a keen mocking glance. "And can't you come either, Mr Fortune?"

"I have a great deal of work, Lady Chantry. It's come rather unexpectedly."

"Indeed, you do look worried. I'm so sorry. I'm sure you ought to take a rest, a long rest." A servant came in. "Won't you really have some tea?"

"No, thank you. Good-bye, Lady Chantry."

He went home and rang up Lomas. Lomas, like the father of Baby Bunting, had gone a-hunting. Lomas was in Leicestershire. Superintendent Bell replied: Did Bell know if they had anything new about the unknown murderer?

"Inquiries are proceeding, sir," said Superintendent Bell.

"Damn it, Bell, I'm not the House of Commons. Have you got anything?"

"Not what you'd call definite, sir, no."

"You'll say that on the Day of Judgement," said Reggie.

It was on the next day that he found a telegram waiting for him when he came home to dress for dinner:

Gerald ill again very anxious beg you will come sending car to meet evening trains.

Warnham
Fernhurst
Blackover.

He scrambled into the last carriage of the half-past six as it drew out of Waterloo.

Mrs Warnham had faithfully obeyed his orders to take Gerald to a quiet place. Blackover stands an equally uncomfortable distance from two main lines, one of which throws out towards it a feeble and spasmodic branch. After two changes Reggie arrived, cold and with a railway sandwich rattling in his emptiness, on the dimly lit platform of Blackover. The porter of all work who took his ticket thought there was a car outside.

In the dark station yard Reggie found only one: "Do you come from Fernhurst?" he called, and the small chauffeur who was half inside the bonnet shut it up and touched his cap and ran round to his seat.

They dashed off into the night, climbing up by narrow winding roads through woodland. Nothing passed them, no house gave a gleam of light. The car stopped on the crest of a hill and Reggie looked out. He could see nothing but white frost and pines. The chauffeur was getting down.

"What's the trouble?" said Reggie, with his head out of the window: and slipped the catch and came out in a bundle.

The chauffeur's face was the face of Lady Chantry. He saw it in the flash of a pistol overhead as he closed with her. "I will, I will," she muttered, and fought him fiercely. Another shot went into the pines. He wrenched her hand round. The third was fired into her face. The struggling body fell away from him, limp.

He carried it into the rays of the headlights and looked close. "That's that," he said with a shrug, and put it into the car.

He lit a cigar and listened. There was no sound anywhere but the sough of the wind in the pines. He climbed into the chauffeur's place and drove away. At the next crossroads he took that which led north and west, and so in a while came out on the Portsmouth road.

That night the frost gathered on a motor-car in a lane between Hindhead and Shottermill. Mr Fortune unobtrusively caught the last train from Haslemere.

When he came out from a matinée with Joan Amber next day, the newsboys were shouting "Motor Car Mystery." Mr Fortune did not buy a paper.

It was on the morning of the second day that Scotland Yard sent for him. Lomas was with Superintendent Bell. The two of them received him with solemnity and curious eyes. Mr Fortune was not pleased. "Dear me, Lomas, can't you keep the peace for a week at a time?" he protested. "What is the reason for your existence?"

"I had all that for breakfast," said Lomas. "Don't talk like the newspapers. Be original."

"'Another Mysterious Murder,'" Reggie murmured, quoting headlines. "'Scotland Yard Baffled Again,' 'Police Mandarins.' No, you haven't a 'good Press,' Lomas old thing."

Lomas said something about the Press. "Do you know who that woman chauffeur was, Fortune?"

"That wasn't in the papers, was it?"

"You haven't guessed?"

Again Reggie Fortune was aware of the grave curiosity in their eyes. "Another of our mysterious murders," he said dreamily. "I wonder. Are you working out the series at last? I told you to look for some one who was always present."

Lomas looked at Superintendent Bell. "Lady Chantry was present at this one, Fortune," he said. "Lady Chantry took out her car the day before yesterday. Yesterday morning the car was found in a lane above Haslemere. Lady Chantry was inside. She wore chauffeur's uniform. She was shot through the head."

"Well, well," said Reggie Fortune.

"I want you to come down and look at the body."

"Is the body the only evidence?"

"We know where she bought the coat and cap. Her own coat and hat were under the front seat. She told her servants she might not be back at night. No one knows what she went out for or where she went."

"Yes. Yes. When a person is shot, it's generally with a gun. Have you found it?"

"She had an automatic pistol in her hand."

Reggie Fortune rose. "I had better see her," he said sadly. "A wearing world, Lomas. Come on. My car's outside."

Two hours later he stood looking down at the slight body and the scorched wound in that pale face while a police surgeon demonstrated to him how the shot was fired. The pistol was gripped with the rigour of death in the woman's right hand, the bullet that was taken from the base of the skull fitted it, the muzzle—remark the stained, scorched flesh—must have been held close to her face when the shot was fired. And Reggie listened and nodded. "Yes, yes. All very clear, isn't it? A straight case." He drew the sheet over the body and paid compliments to the doctor as they went out.

Lomas was in a hurry to meet them. Reggie shook his head. "There's nothing for me, Lomas. And nothing for you. The medical evidence is suicide. Scotland Yard is acquitted without a stain on its character."

"No sort of doubt?" said Lomas.

"You can bring all the College of Surgeons to see her. You'll get nothing else."

And so they climbed into the car again. "Finis, thank God!" said Mr Fortune as the little town ran by.

Lomas looked at him curiously. "Why did she commit suicide, Fortune?" he said.

"There are also other little questions," Reggie murmured. "Why did she murder Bigod? Why did she murder the lady doctor? Why did she try to murder the child?"

Lomas continued to stare at him. "How do you know she did?" he said in a low voice. "You're making very sure."

"Great heavens! You might do some of the work. I know Scotland Yard isn't brilliant, but it might take pains. Who was present at all the murders? Who was the constant force? Haven't you found that out yet?"

"She was staying near Bigod's place. She was at the orphanage. She was at the child's party. And only she was at all three. It staggered me when I got the evidence complete. But what in heaven makes you think she is the murderer?"

Reggie moved uneasily. "There was something malign about her."

"Malign! But she was always doing philanthropic work."

"Yes. It may be a saint who does that—or the other thing. Haven't you ever noticed—some of the people who are always busy about distress they rather like watching distress?"

"Why, yes. But murder! And what possible motive is there for killing these different people? She might have hated one or another. But not all three."

"Oh, there is a common factor. Don't you see? Each one had somebody to feel the death like torture—the girl Bigod was engaged to, the girl who was devoted to the lady doctor, the small Gerald's mother. There was always somebody to suffer horribly—and the person to be killed was always somebody who had a young good life to lose. Not at all nice murders, Lomas. Genus diabolical, species feminine. Say that Lady Chantry had a devilish passion for cruelty—and it ended that night in the motor-car."

"But why commit suicide? Do you mean she was mad?"

"I wouldn't say that. That's for the Day of Judgement. When is cruelty madness? I don't know. Why did she—give herself away—in the end? Perhaps she found she had gone a little too far. Perhaps she knew you and I had begun to look after her. She never liked me much, I fancy. She was a little—odd—with me."

"You're an uncanny fellow, Fortune."

"My dear chap! Oh, my dear chap! I'm wholly normal. I'm the natural man," said Reggie Fortune.

# THE ABSCONDING TREASURER

## J. JEFFERSON FARJEON

Joseph Jefferson Farjeon (1883–1955) came from a distinguished family. His grandfather was the American actor Joseph Jefferson, and his father, Benjamin Farjeon, was a prolific and successful novelist, while his sister Eleanor became renowned for her stories and poetry for young people. Farjeon's crime novels included *No. 17*; originally a stage play, the story was the source for Alfred Hitchcock's 1932 thriller *Number Seventeen*. Dorothy L. Sayers was among his many admirers, saying: "Jefferson Farjeon is quite unsurpassed for creepy skill in mysterious adventures". A striking reminder of the enduring appeal of Golden Age crime writing came in late 2014, when the British Library reissue of Farjeon's *Mystery in White* became a runaway best-seller.

The short stories that Farjeon wrote early in his career are less well known, and not even the British Library possesses a copy of "The Absconding Treasurer". We are therefore indebted to Monte Herridge, a very knowledgeable American enthusiast, for tracing and supplying the text of the story. Monte's researches, published on the excellent Mystery*File website, have revealed that Farjeon wrote no fewer than fifty-seven stories featuring Detective X. Crook which originally appeared in *Flynn's/Detective Fiction Weekly* between 1925 and 1927. They are straightforward stories when compared to Farjeon's later work, but they display his developing craftsmanship as a writer of mysteries.

\* \* \* \* \*

"I be secretary of the Slate Club, d'ye see," said Mr Jenks, nervously rubbing his somewhat stubbly chin, "and so, naterally, I do feel sort o' responsible."

"Naturally," agreed Detective Crook. "But no one suspects you of having run off with the money?"

"'Ow could they?" responded Mr Jenks, frowning heavily. "I *ain't* run off. I be 'ere. Well, then." He rubbed his chin again. "But Mr Parkins, the treasurer—well, 'e ain't 'ere, d'ye see? And 'twas '*im* 'ad the money. And the *money* ain't 'ere."

"So, of course, Mr Parkins is suspected, not you," nodded the detective. "That's quite obvious. When was the sharing out to have been?"

Mr Jenks looked doleful. They were sitting in the back room of his toy-shop, and the blinds were half drawn, as though in mourning for the departed cash.

"To-morrer, it was," he groaned. "And a rare day it was to 'ave been. Ninety-three pound eight-and-twopence—we reckoned it up on'y lars' night, sir. And twenty-six on us to share it, which was more'n three-pound-ten each, and many on us wantin' it badly, you may be sure, sir, and some on us spent it already. And Mrs Mason ill, and countin' on 'er three-pound-ten fer med'cine, and my own son jest lost 'is job, too—"

"Yes, I can imagine it must be a blow to you all," interposed Crook, "but perhaps we may be able to trace the money yet. You say Mr Parkins and you reckoned up the amount last night?"

"That be right. Lars' night, it was," answered the secretary.

"Do you mean you reckoned it out on paper, or actually counted the cash?"

"On paper. But Mr Parkins, 'e 'ad the cash, too, locked away in a drawer. And, I'll allow, we checked the amount."

Mr Jenks' eyes glistened at the memory. It had evidently been a pleasant occasion.

"But how did Mr Parkins happen to have the money there?" was Crook's next question. "Wasn't he in rather a hurry to withdraw it from the bank? Or hadn't it been put in the bank?"

"Oh, 'twas put in the bank, that's right enough," exclaimed the secretary. "Mr Parkins was most methodical. That's why he was chose for treasurer when Mr 'Ardcastle put 'im up, ye see. But 'e got sorter worked up—Christmas excitement, I put it down to—and said 'e'd get the money out, and 'ave plenty o' time to divide it up.

"'Why not wait till tomorrer, Jim,' I said. 'W'ot's the 'arm in takin' it out today?' 'e said. 'Wouldn't ye like to see it?' 'e said. 'Well, I wouldn't mind,' I said. So 'e draws it out, and lars' night round I go to 'is room, and we reckon it up, as I've told ye."

"What is Mr Parkins?"

"Treasurer. 'E be the treasurer—"

"Yes, but what's his job?"

"Oh, I see. 'E was with Mr 'Ardcastle, the grocer—been 'is assistant for well nigh two year."

"Married?"

"No. Nor goin' to be, that I knew on."

"Where was his room? The room where he kept the money?"

"'E 'ad a bedroom over the shop."

"And that's where you last saw him?" asked the detective. Mr Jenks nodded. "What time did you leave his room?"

"'Twas near ten, I reckon. 'Come for a stroll?' I said. 'Walk back with me, Jim?' 'Not it,' ses Jim. 'Not with all this money lyin' about.' And then, when I'm outside, I whistles up to 'is winder, and 'e pops 'is 'ead out, and I said: 'Lock it away, and come round for a drink,' but 'no,' 'e ses, 'I'm not leavin' it.' And then back I come, sir, and that's the lars' we see o' Jim Parkins. Nex' mornin' 'e was gone, 'is bed not slep' in, and the money was gone. too."

A silence fell upon them. It was broken by a small voice from the shop.

"Mr Jenks!" called the small voice.

"That you, Elsie?" exclaimed Mr Jenks, and went to the door.

An odd sensation passed through Detective Crook as he overheard the short ensuing conversation.

"Excuse me," said the small voice, "but mother ses 'as anything been found out, yet, if you please?"

"Nothin'," replied Mr Jenks. "But you go back and tell 'er, we're doin' all we can."

"'Er cough's awful bad today, Mr Jenks."

"That's a shame, that is. Well, you see she takes 'er med'cine reg'ler, then she'll get better."

"Thank you, Mr Jenks."

There was a sound of retreating feet, which suddenly paused as Mr Jenks called out:

"Hey! Wait a minnit! Santa Claus 'e come by 'ere today, and 'e left somethin' for you. Now, what was it? Ah—'twas that stockin' 'anging by the door. Take it down."

"Oh, Mr Jenks!" gasped the child.

"Whoa! Not the big 'un! 'E didn't leave that 'un. 'Twas the—the middle-size 'un. Ay, that be it. Now run along, my dear—I gotter go back and try and find that money!"

When Mr Jenks returned to the little back room, he found his visitor in a very thoughtful mood, and watched him hopefully, without speaking. Detectives should not be interrupted.

"Tell me, was Mr Parkins in financial trouble of any kind?" asked Crook suddenly.

"Not that I knows on."

"Would you say his character was as good as the average?"

"If it 'adn't been, 'e'd not 'ave been made treasurer," responded Mr Jenks. "We always thought 'im honest. Took Mr 'Ardcastle's word for it. But there—you never know, do we?"

"No, you never know," nodded Crook. "Who is this Mr Hardcastle?"

"E's boss, where 'e worked."

"All right, I think I'll go and call on him, and also take a look at Parkins' room."

Mr Jenks opened his eyes wide.

"That be no good!" he exclaimed. "We all on us done that first. There ain't a penny in it!"

"I don't expect there is, Mr Jenks," answered the detective. "But maybe I'll find something else."

## II

Mr Hardcastle, the grocer, received the detective with considerable pleasure. Though he stood to lose his three-pound-ten, he was troubled less about that than about his assistant, for whose honesty, he told the detective, he would have sworn.

"Not that there weren't others who held a different view," he admitted frankly. "You see, not much was known about him when he first come to our town, and he wouldn't have found a job here, not if I hadn't given him a chance."

"Why not?" asked Crook.

"Dunno, sir. Prejudice, I expect. We like our own people, and don't much care about strangers. And then, as I say, we knew next to nothing about him."

"What made *you* give him a chance?"

The grocer rubbed his nose, and looked a little puzzled.

"Danged if I can say, exactly," he answered. "Something about him, I expect. You can't explain it, can you? Anyhow, there it was.

"I took him on, and when my chief assistant got a better job in London, I put Jim in his place."

"And he justified himself?"

"Absolutely." But the detective noted a slight hesitation, despite the definiteness of the word.

"Better tell me everything, Mr Hardcastle, if I'm to help you," he suggested.

"Yes, you're right," frowned the grocer. "It's true, he never did a wrong thing after I promoted him—until this present business, that is—but, before then—well, I *did* catch him over a small matter. Nobody knew it but him and me—and you're the third. He took ten shillings from the till." The grocer paused, and his frown grew. "He'd got a sister—not quite right in her head. He's keeping her in a home somewhere."

"So there's our motive," muttered Crook reflectively. "What happened, after you found him out?"

Mr Hardcastle shifted rather uncomfortably.

"I ought to have kicked him off, of course," he grunted. "But I couldn't, somehow. You know how it is. I said I'd overlook it, and he bucked up wonderful, and when this chance came—well, I thought it might just do the trick and make a man of him. Some of us are only waiting for a bit of trust from other folk to give us the right view of things. Or don't you agree?"

"Of course, I agree," said Crook. "Many a man has gone wrong through mere suspicion."

"Now, there you are! That's how I argued. So I gave him the chance, and I went further, and proposed him for the treasurer of our Slate Club when I'd been asked to take it on and didn't want to."

Crook shook his head slightly.

"You were right to take a risk on the man yourself," he commented, "but were you right to take a risk on other people's money?"

Mr Hardcastle did not reply. Instead, he rose and walked to a desk. For a few seconds he remained there writing, and then he returned to the detective with what he had written.

"There's my check," he said bluntly. "Ninety-three pounds eight-and-twopence. If you don't trace that money, Mr Crook, hand that to Mr Jenks tomorrow."

Crook took the slip of paper, looked at it, and then looked at the grocer.

"You're a white man, Mr Hardcastle," he said.

"Not a bit," came the gruff retort. "It's what I ought to do. When I proposed Jim for treasurer, I said to myself that I'd stand the racket if things did go wrong. Well, I stand by my word, whether it's down on paper or not. So please say no more about it. Only," he added, with a faint smile, "I'm not a millionaire, and if you can catch the silly young devil, I'm not saying I won't be glad."

"I'll do my best," replied the detective. "I'd like to see his room now, if I may."

The room in which Jim Parkins had slept—though not on the night of the theft—was at the back of the building. It was on the first floor, and its small window overlooked a narrow street. There was a side door below the window, and it was out of this side door he had undoubtedly gone, for it had been found open in the morning, and all the other doors were locked.

"He'd naturally go by that door," added the grocer. "Just down one flight of stairs, and passing nobody's bedroom. Easy!"

"The door was found wide open?"

"Wide."

"I should have thought he'd have closed it behind him," commented Crook.

"A man in a hurry don't always think of those things," answered Mr Hardcastle.

"Perhaps not." Crook turned to the bed, and noted its disorder. "You said the bed had not been slept in?"

"Nor had it. It wasn't like that this morning. But we've turned the place upside down, looking for the money."

"You had small hope of finding it!"

"That's right. But there was one or two in here near went off their heads! Ted Blake even ripped up the mattress!" He pointed to a slash in the bedding, and then turned to a small chest in a corner. "And he smashed that drawer, getting it finally open!"

"This chair's broken."

"Ay, and I saw it broke. Joe Binder sat upon it a bit too hard this morning through emotion. A leg was loose."

"There seems to have been a good deal of emotion flying around," smiled Crook. "I shall be quite half an hour in this room, Mr Hardcastle, if you've anything else to do."

### III

Mr Hardcastle took the hint and departed. Left alone, Detective Crook made a thorough examination of the little room, taking his full time over it. Then he descended the narrow flight to the side door, examined that, and emerged into the lane.

A small group of villagers, standing outside a cottage on the opposite side, watched him, and one or two straggled forward.

"Be you a detective?" asked one.

"You never know," replied Crook.

"Haw, haw," guffawed the speaker awkwardly. "Well, if you be, are you goin' to find that money for us?"

"You never know," repeated Crook, smiling.

"'E's a close 'un!" exclaimed the other, nudging his neighbour. "But that's what I'd do, if I was a 'tec!" He turned back to Crook. "'E must 'ave slipped out quiet, mustn't 'e? Ted Blake 'ere never 'eard 'im, and 'e sleeps oppersit."

"Wish I '*ad!*" grunted Blake. "'E'd not 'ave got far, blast 'im!"

"You sleep too 'eavy, Ted," retorted the first speaker. "What's goin' to 'appen to my Christmas turkey?"

"Perhaps I'll find the money for you," said Crook.

Blake whistled. "P'r'aps 'e's got it already," he said with a wink, "and 'll pop it down our chimney into our stockin's, fer a Christmas surprise!"

"Yer never know!" chorused the others. Crook passed on, with a smile, and wended his way to the post office. Here he made a request to the postmaster, and a few minutes later an elderly, keen-eyed man was standing before him. Jerry Lupton had delivered letters in the district for over eighteen years.

"More dust than mud these days, isn't there?" began the detective.

The postman agreed, a little wonderingly.

"Ay, it's been dry, sir, that it has," he nodded.

"All the same," continued Crook, "I see you've got a little red mud on your left foot. Where did you pick that up?"

"Eh?" queried the postman, and gazed down at his boot. "Can't say."

"Don't give up at the start!" reproved Crook. "Have a think."

The postman thought. He thought for three minutes. Again he shook his head.

"Can't say," he repeated.

"Come, come," insisted Crook. "I think better of you than that! No one knows this district better than you! Isn't there a spot somewhere where the ground is slightly reddish? Get pictures into your mind!

"Here's a long, white road—here's a bit of yellow, sandy soil— here's brown earth—this is almost black—and now, here, is some reddish earth. And it must be near water—a spring, or a river, or a brook, for the weather's been dry lately—"

"Got it!" cried the postman, all at once. "Shooter's Wood! That'd be the place now!"

"Well done!" exclaimed Crook, and his eye lightened. "Where is Shooter's Wood? And when were you last there?"

Jerry Lupton told him. It was a small wood at the far end of the town. He only went through it once a day, to deliver letters, when there were any, at a small cottage on the farther edge.

It was just in his district, and many a time he'd wished it weren't. A path ran through the wood to the cottage, and midway the path was traversed by a stream running at right angles to it. Yes, the earth was certainly reddish about there, and he must have trod on a bit of moist bank. That would explain his boot satisfactorily.

Detective Crook thanked him, received directions, and after giving the postman strict instructions to tell no one of their conversation, set out for Shooter's Wood. He walked at a fair pace, yet he gave no appearance of hurry, and his eyes missed nothing on the way.

In less than ten minutes he was in the wood. In another five he had reached the little brook. It ran lazily across the track, disappearing in the thick trees on either side.

Crook stood still for a few seconds, taking in the picture. Then he began to move slowly toward the left, keeping near the bank of the stream. A low branch of one of the trees attracted his attention. It had been snapped off.

The stream led him into a spot where the trees thickened considerably. Crook noticed that the undergrowth was downtrodden. He pursued his way with slow steps, but with a quickening sensation in his heart. Coming round a bush, he stopped.

## IV

Lying on the ground, on its face, was a body.

Crook's lips tightened, but he gave no other outward sign of emotion. Stooping swiftly, he felt the body. It was cold. It had been dead several hours.

The cause of death was apparent. That was, the immediate cause. Beneath the man's head, which the detective gently raised, was the spiked stump of a tree. The man had fallen, or been struck or thrown, and the spike had finished the job.

Carefully and tenderly, Crook lifted the body slightly, turning it a little on its side, and as he did so an exclamation escaped him. Tightly grasped in one hand was a stout brown envelope.

Even before he took the envelope from the dead man's hand, and opened it, the detective knew what it contained. It contained ninety-three pounds in notes, eight shillings in silver, and two coppers.

But there were other things on the envelope which, to the detective's experienced eye, were even more important. There were fingerprints. Some were small. The fingers of the dead man were small. Other of the fingerprints were big.

The detective rose from his examination of the recumbent figure, and gazed around. The wood was ghostly and silent, save for the faint trickling of the water of the stream as it ran along its red bed, to emerge for a moment at a public track that its secret might be revealed, and then lose itself again in the woods beyond.

With the envelope in his pocket, Detective Crook retraced his way back to the track, and returned slowly to the village. Mr Hardcastle raised his head quickly as he saw him coming toward his shop, and exclaimed:

"Ah! I wonder if he's found anything?"

"I wunner," murmured Mr Jenks, who had called to discuss the one and only topic.

A moment later the detective entered.

"Well?" cried Mr Hardcastle and Mr Jenks together.

"I've got your money," replied Crook quietly.

Two mouths opened wide.

"What's that?" exclaimed the grocer. "You've—you've *found* it?"

"Yes. And I've found something else not quite so pleasant, I'm afraid."

"What?"

"I've found Jim Parkins, Mr Hardcastle. He's lying on his face, dead, in Shooter's Wood."

There was a silence. Mr Jenks suddenly choked a little, and Mr Hardcastle stared glassily in front of him.

"What's that you're saying?" he muttered at last. "Jim—dead?"

"Yes. He was holding this envelope." The detective laid the envelope on the table, and they fixed their eyes on it, in fearful fascination.

"The Lord's hand descended on 'im," piped Mr Jenks unsteadily.

"No—not the Lord's," came the detective's gentle voice. "The hand of somebody rather less than the Lord." He turned to the grocer. "You were right in your estimation of your assistant. Mr Hardcastle. He was a white man, like yourself—and it may give you pleasure to remember that it was your kindliness helped to turn him white."

"I—I don't understand this," muttered Mr Hardcastle.

"It's quite simple," answered Crook. "That money was stolen from Jim Parkins last night, shortly after Mr Jenks left him, and Parkins followed the thief and regained the money. But it cost him his life."

"You mean—the thief killed him?" whispered Mr Hardcastle.

"Not intentionally, I imagine. In the struggle—as I picture it— Parkins got the envelope back, and was knocked down, or fell, immediately afterward. He fell on a sharp tree-stump, and, I should say, was killed instantly."

"But, if that be so," exclaimed Mr Jenks. "why didn't the thief take the money back again?"

"Because, at the moment, fear was greater than greed," responded Crook. "When he found out what he had done, he fled. It involves less courage to take a chance on being caught as a thief than as a murderer."

The truth of this sank in.

"How did you come to find poor Jim?" asked Mr Hardcastle quietly.

"Ay, and 'oo done it?" cried Mr Jenks.

There were tears in the old man's indignant voice; and also, Crook noticed, in his eyes.

"Let me tell you my theory," said the detective, "and correct me where you think I am wrong. You remember, Mr Jenks, you whistled up to Jim Parkins' window after you left him last night, and tried to get him to come out with you?" Mr Jenks nodded. "Will you repeat what you called up to him—the words you repeated to me?"

" 'Lock it away,' I said, 'and come round for a drink.'"

"And he replied, 'I'm not leavin' it.' Now, suppose somebody overheard that conversation—"

"They wouldn't know it was money." interposed Mr Hardcastle.

"They might think it was something valuable, all the same," replied Crook, "and they might—if they knew that he was treasurer of the Slate Club—even guess that it was money."

"That's true," admitted Mr Hardcastle. "Well?"

"Suppose the person who overheard whistled up at the window after Mr Jenks had left, and, concealing himself, went on whistling till Jim Parkins came down? It would be easy—Jim Parkins being a small man—to knock him on the head, slip up to his room, and run off with the money. And if Jim came to just as the thief was getting away, he would probably chase him."

"He would," agreed his listeners.

"Then my theory is that Jim chased the thief to Shooter's Wood, the thief trying unsuccessfully to shake him off. When they came to the stream, they turned up along the banks, and at last Jim caught his man, and managed in the struggle to get the money back. But he was killed the next minute, as I've told you."

"Yes, but you ain't told us 'oo killed 'im!" exclaimed Mr Jenks.

"I am coming to that," answered Crook slowly. "It was a man on whose boots I saw traces of the red mud that led me to Shooter's Wood. It was a man who, while I was speaking to him, whistled at one of my remarks, and put an idea into my head—an idea which, in itself, might not have been worth considering, but which *was* worth considering coupled with the red mud.

"The man lives opposite the window of Jim's bedroom, so might easily have overheard the conversation. And he left his finger-marks both on the envelope you are now looking at, and also, I imagine, on the locked drawer he was so anxious to prize open this morning—knowing that he would find nothing in it."

"You mean Ted Blake?" ejaculated Mr Hardcastle.

"Ted Blake killed Jim Parkins," responded Crook. "His enthusiasm when searching Jim's room this morning was merely an obvious and clumsy attempt to divert possible suspicion from himself as far as he could."

"Ted Blake!" repeated Mr Hardcastle, while Mr Jenks murmured, "I never did like that feller, not since 'e broke my toy windmill an' refoosed to pay for the mendin'."

"Can you arrest a man on that?" demanded Mr Hardcastle suddenly. "It's all what you call circumstantial."

"The evidence is circumstantial, but it's strong," replied the detective. "However, Blake himself will supply the final proof. I called at the police station on my way back, and a couple of men are concealed near the dead man's body at this moment. An empty envelope has been substituted for this one. The murderer of Jim Parkins will return for that envelope, when he thinks it is safe enough."

"Lord above us!" muttered Mr Jenks. "Ain't detectives wun'erful?"

Crook laughed.

"And now, I think, my work here is done," he said, "excepting for your check, Mr Hardcastle. Mr Jenks has got his money back, and the sharing can take place tomorrow, as arranged. So—"

Crook took the check from his pocket, but Mr Hardcastle waved it away.

"I don't want it, I don't it!" he exclaimed. "Jim saved our money for us, didn't he? Well, then—I reckon he's earned that for his sister."

Ted Blake went alone into Shooter's Wood that night; but he did not come out alone.

# THE NECKLACE OF PEARLS

## DOROTHY L. SAYERS

Dorothy Leigh Sayers (1893–1957) was one of the outstanding exponents of "Golden Age" detective fiction, and remains celebrated for the creation of Lord Peter Wimsey, the aristocratic sleuth who began life almost as a caricature, but was portrayed in greater depth as Sayers' literary ambition grew. The last novel in which he appeared was *Busman's Honeymoon*, published in 1937, but since 1998, Jill Paton Walsh (a distinguished writer once shortlisted for the Booker Prize) has produced four well-received Wimsey novels with the blessing of the Sayers estate; there could be no better demonstration of the continued popularity of Lord Peter.

Sayers was a gifted writer, who in later life devoted herself to translating Dante and writing theological work, such as the radio play cycle *The Man Born to Be King*, rather than detective fiction. Her short stories are less well known than her novels, but "The Necklace of Pearls", which appeared in the collection *Hangman's Holiday*, is an enjoyable spin on the seasonal mystery.

\*    \*    \*    \*    \*

Sir Septimus Shale was accustomed to assert his authority once in the year and once only. He allowed his young and fashionable wife to fill his house with diagrammatic furniture made of steel; to collect advanced artists and anti-grammatical poets; to believe in cocktails and relativity and to dress as extravagantly as she pleased; but he did insist on an old-fashioned Christmas. He was a simple-hearted man, who really liked plum-pudding and cracker mottoes, and he could not get it out of his head that other people, "at bottom", enjoyed these things also. At Christmas, therefore, he firmly retired to his country house in Essex, called in the servants to hang holly and mistletoe upon the cubist electric fittings; loaded the steel sideboard with delicacies from Fortnum & Mason; hung up stockings at the heads of the polished walnut bedsteads; and even, on this occasion only, had the electric radiators removed from the modernist grates and installed wood fires and a Yule log. He then gathered his family and friends about him, filled them with as much Dickensian good fare as he could persuade them to swallow, and, after their Christmas dinner, set them down to play "Charades" and "Clumps" and "Animal, Vegetable and Mineral" in the drawing-room, concluding these diversions by "Hide-and-Seek" in the dark all over the house. Because Sir Septimus was a very rich man, his guests fell in with this invariable programme, and if they were bored, they did not tell him so.

Another charming and traditional custom which he followed was that of presenting to his daughter Margharita a pearl on each successive birthday—this anniversary happening to coincide with Christmas Eve. The pearls now numbered twenty, and the collection was beginning to enjoy a certain celebrity, and had been photographed in the Society papers. Though not sensationally large—each one being about the size of a marrowfat pea—the pearls were of very great value. They were of exquisite colour and perfect shape and matched to a hair's-weight. On this particular Christmas Eve, the presentation of the twenty-first pearl had been the occasion of a very special ceremony. There was a dance and there were speeches. On the Christmas night following, the more restricted family party took place, with the turkey and the Victorian games. There were eleven guests, in addition to Sir Septimus and Lady Shale and their daughter, nearly all related or connected to them in some way: John Shale, a brother, with his wife and their son and daughter

Henry and Betty; Betty's fiancé, Oswald Truegood, a young man with parliamentary ambitions; George Comphrey, a cousin of Lady Shale's, aged about thirty and known as a man about town; Lavinia Prescott, asked on George's account; Joyce Trivett, asked on Henry Shale's account; Richard and Beryl Dennison, distant relations of Lady Shale, who lived a gay and expensive life in town on nobody precisely knew what resources; and Lord Peter Wimsey, asked, in a touching spirit of unreasonable hope, on Margharita's account. There were also, of course, William Norgate, secretary to Sir Septimus, and Miss Tomkins, secretary to Lady Shale, who had to be there because, without their calm efficiency, the Christmas arrangements could not have been carried through.

Dinner was over—a seemingly endless succession of soup, fish, turkey, roast beef, plum-pudding, mince-pies, crystallized fruit, nuts and five kinds of wine, presided over by Sir Septimus, all smiles, by Lady Shale, all mocking deprecation, and by Margharita, pretty and bored, with the necklace of twenty-one pearls gleaming softly on her slender throat. Gorged and dyspeptic and longing only for the horizontal position, the company had been shepherded into the drawing-room and set to play "Musical Chairs" (Miss Tomkins at the piano), "Hunt the Slipper" (slipper provided by Miss Tomkins), and "Dumb Crambo" (costumes by Miss Tomkins and Mr William Norgate). The back drawing-room (for Sir Septimus clung to these old-fashioned names) provided an admirable dressing-room, being screened by folding doors from the large drawing-room in which the audience sat on aluminium chairs, scrabbling uneasy toes on a floor of black glass under the tremendous illumination of electricity reflected from a brass ceiling.

It was William Norgate who, after taking the temperature of the meeting, suggested to Lady Shale that they should play at something less athletic. Lady Shale agreed and, as usual, suggested bridge. Sir Septimus, as usual, blew the suggestion aside.

"Bridge? Nonsense! Nonsense! Play bridge every day of your lives. This is Christmas time. Something we can all play together. How about 'Animal, Vegetable and Mineral'?"

This intellectual pastime was a favourite with Sir Septimus; he was rather good at putting pregnant questions. After a brief discussion, it became evident that this game was an inevitable part of the programme. The party settled down to it, Sir Septimus undertaking to "go out" first and set the thing going.

Presently they had guessed among other things Miss Tomkins' mother's photograph, a gramophone record of "I want to be happy" (much scientific research into the exact composition of records, settled by William Norgate out of the *Encyclopaedia Britannica*), the smallest stickleback in the stream at the bottom of the garden, the new planet Pluto, the scarf worn by Mrs Dennison (very confusing, because it was not silk, which would be animal, or artificial silk, which would be vegetable, but made of spun glass—mineral, a very clever choice of subject), and had failed to guess the Prime Minister's wireless speech—which was voted not fair, since nobody could decide whether it was animal by nature or a kind of gas. It was decided that they should do one more word and then go on to "Hide-and-Seek". Oswald Truegood had retired into the back room and shut the door behind him while the party discussed the next subject of examination, when suddenly Sir Septimus broke in on the argument by calling to his daughter:

"Hullo, Margy! What have you done with your necklace?"

"I took it off, Dad, because I thought it might get broken in 'Dumb Crambo'. It's over here on this table. No, it isn't. Did you take it, mother?"

"No, I didn't. If I'd seen it, I should have. You are a careless child."

Sir Septimus was horrified, but the guests, having found a leader, backed up Norgate. The door was locked, and the search was conducted—the ladies in the inner room and the men in the outer.

Nothing resulted from it except some very interesting information about the belongings habitually carried about by the average man and woman. It was natural that Lord Peter Wimsey should possess a pair of forceps, a pocket lens and a small folding foot-rule—was he not a Sherlock Holmes in high life? But that Oswald Truegood should have two liver-pills in a screw of paper and Henry Shale a pocket edition of *The Odes of Horace* was unexpected. Why did John Shale distend the pockets of his dress-suit with a stump of red sealing-wax, an ugly little mascot and a five-shilling piece? George Comphrey had a pair of folding scissors, and three wrapped lumps of sugar, of the sort served in restaurants and dining-cars—evidence of a not uncommon form of kleptomania; but that the tidy and exact Norgate should burden himself with a reel of white cotton, three separate lengths of string and twelve safety-pins on a card seemed really remarkable till one remembered that he had superintended all the Christmas decorations. Richard Dennison, amid some confusion and laughter, was found to cherish a lady's garter, a powder-compact and half a potato; the last-named, he said, was a prophylactic against rheumatism (to which he was subject), while the other objects belonged to his wife. On the ladies' side, the more striking exhibits were a little book on palmistry, three invisible hair-pins and a baby's photograph (Miss Tomkins); a Chinese trick cigarette-case with a secret compartment (Beryl Dennison); a *very* private letter and an outfit for mending stocking-ladders (Lavinia Prescott); and a pair of eyebrow tweezers and a small packet of white powder, said to be for headaches (Betty Shale). An agitating moment followed the production from Joyce Trivett's handbag of a small string of pearls—but it was promptly remembered that these had come out of one of the crackers at dinner-time, and they were, in fact, synthetic. In short, the search was unproductive of anything beyond a general shamefacedness and the discomfort always produced by undressing and re-dressing in a hurry at the wrong time of the day.

It was then that somebody, very grudgingly and haltingly, mentioned the horrid word "Police". Sir Septimus, naturally, was appalled by the idea. It was disgusting. He would not allow it. The pearls must be somewhere. They must search the rooms again. Could not Lord Peter Wimsey, with his experience of—er—mysterious happenings, do something to assist them?

"Eh?" said his lordship. "Oh, by Jove, yes—by all means, certainly. That is to say, provided nobody supposes—eh, what? I mean to say, you don't know that I'm not a suspicious character, do you, what?"

Lady Shale interposed with authority.

"We don't think *anybody* ought to be suspected," she said, "but, if we did, we'd know it couldn't be you. You know *far* too much about crimes to want to commit one."

"All right," said Wimsey. "But after the way the place has been gone over——" He shrugged his shoulders.

"Yes, I'm afraid you won't be able to find any footprints," said Margharita. "But we may have overlooked something."

Wimsey nodded.

"I'll try. Do you all mind sitting down on your chairs in the outer room and staying there. All except one of you—I'd better have a witness to anything I do or find. Sir Septimus—you'd be the best person, I think."

He shepherded them to their places and began a slow circuit of the two rooms, exploring every surface, gazing up to the polished brazen ceiling and crawling on hands and knees in the approved fashion across the black and shining desert of the floors. Sir Septimus followed, staring when Wimsey stared, bending with his hands upon his knees when Wimsey crawled, and puffing at intervals with astonishment and chagrin. Their progress rather resembled that of a man taking out a very inquisitive puppy for a very leisurely constitutional. Fortunately, Lady Shale's taste in furnishing made investigation easier; there were scarcely any nooks or corners where anything could be concealed.

They reached the inner drawing-room, and here the dressing-up clothes were again minutely examined, but without result. Finally, Wimsey lay down flat on his stomach to squint under a steel cabinet which was one of the very few pieces of furniture which possessed short legs. Something about it seemed to catch his attention. He rolled up his sleeve and plunged his arm into the cavity, kicked convulsively in the effort to reach farther than was humanly possible, pulled out from his pocket and extended his folding foot-rule, fished with it under the cabinet and eventually succeeded in extracting what he sought.

It was a very minute object—in fact, a pin. Not an ordinary pin, but one resembling those used by entomologists to impale extremely small moths on the setting-board. It was about three-quarters of an inch in length, as fine as a very fine needle, with a sharp point and a particularly small head.

"Bless my soul!" said Sir Septimus. "What's that?"

"Does anybody here happen to collect moths or beetles or anything?" asked Wimsey, squatting on his haunches and examining the pin.

"I'm pretty sure they don't," replied Sir Septimus. "I'll ask them."

"Don't do that." Wimsey bent his head and stared at the floor, from which his own face stared meditatively back at him.

"I see," said Wimsey presently. "That's how it was done. All right, Sir Septimus. I know where the pearls are, but I don't know who took them. Perhaps it would be as well—for every-body's satisfaction—just to find out. In the meantime they are perfectly safe. Don't tell anyone that we've found this pin or that we've discovered anything. Send all these people to bed. Lock the drawing-room door and keep the key, and we'll get our man—or woman—by breakfast-time."

"God bless my soul," said Sir Septimus, very much puzzled.

Lord Peter Wimsey kept careful watch that night upon the draw-ing-room door. Nobody, however, came near it. Either the thief suspected a trap or he felt confident that any time would do to recover the pearls. Wimsey, however, did not feel that he was wast-ing his time. He was making a list of people who had been left alone in the back drawing-room during the playing of "Animal, Vegetable or Mineral". The list ran as follows.

> Sir Septimus Shale
> Lavinia Prescott
> William Norgate
> Joyce Trivett and Henry Shale (together, because they had claimed to be incapable of guessing anything unaided)
> Mrs Dennison
> Betty Shale
> George Comphrey
> Richard Dennison
> Miss Tomkins
> Oswald Truegood.

He also made out a list of the persons to whom pearls might be useful or desirable. Unfortunately, this list agreed in almost all respects with the first (always excepting Sir Septimus) and so was not very helpful. The two secretaries had both come well recommended, but that was exactly what they would have done had they come with ulterior designs; the Dennisons were notorious livers from hand to mouth; Betty Shale carried mysterious white powders in her hand-bag, and was known to be in with a rather rapid set in town; Henry was a harmless dilettante, but Joyce Trivett could twist him round her little finger and was what Jane Austen liked to call "expensive and dissipated"; Comphrey speculated; Oswald Truegood was rather frequently present at Epsom and Newmarket—the search for motives was only too fatally easy.

When the second housemaid and the under-footman appeared in the passage with household implements, Wimsey abandoned his vigil, but he was down early to breakfast. Sir Septimus with his wife and daughter were down before him, and a certain air of tension made itself felt. Wimsey, standing on the hearth before the fire, made conversation about the weather and politics.

The party assembled gradually, but, as though by common consent, nothing was said about pearls until after breakfast, when Oswald Truegood took the bull by the horns.

"Well now!" said he. "How's the detective getting along? Got your man, Wimsey?"

"Not yet," said Wimsey easily.

Sir Septimus, looking at Wimsey as though for his cue, cleared his throat and dashed into speech.

"All very tiresome," he said, "all very unpleasant. Hr'rm. Nothing for it but the police, I'm afraid. Just at Christmas, too. Hr'rm. Spoilt the party. Can't stand seeing all this stuff about the place." He waved his hand towards the festoons of evergreens and coloured paper that adorned the walls. "Take it all down, eh, what? No heart in it. Hr'rm. Burn the lot."

"What a pity, when we worked so hard over it," said Joyce.

"Oh, leave it, Uncle," said Henry Shale. "You're bothering too much about the pearls. They're sure to turn up."

"Shall I ring for James?" suggested William Norgate.

"No," interrupted Comphrey, "let's do it ourselves. It'll give us something to do and take our minds off our troubles."

"That's right," said Sir Septimus. "Start right away. Hate the sight of it."

He savagely hauled a great branch of holly down from the mantelpiece and flung it, crackling, into the fire.

"That's the stuff," said Richard Dennison. "Make a good old blaze!" He leapt up from the table and snatched the mistletoe from the chandelier. "Here goes! One more kiss for somebody before it's too late."

"Isn't it unlucky to take it down before the New Year?" suggested Miss Tomkins.

"Unlucky be hanged. We'll have it all down. Off the stairs and out of the drawing-room too. Somebody go and collect it."

"Isn't the drawing-room locked?" asked Oswald.

"No. Lord Peter says the pearls aren't there, wherever else they are, so it's unlocked. That's right, isn't it, Wimsey?"

"Quite right. The pearls were taken out of these rooms. I can't yet tell you how, but I'm positive of it. In fact, I'll pledge my reputation that wherever they are, they're not up there."

"Oh, well," said Comphrey, "in that case, have at it! Come along, Lavinia—you and Dennison do the drawing-room and I'll do the back room. We'll have a race."

"But if the police are coming in," said Dennison, "oughtn't everything to be left just as it is?"

"Damn the police!" shouted Sir Septimus. "They don't want evergreens."

Oswald and Margharita were already pulling the holly and ivy from the staircase, amid peals of laughter. The party dispersed. Wimsey went quietly upstairs and into the drawing-room, where the work of demolition was taking place at a great rate, George having bet the other two ten shillings to a tanner that they would not finish their part of the job before he finished his.

"You mustn't help," said Lavinia, laughing to Wimsey. "It wouldn't be fair."

Wimsey said nothing, but waited till the room was clear. Then he followed them down again to the hall, where the fire was sending up a great roaring and spluttering, suggestive of Guy Fawkes night. He whispered to Sir Septimus, who went forward and touched George Comphrey on the shoulder.

"Lord Peter wants to say something to you, my boy," he said.

Comphrey started and went with him a little reluctantly, as it seemed. He was not looking very well.

"Mr Comphrey," said Wimsey, "I fancy these are some of your property." He held out the palm of his hand, in which rested twenty-two fine, small-headed pins.

"Ingenious," said Wimsey, "but something less ingenious would have served his turn better. It was very unlucky, Sir Septimus, that you should have mentioned the pearls when you did. Of course, he hoped that the loss wouldn't be discovered till we'd chucked guessing games and taken to 'Hide-and-Seek'. Then the pearls might have been any-where in the house, we shouldn't have locked the drawing-room door, and he could have recovered them at his leisure. He had had this pos-sibility in his mind when he came here, obviously, and that was why he brought the pins, and Miss Shale's taking off the necklace to play 'Dumb Crambo' gave him his opportunity.

"He had spent Christmas here before, and knew perfectly well that 'Animal, Vegetable and Mineral' would form part of the entertainment. He had only to gather up the necklace from the table when it came to his turn to retire, and he knew he could count on at least five minutes by himself while we were all arguing about the choice of a word. He had only to snip the pearls from the string with his pocket-scissors, burn the string in the grate and fasten the pearls to the mistletoe with the fine pins. The mistletoe was hung on the chandelier, pretty high—it's a lofty room—but he could easily reach it by standing on the glass table, which wouldn't show footmarks, and it was almost certain that nobody would think of examining the mistletoe for extra berries. I shouldn't have thought of it myself if I hadn't found that pin which he had dropped. That gave me the idea that the pearls had been separated and the rest was easy. I took the pearls off the mistletoe last night—the clasp was there, too, pinned among the holly-leaves. Here they are. Comphrey must have got a nasty shock this morning. I knew he was our man when he suggested that the guests should tackle the decorations themselves and that he should do the back drawing-room—but I wish I had seen his face when he came to the mistletoe and found the pearls gone."

"And you worked it all out when you found the pin?" said Sir Septimus.

"Yes; I knew then where the pearls had gone to."

"But you never even looked at the mistletoe."

"I saw it reflected in the black glass floor, and it struck me then how much the mistletoe berries looked like pearls."

# THE CASE IS ALTERED

## Margery Allingham

Margery Allingham (1904–1966) was the daughter of two writers, and she wrote steadily throughout her schooldays, publishing an adventure story, *Blackerchief Dick*, when she was only seventeen. Albert Campion, the enigmatic detective who became her main series character, first appeared in a subordinate role in *The Crime at Black Dudley* (1928).

Allingham regarded the mystery novel as a box with four sides – "a Killing, a Mystery, an Enquiry and a Conclusion with an element of satisfaction in it", and liked to distinguish between her "right hand writing" which she did for pleasure and creative satisfaction, and her "left hand writing" which was commercially orientated. Three of her (now very hard to find) mysteries which were written under the name Maxwell March, were examples of the latter approach. "The Case is Altered" is a case of "right hand writing".

\* \* \* \* \*

Mr Albert Campion, sitting in a first-class smoking compartment, was just reflecting sadly that an atmosphere of stultifying decency could make even Christmas something of a stuffed-owl occasion, when a new hogskin suitcase of distinctive design hit him on the knees. At that same moment a golf bag bruised the shins of the shy young man opposite, an armful of assorted magazines burst over the pretty girl in the far corner, and a blast of icy air swept round the carriage. There was the familiar rattle and lurch which indicates that the train has started at last, a squawk from a receding porter, and Lance Feering arrived before him apparently by rocket.

"Caught it," said the newcomer with the air of one confidently expecting congratulations, but as the train bumped jerkily he tee- tered back on his heels and collapsed between the two young people on the opposite seat.

"My dear chap, so we noticed," murmured Campion, and he smiled apologetically at the girl, now disentangling herself from the shellburst of newsprint. It was his own disarming my-poor-friend- is-afflicted variety of smile that he privately considered infallible, but on this occasion it let him down.

The girl, who was in the early twenties and was slim and fair, with eyes like licked brandy-balls, as Lance Feering inelegantly put it after- wards, regarded him with grave interest. She stacked the magazines into a neat bundle and placed them on the seat opposite before returning to her own book. Even Mr Feering, who was in one of his more exuberant moods, was aware of that chilly protest. He began to apologize.

Campion had known Feering in his student days, long before he had become one of the foremost designers of stage décors in Europe, and was used to him, but now even he was impressed. Lance's apolo- gies were easy but also abject. He collected his bag, stowed it on a clear space on the rack above the shy young man's head, thrust his golf things under the seat, positively blushed when he claimed his magazines, and regarded the girl with pathetic humility. She glanced at him when he spoke, nodded coolly with just enough graciousness not to be gauche, and turned over a page.

Campion was secretly amused. At the top of his form Lance was reputed to be irresistible. His dark face with the long mourn- ful nose and bright eyes were unhandsome enough to be interesting and the quick gestures of his short painter's hands made his con- versation picturesque. His singular lack of success on this occasion clearly astonished him and he sat back in his corner eyeing the young woman with covert mistrust.

Campion resettled himself to the two hours' rigid silence which etiquette demands from first-class travellers who, although they are more than probably going to be asked to dance a reel together if not to share a bathroom only a few hours hence, have not yet been introduced.

There was no way of telling if the shy young man and the girl with the brandy-ball eyes knew each other, and whether they too were en route for Underhill, Sir Philip Cookham's Norfolk place. Campion was inclined to regard the coming festivities with a certain amount of lugubrious curiosity. Cookham himself was a magnificent old boy, of course, "one of the more valuable pieces in the Cabinet", as someone had once said of him, but Florence was a different kettle of fish. Born to wealth and breeding, she had grown blasé towards both of them and now took her delight in notabilities, a dangerous affectation in Campion's experience. She was some sort of remote aunt of his.

He glanced again at the young people, caught the boy unaware, and was immediately interested.

The illustrated magazine had dropped from the young man's hand and he was looking out of the window, his mouth drawn down at the corners and a narrow frown between his thick eyebrows. It was not an unattractive face, too young for strong character but decent and open enough in the ordinary way. At that particular moment, however, it wore a revealing expression. There was recklessness in the twist of the mouth and sullenness in the eyes, while the hand which lay upon the inside arm-rest was clenched.

Campion was curious. Young people do not usually go away for Christmas in this top-step-at-the-dentist's frame of mind. The girl looked up from her book.

"How far is Underhill from the station?" she inquired.

"Five miles. They'll meet us." The shy young man turned to her so easily and with such obvious affection that any romantic theory Campion might have formed was knocked on the head instantly. The youngster's troubles evidently had nothing to do with love.

Lance had raised his head with bright-eyed interest at the gratuitous information and now a faintly sardonic expression appeared upon his lips. Campion sighed for him. For a man who fell in and out of love with the abandonment of a seal round a pool, Lance Feering was an impossible optimist. Already he was regarding the girl with that shy despair which so many ladies had found too piteous to be allowed to persist. Campion washed his hands of him and turned away just in time to notice a stranger glancing in at them from the corridor. It was a dark and arrogant young face and he recognized it instantly, feeling at the same time a deep wave of sympathy for old Cookham. Florence, he gathered, had done it again.

Young Victor Preen, son of old Preen of the Preen Aero Company, was certainly notable, not to say notorious. He had obtained much publicity in his short life for his sensational flights, but a great deal more for adventures less creditable; and when angry old gentlemen in the armchairs of exclusive clubs let themselves go about the blackguardliness of the younger generation, it was very often of Victor Preen that they were thinking.

He stood now a little to the left of the compartment window, leaning idly against the wall, his chin up and his heavy lids drooping. At first sight he did not appear to be taking any interest in the occupants of the compartment, but when the shy young man looked up, Campion happened to see the swift glance of recognition, and of something else, which passed between them. Presently, still with the same elaborate casualness, the man in the corridor wandered away, leaving the other staring in front of him, the same sullen expression still in his eyes.

The incident passed so quickly that it was impossible to define the exact nature of that second glance, but Campion was never a man to go imagining things, which was why he was surprised when they arrived at Minstree station to hear Henry Boule, Florence's private secretary, introducing the two and to notice that they met as strangers.

It was pouring with rain as they came out of the station, and Boule, who, like all Florence's secretaries, appeared to be suffering from an advanced case of nerves, bundled them all into two big Daimlers, a smaller car and a shooting-brake. Campion looked round him at Florence's Christmas bag with some dismay. She had surpassed herself. Besides Lance there were at least half a dozen celebrities: a brace of political high-lights, an angry-looking lady novelist, Nadja from the ballet, a startled R.A., and Victor Preen, as well as some twelve or thirteen unfamiliar faces who looked as if they might belong to Art, Money, or even mere Relations.

Campion became separated from Lance and was looking for him anxiously when he saw him at last in one of the cars, with the novelist on one side and the girl with brandy-ball eyes on the other, Victor Preen making up the ill-assorted four.

Since Campion was an unassuming sort of person he was relegated to the brake with Boule himself, the shy young man and the whole of the luggage. Boule introduced them awkwardly and collapsed into a seat, wiping the beads from off his forehead with a relief which was a little too blatant to be tactful.

Campion, who had learned that the shy young man's name was Peter Groome, made a tentative inquiry of him as they sat jolting shoulder to shoulder in the back of the car. He nodded.

"Yes, it's the same family," he said. "Cookham's sister married a brother of my father's. I'm some sort of relation, I suppose."

The prospect did not seem to fill him with any great enthusiasm and once again Campion's curiosity was piqued. Young Mr Groome was certainly not in seasonable mood.

In the ordinary way Campion would have dismissed the matter from his mind, but there was something about the youngster which attracted him, something indefinable and of a despairing quality, and moreover there had been that curious intercepted glance in the train.

They talked in a desultory fashion throughout the uncomfortable journey. Campion learned that young Groome was in his father's firm of solicitors, that he was engaged to be married to the girl with the brandy-ball eyes, who was a Miss Patricia Bullard of an old north country family, and that he thought Christmas was a waste of time.

"I hate it," he said with a sudden passionate intensity which startled even his mild inquisitor. "All this sentimental good-will-to-all-men-business is false and sickening. There's no such thing as good-will. The world's rotten."

He blushed as soon as he had spoken and turned away.

"I'm sorry," he murmured, "but all this bogus Dickensian stuff makes me writhe."

Campion made no direct comment. Instead he asked with affable inconsequence, "Was that young Victor Preen I saw in the other car?"

Peter Groome turned his head and regarded him with the steady stare of the wilfully obtuse.

"I was introduced to someone with a name like that, I think," he said carefully. "He was a little baldish man, wasn't he?"

"No, that's Sir George." The secretary leaned over the luggage to give the information. "Preen is the tall young man, rather handsome, with the very curling hair. He's *the* Preen, you know." He sighed. "It seems very young to be a millionaire, doesn't it?"

"Obscenely so," said Mr Peter Groome abruptly, and returned to his despairing contemplation of the landscape.

Underhill was *en fête* to receive them. As soon as Campion observed the preparations, his sympathy for young Mr Groome increased, for to a jaundiced eye Lady Florence's display might well have proved as dispiriting as Preen's bank balance. Florence had "gone all Dickens", as she said herself at the top of her voice, linking her arm through Campion's, clutching the R.A. with her free hand, and capturing Lance with a bright birdlike eye.

The great Jacobean house was festooned with holly. An eighteen-foot tree stood in the great hall. Yule logs blazed on iron dogs in the wide hearths and already the atmosphere was thick with that curious Christmas smell which is part cigar smoke and part roasting food.

Sir Philip Cookham stood receiving his guests with pathetic bewilderment. Every now and again his features broke into a smile of genuine welcome as he saw a face he knew. He was a distinguished-looking old man with a fine head and eyes permanently worried by his country's troubles.

"My dear boy, delighted to see you. Delighted," he said, grasping Campion's hand. "I'm afraid you've been put over in the Dower House. Did Florence tell you? She said you wouldn't mind, but I insisted that Feering went over there with you and also young Peter." He sighed and brushed away the visitor's hasty reassurances. "I don't know why the dear girl never feels she has a party unless the house is so overcrowded that our best friends have to sleep in the annex," he said sadly.

The "dear girl", looking not more than fifty-five or her sixty years, was clinging to the arm of the lady novelist at that particular moment and the two women were emitting mirthless parrot cries at each other. Cookham smiled.

"She's happy, you know," he said indulgently. "She enjoys this sort of thing. Unfortunately I have a certain amount of urgent work to do this weekend, but we'll get in a chat, Campion, some time over the holiday. I want to hear your news. You're a lucky fellow. You can tell your adventures."

The lean man grimaced. "More secret sessions, sir?" he inquired.

The Cabinet Minister threw up his hands in a comic but expressive little gesture before he turned to greet the next guest.

As he dressed for dinner in his comfortable room in the small Georgian dower house across the park, Campion was inclined to congratulate himself on his quarters. Underhill itself was a little too much of the ancient monument for strict comfort.

He had reached the tie stage when Lance appeared. He came in very elegant indeed and highly pleased with himself. Campion diagnosed the symptoms immediately and remained irritatingly incurious.

Lance sat down before the open fire and stretched his sleek legs.

"It's not even as if I were a good-looking blighter, you know," he observed invitingly when the silence had become irksome to him. "In fact, Campion, when I consider myself I simply can't understand it. Did I so much as speak to the girl?"

"I don't know," said Campion, concentrating on his dressing. "Did you?"

"No." Lance was passionate in his denial. "Not a word. The hard-faced female with the inky fingers and the walrus mustache was telling me her life story all the way home in the car. This dear little poppet with the eyes was nothing more than a warm bundle at my side. I give you my dying oath on that, And yet—well, it's extraordinary, isn't it?"

Campion did not turn round. He could see the artist quite well through the mirror in front of him. Lance had a sheet of note-paper in his hand and was regarding it with that mixture of feigned amusement and secret delight which was typical of his eternally youthful spirit.

"Extraordinary," he repeated, glancing at Campion's unresponsive back. "She had nice eyes. Like licked brandy-balls."

"Exactly," agreed the lean man by the dressing table. "I thought she seemed very taken up with her fiancé, young Master Groome, though," he added tactlessly.

"Well, I noticed that, you know," Lance admitted, forgetting his professions of disinterest. "She hardly recognized my existence in the train. Still, there's absolutely no accounting for women. I've studied 'em all my life and never understood 'em yet. I mean to say, take this case in point. That kid ignored me, avoided me, looked through me. And yet look at this. I found it in my room when I came up to change just now."

Campion took the note with a certain amount of distaste. Lovely women were invariably stooping to folly, it seemed, but even so he could not accustom himself to the spectacle. The message was very brief. He read it at a glance and for the first time that day he was conscious of that old familiar flicker down the spine as his experienced nose smelled trouble. He re-read the five lines.

"There is a sundial on a stone pavement just off the drive. We saw it from the car. I'll wait ten minutes there for you half an hour after the party breaks up tonight."

There was neither signature nor initial, and the summons broke off as baldly as it had begun.

"Amazing, isn't it?" Lance had the grace to look shamefaced.

"Astounding." Campion's tone was flat. "Staggering, old boy. Er—fishy."

"Fishy?"

"Yes, don't you think so?" Campion was turning over the single sheet thoughtfully and there was no amusement in the pale eyes behind his horn-rimmed spectacles. "How did it arrive?"

"In an unaddressed envelope. I don't suppose she caught my name. After all, there must be some people who don't know it yet." Lance was grinning impudently. "She's batty, of course. Not safe out and all the rest of it. But I liked her eyes and she's very young."

Campion perched himself on the edge of the table. He was still very serious.

"It's disturbing, isn't it?" he said, "Not nice. Makes one wonder."

"Oh, I don't know." Lance retrieved his property and tucked it into his pocket. "She's young and foolish, and it's Christmas."

Campion did not appear to have heard him. "I wonder," he said. "I should keep the appointment, I think. It may be unwise to interfere, but yes, I rather think I should."

"You're telling me." Lance was laughing. "I may be wrong, of course," he added defensively, "but I think that's a cry for help. The poor girl evidently saw that I looked a dependable sort of chap and —er— having her back against the wall for some reason or other she turned instinctively to the stranger with the kind face. Isn't that how you read it?"

"Since you press me, no. Not exactly," said Campion, and as they walked over to the house together he remained thoughtful and irritatingly uncommunicative.

Florence Cookham excelled herself that evening. Her guests were exhorted "to be young again", with the inevitable result that Underhill contained a company of irritated and exhausted people long before midnight.

One of her ladyship's more erroneous beliefs was that she was a born organizer, and that the real secret of entertaining people lay in giving everyone something to do. Thus Lance and the R.A.—now even more startled-looking than ever—found themselves superintending the decoration of the great tree, while the girl with the brandy-ball eyes conducted a small informal dance in the drawing-room, the lady novelist scowled over the bridge table, and the ballet star refused flatly to arrange amateur theatricals.

Only two people remained exempt from this tyranny. One was Sir Philip himself, who looked in every now and again, ready to plead urgent work awaiting him in his study whenever his wife pounced upon him, and the other was Mr Campion, who had work to do on his own account and had long mastered the difficult art of self-effacement. Experience had taught him that half the secret of this manoeuvre was to keep discreetly on the move and he strolled from one party to another, always ready to look as if he belonged to any one of them should his hostess' eye ever come to rest upon him inquiringly.

For once his task was comparatively simple. Florence was in her element as she rushed about surrounded by breathless assistants, and at one period the very air in her vicinity seemed to have become thick with coloured paper-wrappings, yards of red ribbons and a coloured snowstorm of little address tickets as she directed the packing of the presents for the Tenants' Tree, a second monster which stood in the ornamental barn beyond the kitchens.

Campion left Lance to his fate, which promised to be six or seven hours' hard labour at the most moderate estimate, and continued his purposeful meandering. His lean figure drifted among the company with an apparent aimlessness which was deceptive. There was hidden urgency in his lazy movements and his pale eyes behind his spectacles were inquiring and unhappy.

He found Patricia Bullard dancing with young Preen and paused to watch them as they swung gracefully by him. The man was in a somewhat flamboyant mood, flashing his smile and his noisy witticisms about him after the fashion of his kind, but the girl was not so content. As Campion caught sight of her pale face over her partner's sleek shoulder his eyebrows rose. For an instant he almost believed in Lance's unlikely suggestion. The girl actually did look as though she had her back to the wall. She was watching the doorway nervously and her shiny eyes were afraid.

Campion looked about him for the other young man who should have been present, but Peter Groome was not in the ballroom, nor in the great hall, nor yet among the bridge tables in the drawing-room, and half an hour later he had still not put in an appearance.

Campion was in the hall himself when he saw Patricia slip into the anteroom which led to Sir Philip's private study, that holy of holies which even Florence treated with a wholesome awe. Campion had paused for a moment to enjoy the spectacle of Lance, wild-eyed and tight-lipped, wrestling with the last of the blue glass balls and tinsel streamers on the Guests' Tree, when he caught sight of the flare of her silver skirt disappearing round a familiar doorway under one branch of the huge double staircase.

It was what he had been waiting for, and yet when it came his disappointment was unexpectedly acute, for he too had liked her smile and her brandy-ball eyes. The door was ajar when he reached it, and he pushed it open an inch or so farther, pausing on the threshold to consider the scene within. Patricia was on her knees before the panelled door which led into the inner room and was trying somewhat ineffectually to peer through the keyhole.

Campion stood looking at her regretfully, and when she straightened herself and paused to listen, with every line of her young body taut with the effort of concentration, he did not move.

Sir Philip's voice amid the noisy chatter behind him startled him, however, and he swung round to see the old man talking to a group on the other side of the room. A moment later the girl brushed past him and hurried away.

Campion went quietly into the anteroom. The study door was still closed and he moved over to the enormous period fireplace which stood beside it. This particular fireplace, with its carved and painted front, its wrought iron dogs and deeply recessed inglenooks, was one of the showpieces of Underhill.

At the moment the fire had died down and the interior of the cavern was dark, warm, and inviting. Campion stepped inside and sat down on the oak settle, where the shadows swallowed him. He had no intention of being unduly officious, but his quick ears had caught a faint sound in the inner room and Sir Philip's private sanctum was no place for furtive movements when its master was out of the way. He had not long to wait.

A few moments later the study door opened very quietly and someone came out. The newcomer moved across the room with a nervous, unsteady tread, and paused abruptly, his back to the quiet figure in the inglenook.

Campion recognized Peter Groome and his thin mouth narrowed. He was sorry. He had liked the boy.

The youngster stood irresolute. He had his hands behind him, holding in one of them a flamboyant parcel wrapped in the colored paper and scarlet ribbon which littered the house. A sound from the hall seemed to fluster him. for he spun round, thrust the parcel into the inglenook which was the first hiding place to present itself, and returned to face the new arrival. It was the girl again. She came slowly across the room, her hands outstretched and her face raised to Peter's.

In view of everything, Campion thought it best to stay where he was, nor had he time to do anything else. She was speaking urgently, passionate sincerity in her low voice.

"Peter, I've been looking for you. Darling, there's something I've got to say and if I'm making an idiotic mistake then you've got to forgive me. Look here, you wouldn't go and do anything silly, would you? Would you, Peter? Look at me."

"My dear girl." He was laughing unsteadily and not very convincingly with his arms around her. "What on earth are you talking about?"

She drew back from him and peered earnestly into his face.

"You wouldn't, would you? Not even if it meant an awful lot. Not even if for some reason or other you felt you *had* to. Would you?"

He turned from her helplessly, a great weariness in the lines of his sturdy back, but she drew him round, forcing him to face her.

"Would he what, my dear?"

Florence's arch inquiry from the doorway separated them so hurriedly that she laughed delightedly and came briskly into the room, her gray curls a trifle dishevelled and her draperies flowing.

"Too divinely young. I love it!" she said devastatingly. "I must kiss you both. Christmas is the time for love and youth and all the other dear charming things, isn't it? That's why I adore it. But, my dears, not here. Not in this silly poky little room. Come along and help me, both of you, and then you can slip away and dance together later on. But don't come in this room. This is Philip's dull part of the house. Come along this minute. Have you seen my precious tree? Too incredibly distinguished, my darlings, with two great artists at work on it. You shall both tie on a candle. Come along."

She swept them away like an avalanche. No protest was possible. Peter shot a single horrified glance towards the fireplace, but Florence was gripping his arm; he was thrust out into the hall and the door closed firmly behind him.

Campion was left in his corner with the parcel less than a dozen feet away from him on the opposite bench. He moved over and picked it up. It was a long flat package wrapped in holly-printed tissue. Moreover, it was unexpectedly heavy and the ends were unbound.

He turned it over once or twice, wrestling with a strong disinclination to interfere, but a vivid recollection of the girl with the brandy-ball eyes, in her silver dress, her small pale face alive with anxiety, made up his mind for him and, sighing, he pulled the ribbon.

The typewritten folder which fell on to his knees surprised him at first, for it was not at all what he had expected, nor was its title, "Report on Messrs. Anderson and Coleridge, Messrs. Saunders, Duval and Berry, and Messrs. Birmingham and Rose," immediately enlightening, and when he opened it at random a column of incomprehensible figures confronted him. It was a scribbled pencil note in a precise hand at the foot of one of the pages which gave him his first clue.

"These figures are estimated by us to be a reliable forecast of this firm's full working capacity."

Two hours later it was bitterly cold in the garden and a thin white mist hung over the dark shrubbery which lined the drive when Mr Campion, picking his way cautiously along the clipped grass verge, came quietly down to the sundial walk. Behind him the gabled roofs of Underhill were shadowy against a frosty sky. There were still a few lights in the upper windows, but below stairs the entire place was in darkness.

Campion hunched his greatcoat about him and plodded on, unwonted severity in the lines of his thin face.

He came upon the sundial walk at last and paused, straining his eyes to see through the mist. He made out the figure standing by the stone column, and heaved a sigh of relief as he recognized the jaunty shoulders of the Christmas tree decorator. Lance's incurable romanticism was going to be useful at last, he reflected with wry amusement.

He did not join his friend but withdrew into the shadows of a great clump of rhododendrons and composed himself to wait. He intensely disliked the situation in which he found himself. Apart from the extreme physical discomfort involved, he had a natural aversion towards the project on hand, but little fair-haired girls with shiny eyes can be very appealing.

It was a freezing vigil. He could hear Lance stamping about in the mist, swearing softly to himself, and even that supremely comic phenomenon had its unsatisfactory side.

They were both shivering and the mist's damp fingers seemed to have stroked their very bones when at last Campion stiffened. He had heard a rustle behind him and presently there was a movement in the wet leaves, followed by the sharp ring of feet on the stones. Lance swung round immediately, only to drop back in astonishment as a tall figure bore down.

"Where is it?"

Neither the words nor the voice came as a complete surprise to Campion, but the unfortunate Lance was taken entirely off his guard.

"Why, hello, Preen," he said involuntarily. "What the devil are you doing here?"

The newcomer had stopped in his tracks, his face a white blur in the uncertain light. For a moment he stood perfectly still and then, turning on his heel, he made off without a word.

"Ah, but I'm afraid it's not quite so simple as that, my dear chap."

Campion stepped out of his friendly shadows and as the younger man passed, slipped an arm through his and swung him round to face the startled Lance, who was coming up at the double.

"You can't clear off like this," he went on, still in the same affable, conversational tone. "You have something to give Peter Groome, haven't you? Something he rather wants?"

"Who the hell are you?" Preen jerked up his arm as he spoke and might have wrenched himself free had it not been for Lance, who had recognized Campion's voice and, although completely in the dark, was yet quick enough to grasp certain essentials.

"That's right, Preen," he said, seizing the man's other arm in a bear's hug. "Hand it over. Don't be a fool. Hand it over."

This line of attack appeared to be inspirational, since they felt the powerful youngster stiffen between them.

"Look here, how many people know about this?"

"The world—" Lance was beginning cheerfully when Campion forstalled him.

"We three and Peter Groome," he said quietly. "At the moment Sir Philip has no idea that Messrs. Preen's curiosity concerning the probably placing of Government orders for aircraft parts has overstepped the bounds of common sense. You're acting alone, I suppose?"

"Oh, lord, yes, of course." Preen was cracking dangerously, "If my old man gets to hear of this I — oh, well, I might as well go and crash."

"I thought so." Campion sounded content. "Your father has a reputation to consider. So has our young friend Groome. You'd better hand it over."

"What?"

"Since you force me to be vulgar, whatever it was you were attempting to use as blackmail, my precious young friend," he said.

"Whatever it may be, in fact, that you hold over young Groome and were trying to use in your attempt to force him to let you have a look at a confidential Government report concerning the orders which certain aircraft firms were likely to receive in the next six months. In your position you could have made pretty good use of them, couldn't you? Frankly, I haven't the faintest idea what this incriminating document may be. When I was young, objectionably wealthy youths accepted I.O.U.s from their poorer companions, but now that's gone out of fashion. What's the modern equivalent? An R.D. check, I suppose?"

Preen said nothing. He put his hand in an inner pocket and drew out an envelope which he handed over without a word. Campion examined the slip of pink paper within by the light of a pencil torch.

"You kept it for quite a time before trying to cash it, didn't you?" he said. "Dear me, that's rather an old trick and it was never admired. Young men who are careless with their accounts have been caught out like that before. It simply wouldn't have looked good to his legal-minded old man, I take it? You two seem to be hampered by your respective papas' integrity. Yes, well, you can go now."

Preen hesitated, opened his mouth to protest, but thought better of it. Lance looked after his retreating figure for some little time before he returned to his friend.

"Who wrote that blinking note?" he demanded.

"He did, of course," said Campion brutally. "He wanted to see the report but was making absolutely sure that young Groome took all the risks of being found with it."

"Preen wrote the note," Lance repeated blankly.

"Well, naturally," said Campion absently. "That was obvious as soon as the report appeared in the picture. He was the only man in the place with the necessary special information to make use of it."

Lance made no comment. He pulled his coat collar more closely about his throat and stuffed his hands into his pockets.

All the same the artist was not quite satisfied, for, later still, when Campion was sitting in his dressing-gown writing a note at one of the little escritoires which Florence so thoughtfully provided in her guest bedrooms, he came padding in again and stood warming himself before the fire.

"Why?" he demanded suddenly. "Why did I get the invitation?"

"Oh, that was a question of luggage." Campion spoke over his shoulder. "That bothered me at first, but as soon as we fixed it on to Preen that little mystery became blindingly clear. Do you remember falling into the carriage this afternoon? Where did you put your elegant piece of gent's natty suitcasing? Over young Groome's head. Preen saw it from the corridor and assumed that the chap was sitting *under his own bag*! He sent his own man over here with the note, told him not to ask for Peter by name but to follow the nice new pigskin suitcase upstairs."

Lance nodded regretfully. "Very likely," he said sadly. "Funny thing. I was sure it was the girl."

After a while he came over to the desk. Campion put down his pen and indicated the written sheet.

"Dear Groome," it ran, "I enclose a little matter that I should burn forthwith. The package you left in the inglenook is still there, right at the back on the left-hand side, cunningly concealed under a pile of logs. It has not been seen by anyone who could possibly understand it. If you nipped over very early this morning you could return it to its appointed place without any trouble. If I may venture a word of advice, it is never worth it."

The author grimaced. "It's a bit avuncular," he admitted awkwardly, "but what else can I do? His light is still on, poor chap. I thought I'd stick it under his door."

Lance was grinning wickedly.

"That's fine," he murmured. "The old man does his stuff for reckless youth. There's just the signature now and that ought to be as obvious as everything else has been to you. I'll write it for you. 'Merry Christmas. Love from Santa Claus.'"

"You win," said Mr Campion.

# WAXWORKS

## ETHEL LINA WHITE

Ethel Lina White (1876–1944) grew up in Abergavenny. A few years after she was born, her father, a local master builder called William White, built an imposing family home, "Fairlea", in a Mock Tudor style. He invented a product called "White's Hygeia Rock", which he used to soundproof and waterproof the house. Ethel eventually left Wales, and worked for the Ministry of Pensions in London, but like her father, she possessed a creative streak.

She turned to crime fiction quite late in life, publishing her first mystery novel, *Put out the Light*, in 1931 — although by then, "Waxworks" had already appeared in print. Her most famous book, *The Wheel Spins,* became one of Alfred Hitchcock's most popular movies, *The Lady Vanishes*, while *Some Must Watch* (set in a house inspired by "Fairlea") was also filmed successfully, as *The Spiral Staircase*. Like the American Mary Roberts Rinehart before her, and many authors since, she wrote about women in jeopardy, but – as "Waxworks" shows – in a way that made the most of her ability to build relentless suspense.

\* \* \* \* \*

Sonia made her first entry in her notebook:

> Eleven o'clock. The lights are out. The porter has just locked the door. I can hear his footsteps echoing down the corridor. They grow fainter. Now there is silence. I am alone.

She stopped writing to glance at her company. Seen in the light from the street-lamp, which streamed in through the high window, the room seemed to be full of people. Their faces were those of men and women of character and intelligence. They stood in groups, as though in conversation, or sat apart, in solitary reverie.

But they neither moved nor spoke.

When Sonia had last seen them in the glare of the electric globes, they had been a collection of ordinary waxworks, some of which were the worse for wear. The black velvet which lined the walls of the Gallery was alike tawdry and filmed with dust.

The side opposite to the window was built into alcoves, which held highly moral tableaux, depicting contrasting scenes in the career of Vice and Virtue. Sonia had slipped into one of these recesses, just before closing-time, in order to hide for her vigil.

It had been a simple affair. The porter had merely rung his bell, and the few courting couples which represented the Public had taken his hint and hurried towards the exit.

No one was likely to risk being locked in, for the Waxwork Collection of Oldhampton, had lately acquired a sinister reputation. The foundation for this lay in the fate of a stranger to the town—a commercial traveller—who had cut his throat in the Hall of Horrors.

Since then, two persons had, separately, spent the night in the Gallery and, in the morning, each had been found dead.

In both cases the verdict had been "Natural death, due to heart failure". The first victim—a local alderman—had been addicted to alcoholism, and was in very bad shape. The second—his great friend—was a delicate little man, a martyr to asthma, and slightly unhinged through unwise absorption in spiritualism.

While the coincidence of the tragedies stirred up a considerable amount of local superstition, the general belief was that both deaths were due to the power of suggestion, in conjunction with macabre surroundings. The victims had let themselves be frightened to death by the Waxworks.

Sonia was there, in the Gallery, to test its truth.

She was the latest addition to the staff of the *Oldhampton Gazette*. Bubbling with enthusiasm, she made no secret of her literary ambitions, and it was difficult to feed her with enough work. Her colleagues listened to her with mingled amusement and boredom, but they liked her as a refreshing novelty. As for her fine future, they looked to young Wells—the Sporting Editor—to effect her speedy and painless removal from the sphere of journalism.

On Christmas Eve, Sonia took them all into her confidence over her intention to spend a night in the Waxworks, on the last night of the old year.

"Copy there," she declared. "I'm not timid and I have fairly sensitive perceptions, so I ought to be able to write up the effect of imagination on the nervous system. I mean to record my impressions, every hour, while they're piping-hot."

Looking up suddenly, she had surprised a green glare in the eyes of Hubert Poke.

When Sonia came to work on the *Gazette*, she had a secret fear of unwelcome amorous attentions, since she was the only woman on the staff. But the first passion she awoke was hatred.

Poke hated her impersonally, as the representative of a Force, numerically superior to his own sex, which was on the opposing side in the battle for existence. He feared her, too, because she was the unknown element, and possessed the unfair weapon of charm.

Before she came, he had been the star turn on the *Gazette*. His own position on the staff gratified his vanity and entirely satisfied his narrow ambition. But Sonia had stolen some of his thunder. On more than one occasion she had written up a story he had failed to cover, and he had to admit that her success was due to a quicker wit.

For some time past he had been playing with the idea of spending a night in the Waxworks, but was deterred by the knowledge that his brain was not sufficiently temperate for the experiment. Lately he had been subject to sudden red rages, when he had felt a thick hot taste in his throat, as though of blood. He knew that his jealousy of Sonia was accountable. It had almost reached the stage of mania, and trembled on the brink of homicidal urge.

While his brain was still creaking with the idea of first-hand experience in the ill-omened Gallery, Sonia had nipped in with her ready-made plan.

Controlling himself with an effort, he listened while the sub-editor issued a warning to Sonia.

"Bon idea, young woman, but you will find the experience a bit raw. You've no notion how uncanny these big deserted buildings can be."

"That's so," nodded young Wells, "I once spent a night in a haunted house."

Sonia looked at him with her habitual interest. He was short and thick-set, with a three-cornered smile which appealed to her.

"Did you see anything?" she asked.

"No, I cleared out before the show came on. Windy. After a bit, one can imagine *anything*."

It was then that Poke introduced a new note into the discussion by his own theory of the mystery deaths.

Sitting alone in the deserted Gallery, Sonia preferred to forget his words. She resolutely drove them from her mind while she began to settle down for the night.

Her first action was to cross to the figure of Cardinal Wolsey and unceremoniously raise his heavy scarlet robe. From under its voluminous folds, she drew out her cushion and attaché-case, which she had hidden earlier in the evening.

Mindful of the fact that it would grow chilly at dawn, she carried on her arm her thick white tennis-coat. Slipping it on, she placed her cushion in the angle of the wall, and sat down to await developments.

The Gallery was far more mysterious now that the lights were out. At either end, it seemed to stretch away into impenetrable black tunnels. But there was nothing uncanny about it, or about the figures, which were a tame and conventional collection of historical personages. Even the adjoining Hall of Horrors contained no horrors, only a selection of respectable-looking poisoners.

Sonia grinned cheerfully at the row of waxworks which were visible in the lamplight from the street.

"So you are the villains of the piece," she murmured. "Later on, if the office is right, you will assume unpleasant mannerisms to try to cheat me into believing you are alive. I warn you, old sports, you'll have your work cut out for you … And now I think I'll get better acquainted with you. Familiarity breeds contempt."

She went the round of the figures, greeting each with flippancy or criticism. Presently she returned to her corner and opened her notebook ready to record her impressions.

Twelve o'clock. The first hour has passed almost too quickly. I've drawn a complete blank. Not a blessed thing to record. Not a vestige of reaction. The waxworks seem a commonplace lot, without a scrap of hypnotic force. In fact, they're altogether too matey.

Sonia had left her corner, to write her entry in the light which streamed through the window. Smoking was prohibited in the building, and, lest she should yield to temptation, she had left both her cigarettes and matches behind her, on the office table.

At this stage she regretted the matches. A little extra light would be a boon. It was true she carried an electric torch, but she was saving it, in case of emergency.

It was a loan from young Wells. As they were leaving the office together, he spoke to her confidentially.

"Did you notice how Poke glared at you? Don't get up against him. He's a nasty piece of work. He's so mean he'd sell his mother's shroud for old rags. And he's a cruel little devil, too. He turned out his miserable pup, to starve in the streets, rather than cough up for the licence."

Sonia grew hot with indignation.

"What he needs to cure his complaint is a strong dose of rat-poison," she declared.

"What became of the poor little dog?"

"Oh, he's all right. He was a matey chap, and he soon chummed up with a mongrel of his own class."

"You?" asked Sonia, her eyes suddenly soft.

"A mongrel, am I?" grinned Wells. "Well, anyway, the pup will get a better Christmas than his first, when Poke went away and left him on the chain … We're both of us going to over-eat and over-drink. You're on your own, too. Won't you join us?"

"I'd love to."

Although the evening was warm and muggy the invitation suffused Sonia with the spirit of Christmas. The shade of Dickens seemed to be hovering over the parade of the streets. A red-nosed Santa Claus presided over a spangled Christmas tree outside a toy-shop. Windows were hung with tinselled balls and coloured paper festoons. Pedestrians, laden with parcels, called out seasonable greetings.

"Merry Christmas."

Young Wells' three-cornered smile was his tribute to the joyous feeling of festival. His eyes were eager as he turned to Sonia.

"I've an idea. Don't wait until after the holidays to write up the Waxworks. Make it a Christmas stunt, and go there tonight."

"I will," declared Sonia.

It was then that he slipped the torch into her hand.

"I know you belong to the stronger sex," he said. "But even your nerve might crash. If it does, just flash this torch under the window. Stretch out your arm above your head, and the light will be seen from the street."

"And what will happen then?" asked Sonia.

"I shall knock up the miserable porter and let you out."

"But how will *you* see the light?"

"I shall be in the street."

"All night?"

"Yes: I sleep there." Young Wells grinned. "Understand," he added loftily, 'that this is a matter of principle. I could not let any woman— even one so aged and unattractive as yourself—feel beyond the reach of help."

He cut into her thanks as he turned away with a parting warning.

"Don't use the torch for light, or the juice may give out. It's about due for a new battery."

As Sonia looked at the torch, lying by her side, it seemed a link with young Wells. At this moment he was patrolling the street, a sturdy figure in old tweed overcoat, with his cap pulled down over his eyes.

As she tried to pick out his footsteps from among those of the other passers-by, it struck her that there was plenty of traffic, considering that it was past twelve o'clock.

"The witching hour of midnight is another lost illusion," she reflected. "Killed by night-clubs. I suppose."

It was cheerful to know that so many citizens were abroad, to keep her company. Some optimists were still singing carols. She faintly heard the strains of "Good King Wenceslas". It was in a tranquil frame of mind that she unpacked her sandwiches and thermos.

"It's Christmas Day," she thought, as she drank hot coffee. "And I'm spending it with Don and the pup."

At that moment her career grew misty, and the flame of her literary ambition dipped as the future glowed with the warm firelight of home. In sudden elation, she held up her flask and toasted the waxworks.

"Merry Christmas to you all! And many of them."

The faces of the illuminated figures remained stolid. but she could almost swear that a low murmur of acknowledgment seemed to swell from the rest of her company—invisible in the darkness.

She spun out her meal to its limit, stifling her craving for a cigarette. Then, growing bored, she counted the visible waxworks, and tried to memorize them.

"Twenty-one, twenty-two ... Wolsey. Queen Elizabeth, Guy Fawkes, Napoleon ought to go on a diet. Ever heard of eighteen days, Nap? Poor old Julius Caesar looks as though he'd been sun-bathing on the Lido. He's about due for the melting-pot."

In her eyes they were a second-rate set of dummies. The local theory that they could terrorize a human being to death or madness seemed a fantastic notion.

"No," concluded Sonia. "There's really more in Poke's bright idea."

Again she saw the sun-smitten office—for the big unshielded window faced south—with its blistered paint, faded wall-paper, ink-stained desks, typewriters, telephones, and a huge fire in the untidy grate. Young Wells smoked his big pipe, while the sub-editor—a ginger, pig-headed young man—laid down the law about the mystery deaths.

And then she heard Poke's toneless deadman's voice.

"You may be right about the spiritualist. He died of fright—but not of the waxworks. My belief is that he established contact with the spirit of his dead friend, the alderman, and so learned his real fate."

"What fate?" snapped the sub-editor.

"I believe that the alderman was murdered," replied Poke.

He clung to his point like a limpet in the face of all counter-arguments.

"The alderman had enemies," he said. "Nothing would be easier than for one of them to lie in wait for him. In the present circumstances, *I* could commit a murder in the Waxworks, and get away with it."

"How?" demanded young Wells.

"How? To begin with, the Gallery is a one-man show and the porter's a bonehead. Anyone could enter, and leave, the Gallery without his being wise to it."

"And the murder?" plugged young Wells.

With a shudder Sonia remembered how Poke had glanced at his long knotted fingers.

"If I could not achieve my object by fright, which is the foolproof way," he replied, "I should try a little artistic strangulation."

"And leave your marks?"

"Not necessarily. Every expert knows that there are methods which show no trace."

Sonia fumbled in her bag for the cigarettes which were not there.

"Why did I let myself think of that, just now?" she thought. "Really too stupid."

As she reproached herself for her morbidity, she broke off to stare at the door which led to the Hall of Horrors.

When she had last looked at it, she could have sworn that it was tightly closed ... But now it gaped open by an inch.

She looked at the black cavity, recognizing the first test of her nerves. Later on, there would be others. She realized the fact that, within her cool, practical self, she carried a hysterical, neurotic passenger, who would doubtless give her a lot of trouble through officious suggestions and uncomfortable reminders.

She resolved to give her second self a taste of her quality, and so quell her at the start.

"That door was merely closed," she remarked as, with a firm step, she crossed to the Hall of Horrors and shut the door.

One o'clock. I begin to realize that there is more in this than I thought. Perhaps I'm missing my sleep. But I'm keyed up and horribly expectant. Of what? I don't know. But I seem to be waiting for—something. I find myself listening—listening. The place is full of mysterious noises. I know they're my fancy … And things appear to move. I can distinguish footsteps and whispers, as though those waxworks which I cannot see in the darkness are beginning to stir to life.

Sonia dropped her pencil at the sound of a low chuckle. It seemed to come from the end of the Gallery which was blacked out by shadows.

As her imagination galloped away with her, she reproached herself sharply.

"Steady, don't be a fool. There must be a cloak-room here. That chuckle is the air escaping in a pipe—or something. I'm betrayed by my own ignorance of hydraulics."

In spite of her brave words, she returned rather quickly to her corner.

With her back against the wall she felt less apprehensive. But she recognized her cowardice as an ominous sign.

She was desperately afraid of someone—or something—creeping up behind her and touching her.

"I've struck the bad patch," she told herself. "It will be worse at three o'clock and work up to a climax. But when I make my entry, at three, I shall have reached the peak. After that every minute will be bringing the dawn nearer."

But of one fact she was ignorant. There would be no recorded impression at three o'clock.

Happily unconscious, she began to think of her copy. When she returned to the office—sunken-eyed, and looking like nothing on earth—she would then rejoice over every symptom of groundless fear.

"It's a story all right," she gloated, looking at Hamlet. His gnarled, pallid features and dark smouldering eyes were strangely familiar to her.

Suddenly she realized that he reminded her of Hubert Poke.

Against her will, her thoughts again turned to him. She told herself that he was exactly like a waxwork. His yellow face—symptomatic of heart-trouble—had the same cheesy hue, and his eyes were like dull black glass. He wore a denture which was too large for him, and which forced his lips apart in a mirthless grin.

He always seemed to smile—even over the episode of the lift—which had been no joke.

It happened two days before. Sonia had rushed into the office in a state of molten excitement because she had extracted an interview from a Personage who had just received the Freedom of the City. This distinguished freeman had the reputation of shunning newspaper publicity, and Poke had tried his luck, only to be sent away with a flea in his ear.

At the back of her mind, Sonia knew that she had not fought level, for she was conscious of the effect of violet-blue eyes and a

dimple upon a reserved but very human gentleman. But in her elation she had been rather blatant about her score.

She transcribed her notes, rattling away at her typewriter in a tremendous hurry, because she had a dinner-engagement. In the same
breathless speed she had rushed towards the automatic lift.

She was just about to step into it when young Wells had leaped
the length of the passage and dragged her back.

"Look, where you're going," he shouted.

Sonia looked—and saw only the well of the shaft. The lift was not
waiting in its accustomed place.

"Out of order," explained Wells before he turned to blast Hubert
Poke, who stood by.

"You almighty chump, why didn't you grab Miss Fraser, instead of
standing by like a stuck pig?"

At the time Sonia had vaguely remarked how Poke had stam-
mered and sweated, and she accepted the fact that he had been petrified by shock and had lost his head.

For the first time, she realized that his inaction had been deliberate.
She remembered the flame of terrible excitement in his eyes and his
stretched ghastly grin.

"He *hates* me," she thought. "It's my fault. I've been tactless and
cocksure."

Then a flood of horror swept over her.

"But he wanted to see me crash. It's almost *murder*."

As she began to tremble, the jumpy passenger she carried
reminded her of Poke's remark about the alderman.

"He had enemies."

Sonia shook away the suggestion angrily.

"My memory's uncanny," she thought. "I'm stimulated and all
strung up. It must be the atmosphere … Perhaps there's some gas

in the air that accounts for these brainstorms. It's hopeless to be so utterly unscientific. Poke would have made a better job of this."

She was back again to Hubert Poke. He had become an obsession.

Her head began to throb and a tiny gong started to beat in her temples. This time, she recognized the signs without any mental ferment.

"Atmospherics. A storm's coming up. It might make things rather thrilling. I must concentrate on my story. Really, my luck's in."

She sat for some time, forcing herself to think of pleasant subjects—of arguments with young Wells and the Tennis Tournament. But there was always a point when her thoughts gave a twist and led her back to Poke.

Presently she grew cramped and got up to pace the illuminated aisle in front of the window. She tried again to talk to the waxworks, but, this time, it was not a success.

They seemed to have grown remote and secretive, as though they were removed to another plane, where they possessed a hidden life.

Suddenly she gave a faint scream. Someone—or something—had crept up behind her, for she felt the touch of cold fingers upon her arm.

Two o'clock. They're only wax. They shall not frighten me. But they're trying to. One by one they're coming to life … Charles the Second no longer looks sour dough. He is beginning to leer at me. His eyes remind me of Hubert Poke.

Sonia stopped writing, to glance uneasily at the image of the Stuart monarch. His black velveteen suit appeared to have a richer pile. The swart curls which fell over his lace collar looked less like horse-hair. There really seemed a gleam of amorous interest lurking at the back of his glass optics.

Absurdly, Sonia spoke to him, in order to reassure herself.

"Did *you* touch me? At the first hint of a liberty, Charles Stuart, I'll smack your face. You'll learn a modern journalist has not the manners of an orange-girl."

Instantly the satyr reverted to a dummy in a moth-eaten historical costume.

Sonia stood, listening for young Wells' footsteps. But she could not hear them, although the street now was perfectly still. She tried to picture him, propping up the opposite building, solid and immovable as the Rock of Gibraltar.

But it was no good. Doubts began to obtrude.

"I don't believe he's there. After all, why should he stay? He only pretended, just to give me confidence. He's gone."

She shrank back to her corner, drawing her tennis-coat closer, for warmth. It was growing colder, causing her to think of tempting things—of a hot-water bottle and a steaming tea-pot.

Presently she realized that she was growing drowsy. Her lids felt as though weighted with lead, so that it required an effort to keep them open.

This was a complication which she had not foreseen. Although she longed to drop off to sleep, she sternly resisted the temptation.

"No. It's not fair. I've set myself the job of recording a night spent in the Waxworks. It *must* be the genuine thing."

She blinked more vigorously, staring across to where Byron drooped like a sooty flamingo.

"Mercy, how he yearns! He reminds me of—— No, I won't think of *him* ... I must keep awake ... Bed ... blankets, pillows ... No."

Her head fell forward, and for a minute she dozed. In that space of time, she had a vivid dream.

She thought that she was still in her corner in the Gallery, watching the dead alderman as he paced to and fro, before the window. She had never seen him, so he conformed to her own idea of an alderman—stout, pompous, and wearing the dark-blue, fur-trimmed robe of his office.

"He's got a face like a sleepy pear," she decided. "Nice old thing, but brainless."

And then, suddenly, her tolerant derision turned to acute apprehension on his account, as she saw that he was being followed. A shape was stalking him as a cat stalks a bird.

Sonia tried to warn him of his peril, but, after the fashion of nightmares, she found herself voiceless. Even as she struggled to scream, a grotesquely long arm shot out and monstrous fingers gripped the alderman's throat.

In the same moment, she saw the face of the killer. It was Hubert Poke. She awoke with a start, glad to find that it was but a dream. As she looked around her with dazed eyes, she saw a faint flicker of light. The mutter of very faint thunder, together with a patter of rain, told her that the storm had broken.

It was still a long way off, for Oldhampton seemed to be having merely a reflection and an echo.

"It'll clear the air," thought Sonia.

Then her heart gave a violent leap. One of the waxworks had come to life. She distinctly saw it move, before it disappeared into the darkness at the end of the Gallery.

She kept her head, realizing that it was time to give up.

"My nerve's crashed," she thought. "That figure was only my fancy. I'm just like the others. Defeated by wax."

Instinctively, she paid the figures her homage. It was the cumulative effect of their grim company, with their simulated life and sinister associations, that had rushed her defences.

Although it was bitter to fail, she comforted herself with the reminder that she had enough copy for her article. She could even make capital out of her own capitulation to the force of suggestion.

With a slight grimace, she picked up her notebook. There would be no more on-the-spot impressions. But young Wells, if he was still there, would be grateful for the end of his vigil, whatever the state of mind of the porter.

She groped in the darkness for her signal-lamp. But her fingers only scraped bare polished boards.

The torch had disappeared.

In a panic, she dropped down on her knees, and searched for yards around the spot where she was positive it had lain.

It was the instinct of self-preservation which caused her to give up her vain search.

"I'm in danger," she thought. "And I've no one to help me now. I must see this through myself."

She pushed back her hair from a brow which had grown damp.

"There's a brain working against mine. When I was asleep, someone—or something—stole my torch."

*Something?* The waxworks became instinct with terrible possibility as she stared at them. Some were merely blurred shapes—their faces opaque oblongs or ovals. But others—illuminated from the street—were beginning to reveal themselves in a new guise.

Queen Elizabeth, with peaked chin and fiery hair, seemed to regard her with intelligent malice. The countenance of Napoleon was heavy with brooding power, as though he were willing her to submit. Cardinal Wolsey held her with a glittering eye.

Sonia realized that she was letting herself be hypnotized by creatures of wax—so many pounds of candles moulded to human form.

"This is what happened to those others," she thought. "*Nothing happened*. But I'm afraid of them. I'm terribly afraid … There's only one thing to do. I must count them again."

She knew that she must find out whether her torch had been stolen through human agency; but she shrank from the experiment, not knowing which she feared more—a tangible enemy or the unknown.

As she began to count, the chilly air inside the building seemed to throb with each thud of her heart.

"Seventeen, eighteen." She was scarcely conscious of the numerals she murmured. 'Twenty-two, twenty-three.'

She stopped. Twenty-three? If her tally were correct, there was an extra waxwork in the Gallery.

On the shock of the discovery came a blinding flash of light, which veined the sky with fire. It seemed to run down the figure of Joan of Arc like a flaming torch. By a freak of atmospherics, the storm, which had been a starved, whimpering affair of flicker and murmur, culminated, and ended, in what was apparently a thunderbolt.

The explosion which followed was stunning; but Sonia scarcely noticed it, in her terror.

The unearthly violet glare had revealed to her a figure which she had previously overlooked.

It was seated in a chair, its hand supporting its peaked chin, and its pallid, clean-shaven features nearly hidden by a familiar broad-brimmed felt hat, which—together with the black cape—gave her the clue to its identity.

It was Hubert Poke.

*Three o'clock.*

Sonia heard it strike, as her memory began to reproduce, with horrible fidelity, every word of Poke's conversation on murder.

"Artistic strangulation." She pictured the cruel agony of life leaking—bubble by bubble, gasp by gasp. It would be slow—for he had boasted of a method which left no tell-tale marks.

"Another death," she thought dully. "If it happens everyone will say that the Waxworks have killed me. What a story ... Only, I shall not write it up."

The tramp of feet rang out on the pavement below. It might have been the policeman on his beat; but Sonia wanted to feel that young Wells was still faithful to his post.

She looked up at the window, set high in the wall, and, for a moment, was tempted to shout. But the idea was too desperate. If she failed to attract outside attention, she would seal her own fate, for Poke would be prompted to hasten her extinction.

"Awful to feel he's so near, and yet I cannot reach him," she thought. "It makes it so much worse."

She crouched there, starting and sweating at every faint sound in the darkness. The rain, which still pattered on the sky-light, mimicked footsteps and whispers. She remembered her dream and the nightmare spring and clutch.

It was an omen. At any moment it would come...

Her fear jolted her brain. For the first time she had a glimmer of hope.

"I didn't see him before the flash, because he looked exactly like one of the waxworks. Could I hide among them, too?" she wondered.

She knew that her white coat alone revealed her position to him. Holding her breath, she wriggled out of it, and hung it on the effigy of Charles II. In her black coat, with her handkerchief-scarf tied over her face, burglar fashion, she hoped that she was invisible against the sable-draped walls.

Her knees shook as she crept from her shelter. When she had stolen a few yards, she stopped to listen … In the darkness, someone was astir. She heard a soft padding ding of feet, moving with the certainty of one who sees his goal.

Her coat glimmered in her deserted corner.

In a sudden panic, she increased her pace, straining her ears for other sounds. She had reached the far end of the Gallery where no gleam from the window penetrated the gloom. Blindfolded and muffled, she groped her way towards the alcoves which held the tableaux.

Suddenly she stopped, every nerve in her body quivering. She had heard a thud, like rubbered soles alighting after a spring.

"He knows now." Swift on the trail of her thought flashed another. "He will look for me. Oh, *quick*!"

She tried to move, but her muscles were bound, and she stood as though rooted to the spot, listening. It was impossible to locate the footsteps. They seemed to come from every quarter of the Gallery. Sometimes they sounded remote, but, whenever she drew a freer breath, a sudden creak of the boards close to where she stood made her heart leap.

At last she reached the limit of endurance. Unable to bear the suspense of waiting, she moved on.

Her pursuer followed her at a distance. He gained on her, but still withheld his spring. She had the feeling that he held her at the end of an invisible string.

"He's playing with me, like a cat with a mouse," she thought.

If he had seen her, he let her creep forward until the darkness was no longer absolute. There were gradations in its density, so that she was able to recognize the first alcove. Straining her eyes, she could distinguish the outlines of the bed where the Virtuous Man made his triumphant exit from life, surrounded by a flock of his sorrowing family and their progeny.

Slipping inside the circle, she added one more mourner to the tableau.

The minutes passed, but nothing happened. There seemed no sound save the tiny gong beating inside her temples. Even the raindrops had ceased to patter on the sky-light.

Sonia began to find the silence more deadly than noise. It was like the lull before the storm. Question after question came rolling into her mind.

"Where is he? What will he do next? Why doesn't he strike a light?"

As though someone were listening in to her thoughts, she suddenly heard a faint splutter as of an ignited match. Or it might have been the click of an exhausted electric torch.

With her back turned to the room, she could see no light. She heard the half-hour strike, with a faint wonder that she was still alive.

"What will have happened before the next quarter?" she asked.

Presently she began to feel the strain of her pose, which she held as rigidly as any artist's model. For the time—if her presence were not already detected—her life depended on her immobility.

As an overpowering weariness began to steal over her a whisper stirred in her brain:

"The alderman was found dead on a bed."

The newspaper account had not specified which especial tableau had been the scene of the tragedy, but she could not remember another alcove which held a bed. As she stared at the white dimness of the quilt she seemed to see it blotched with a dark, sprawling form, writhing under the grip of long fingers.

To shut out the suggestion of her fancy, she closed her eyes. The cold, dead air in the alcove was sapping her exhausted vitality, so that once again she began to nod. She dozed as she stood, rocking to and fro on her feet.

Her surroundings grew shadowy. Sometimes she knew that she was in the alcove, but at others she strayed momentarily over strange borders … She was back in the summer, walking in a garden with young Wells. Roses and sunshine…

She awoke with a start at the sound of heavy breathing. It sounded close to her—almost by her side. The figure of a mourner kneeling by the bed seemed to change its posture slightly.

Instantly maddened thoughts began to flock and flutter wildly inside her brain.

"Who was it? Was it Hubert Poke? Would history be repeated? Was she doomed also to be strangled inside the alcove? Had Fate led her there?"

She waited, but nothing happened. Again she had the sensation of being played with by a master mind—dangled at the end of his invisible string.

Presently she was emboldened to steal from the alcove, to seek another shelter. But though she held on to the last flicker of her will, she had reached the limit of endurance. Worn out with the violence of her emotions and physically spent from the strain of long periods of standing, she staggered as she walked.

She blundered round the Gallery, without any sense of direction, colliding blindly with the groups of waxwork figures. When she reached the window her knees shook under her and she sank to the ground—dropping immediately into a sleep of utter exhaustion.

She awoke with a start as the first grey gleam of dawn was stealing into the Gallery. It fell on the row of waxworks, imparting a sickly hue to their features, as though they were creatures stricken with plague.

It seemed to Sonia that they were waiting for her to wake. Their peaked faces were intelligent and their eyes held interest, as though they were keeping some secret.

She pushed back her hair, her brain still thick with clouded memories. Disconnected thoughts began to stir, to slide about ... Then suddenly her mind cleared, and she sprang up—staring at a figure wearing a familiar black cape.

Hubert Poke was also waiting for her to wake.

He sat in the same chair, and in the same posture, as when she had first seen him, in the flash of lightning. He looked as though he had never moved from his place—as though he could not move. His face had not the appearance of flesh.

As Sonia stared at him, with the feeling of a bird hypnotized by a snake, a doubt began to gather in her mind. Growing bolder, she crept closer to the figure.

It was a waxwork—a libellous representation of the actor—Kean.

Her laugh rang joyously through the Gallery as she realized that she had passed a night of baseless terrors, cheated by the power of imagination. In her relief she turned impulsively to the waxworks.

"My congratulations," she said. "You are my masters."

They did not seem entirely satisfied by her homage, for they continued to watch her with an expression half-benevolent and half-sinister.

"*Wait!*" they seemed to say.

Sonia turned from them and opened her bag to get out her mirror and comb. There, among a jumble of notes, letters, lipsticks and powder-compresses, she saw the electric torch.

"*Of course!*" she cried. "I remember now, I put it there. I was too windy to think properly ... Well, I have my story. I'd better get my coat."

The Gallery seemed smaller in the returning light. As she approached Charles Stuart, who looked like an umpire in her white coat, she glanced down the far end of the room, where she had groped in its shadows before the pursuit of imaginary footsteps.

A waxwork was lying prone on the floor. For the second time she stood and gazed down upon a familiar black cape—a broad-brimmed conspirator's hat. Then she nerved herself to turn the figure so that its face was visible.

She gave a scream. There was no mistaking the glazed eyes and ghastly grin. She was looking down on the face of a dead man.

It was Hubert Poke.

The shock was too much for Sonia. She heard a singing in her ears, while a black mist gathered before her eyes. For the first time in her life she fainted.

When she recovered consciousness she forced herself to kneel beside the body and cover it with its black cape. The pallid face resembled a death-mask, which revealed only too plainly the lines of egotism and cruelty in which it had been moulded by a gross spirit.

Yet Sonia felt no repulsion—only pity. It was Christmas morning, and he was dead, while her own portion was life triumphant. Closing her eyes, she whispered a prayer of supplication for his warped soul.

Presently, as she grew calmer, her mind began to work on the problem of his presence. His motive seemed obvious. Not knowing that she had changed her plan, he had concealed himself in the Gallery, in order to poach her story.

"He was in the Hall of Horrors at first," she thought, remembering the opened door. "When he came out he hid at this end. We never saw each other, because of the waxworks between us; but we heard each other."

She realized that the sounds which had terrified her had not all been due to imagination, while it was her agency which had converted the room into a whispering gallery of strange murmurs and voices. The clue to the cause of death was revealed by his wrist-watch, which had smashed when he fell. Its hands had stopped at three minutes to three, proving that the flash and explosion of the thunderbolt had been too much for his diseased heart—already overstrained by superstitious fears.

Sonia shuddered at a mental vision of his face, distraught with terror and pulped by raw primal impulses, after a night spent in a madman's world of phantasy.

She turned to look at the waxworks. At last she understood what they seemed to say.

"*But for Us, you should have met—at dawn.*"

"Your share shall be acknowledged, I promise you," she said, as she opened her notebook.

Eight o'clock. The Christmas bells are ringing and it is wonderful just to be alive. I'm through the night, and none the worse for the experience, although I cracked badly after three o'clock. A colleague who, unknown to me, was also concealed in the Gallery has met with a tragic fate, caused, I am sure, by the force of suggestion. Although his death is due to heart-failure, the superstitious will certainly claim it is another victory for the Waxworks.

# CAMBRIC TEA

## Marjorie Bowen

Marjorie Bowen was one of the pen-names used by Gabrielle Margaret Vere Long (1885–1952). She wrote her first novel, *The Viper of Milan*, in her teens, and the need to earn money for her impoverished family caused her to become exceptionally productive. Eventually, she became so prolific that she found it necessary to adopt a string of (predominantly male) pseudonyms, including George R. Preedy, John Winch and Robert Paye.

Bowen's output was varied, both in content and quality, but much of the best work published under her own name touched on the supernatural. She had the knack of creating an atmosphere of gothic horror, and Graham Greene cited her as an influence. "Cambric Tea" is a well-known story, and one of her finest.

\* \* \* \* \*

The situation was bizarre; the accurately trained mind of Bevis Holroyd was impressed foremost by this; that the opening of a door would turn it into tragedy.

"I am afraid I can't stay," he had said pleasantly, humouring a sick man; he was too young and had not been long enough completely successful to have a professional manner but a certain balanced tolerance just showed in his attitude to this prostrate creature.

"I've got a good many claims on my time," he added, "and I'm afraid it would be impossible. And it isn't the least necessary, you know. You're quite all right. I'll come back after Christmas if you really think it worth while."

The patient opened one eye; he was lying flat on his back in a deep, wide-fashioned bed hung with a thick, dark, silk-lined tapestry; the room was dark for there were thick curtains of the same material drawn half across the windows, rigidly excluding all save a moiety of the pallid winter light; to make his examination Dr Holroyd had had to snap on the electric light that stood on the bedside table; he thought it a dreary unhealthy room, but had hardly found it worth while to say as much.

The patient opened one eye; the other lid remained fluttering feebly over an immobile orb.

He said in a voice both hoarse and feeble:

"But, doctor, I'm being poisoned."

Professional curiosity and interest masked by genial incredulity instantly quickened the doctor's attention.

"My dear sir," he smiled, "poisoned by this nasty bout of 'flu you mean, I suppose—"

"No," said the patient, faintly and wearily dropping both lids over his blank eyes, "by my wife."

"That's an ugly sort of fancy for you to get hold of," replied the doctor instantly. "Acute depression—we must see what we can do for you—"

The sick man opened both eyes now; he even slightly raised his head as he replied, not without dignity:

"I fetched you from London, Dr Holroyd, that you might deal with my case impartially—from the local man there is no hope of that, he is entirely impressed by my wife."

Dr Holroyd made a movement as if to protest but a trembling sign from the patient made him quickly subsist.

"Please let me speak. *She* will come in soon and I shall have no chance. I sent for you secretly, she knows nothing about that. I had heard you very well spoken of—as an authority on this sort of thing. You made a name over the Pluntre murder case as witness for the Crown."

"I don't specialize in murder," said Dr Holroyd, but his keen handsome face was alight with interest. "And I don't care much for this kind of case—Sir Harry."

"But you've taken it on," murmured the sick man. "You couldn't abandon me now."

"I'll get you into a nursing home," said the doctor cheerfully, "and there you'll dispel all these ideas."

"And when the nursing home has cured me I'm to come back to my wife for her to begin again?"

Dr Holroyd bent suddenly and sharply over the sombre bed. With his right hand he deftly turned on the electric lamp and tipped back the coral silk shade so that the bleached acid light fell full over the patient lying on his back on the big fat pillows.

"Look here," said the doctor, "what you say is pretty serious."

And the two men stared at each other, the patient examining his physician as acutely as his physician examined him.

Bevis Holroyd was still a young man with a look of peculiar energy and austere intelligence that heightened by contrast purely physical dark good looks that many men would have found sufficient passport to success; resolution, dignity and a certain masculine sweetness, serene and strong, different from feminine sweetness, marked his demeanour which was further softened by a quick humour and a sensitive judgment.

The patient, on the other hand, was a man of well past middle age, light, flabby and obese with a flaccid, fallen look about his large face which was blurred and dimmed by the colours of ill health, being one pasty livid hue that threw into unpleasant relief the grey speckled red of his scant hair.

Altogether an unpleasing man, but of a certain fame and importance that had induced the rising young doctor to come at once when hastily summoned to Strangeways Manor House; a man of a fine, renowned family, a man of repute as a scholar, an essayist who had once been a politician who was rather above politics; a man whom Dr Holroyd only knew vaguely by reputation, but who seemed to him symbolical of all that was staid, respectable and stolid.

And this man blinked up at him and whimpered:

"My wife is poisoning me."

Dr Holroyd sat back and snapped off the electric light.

"What makes you think so?" he asked sharply.

"To tell you that," came the laboured voice of the sick man. "I should have to tell you my story."

"Well, if you want me to take this up—"

"I sent for you to do that, doctor."

"Well, how do you think you are being poisoned?"

"Arsenic, of course."

"Oh? And how administered?"

Again the patient looked up with one eye, seeming too fatigued to open the other.

"Cambric tea," he replied.

And Dr Holroyd echoed:

"Cambric tea!" with a soft amazement and interest.

Cambric tea had been used as the medium for arsenic in the Pluntre case and the expression had become famous; it was Bevis Holroyd who had discovered the doses in the cambric tea and who had put his finger on this pale beverage as the means of murder.

"Very possibly," continued Sir Harry, "the Pluntre case made her think of it."

"For God's sake, don't," said Dr Holroyd; for in that hideous affair the murderer had been a woman; and to see a woman on trial for her life, to see a woman sentenced to death, was not an experience he wished to repeat.

"Lady Strangeways," continued the sick man, "is much younger than I—I overpersuaded her to marry me, she was at that time very much attracted by a man of her own age, but he was in a poor position and she was ambitious."

He paused, wiped his quivering lips on a silk handkerchief, and added faintly:

"Lately our marriage has been extremely unhappy. The man she preferred is now prosperous, successful and unmarried—she wishes to dispose of me that she may marry her first choice."

"Have you proof of any of this?"

"Yes. I know she buys arsenic. I know she reads books on poisons. I know she is eating her heart out for this other man."

"Forgive me, Sir Harry," replied the doctor, "but have you no near friend nor relation to whom you can confide your—suspicions?"

"No one," said the sick man impatiently. "I have lately come from the East and am out of touch with people. Besides I want a doctor, a doctor with skill in this sort of thing. I thought from the first of the Pluntre case and of you."

Bevis Holroyd sat back quietly; it was then that he thought of the situation as bizarre; the queerness of the whole thing was vividly before him, like a twisted figure on a gem—a carving at once writhing and immobile.

"Perhaps," continued Sir Harry wearily, "you are married, doctor?"

"No." Dr Holroyd slightly smiled; his story was something like the sick man's story but taken from another angle; when he was very poor and unknown he had loved a girl who had preferred a wealthy man; she had gone out to India, ten years ago, and he had never seen her since; he remembered this, with sharp distinctness, and in the same breath he remembered that he still loved this girl; it was, after all, a commonplace story.

Then his mind swung to the severe professional aspect of the case; he had thought that his patient, an unhealthy type of man, was struggling with a bad attack of influenza and the resultant depression and weakness, but then he had never thought, of course, of poison, nor looked nor tested for poison.

The man might be lunatic, he might be deceived, he might be speaking the truth; the fact that he was a mean, unpleasant beast ought not to weigh in the matter; Dr Holroyd had some enjoyable Christmas holidays in prospect and now he was beginning to feel that he ought to give these up to stay and investigate this case; for he could readily see that it was one in which the local doctor would be quite useless.

"You must have a nurse," he said, rising.

But the sick man shook his head.

"I don't wish to expose my wife more than need be," he grumbled. "Can't you manage the affair yourself?"

As this was the first hint of decent feeling he had shown, Bevis Holroyd forgave him his brusque rudeness.

"Well, I'll stay the night anyhow," he conceded.

And then the situation changed, with the opening of a door, from the bizarre to the tragic.

This door opened in the far end of the room and admitted a bloom of bluish winter light from some uncurtained, high windowed corridor; the chill impression was as if invisible snow had entered the shaded, dun, close apartment.

And against this background appeared a woman in a smoke-coloured dress with some long lace about the shoulders and a high comb; she held a little tray carrying jugs and a glass of crystal in which the cold light splintered.

Dr Holroyd stood in his usual attitude of attentive courtesy, and then, as the patient, feebly twisting his gross head from the fat pillow, said:

"My wife—doctor—" he recognized in Lady Strangeways the girl to whom he had once been engaged in marriage, the woman he still loved.

"This is Doctor Holroyd," added Sir Harry. "Is that cambric tea you have there?"

She inclined her head to the stranger by her husband's bed as if she had never seen him before, and he, taking his cue, and for many other reasons, was silent.

"Yes, this is your cambric tea," she said to her husband. "You like it just now, don't you? How do you find Sir Harry, Dr Holroyd?"

There were two jugs on the tray; one of crystal half full of cold milk, and one of white porcelain full of hot water; Lady Strangeways proceeded to mix these fluids in equal proportions and gave the resultant drink to her husband, helping him first to sit up in bed.

"I think that Sir Harry has a nasty turn of influenza," answered the doctor mechanically. "He wants me to stay. I've promised till the morning, anyhow."

"That will be a pleasure and a relief," said Lady Strangeways gravely. "My husband has been ill some time and seems so much worse than he need—for influenza."

The patient, feebly sipping his cambric tea, grinned queerly at the doctor.

"So much worse—you see, doctor!" he muttered.

"It is good of you to stay," continued Lady Strangeways equally. "I will see about your room, you must be as comfortable as possible."

She left as she had come, a shadow-coloured figure retreating to a chill light.

The sick man held up his glass as if he gave a toast.

"You see! Cambric tea!"

And Bevis Holroyd was thinking: does she not want to know me? Does he know what we once were to each other? How comes she to be married to this man—her husband's name was Custiss—and the horror of the situation shook the calm that was his both from character and training; he went to the window and looked out on the bleached park; light, slow snow was falling, a dreary dance over the frozen grass and before the grey corpses that paled, one behind the other, to the distance shrouded in colourless mist.

The thin voice of Harry Strangeways recalled him to the bed.

"Would you like to take a look at this, doctor?" He held out the half drunk glass of milk and water.

"I've no means of making a test here," said Dr Holroyd, troubled. "I brought a few things, nothing like that."

"You are not so far from Harley Street," said Sir Harry. "My car can fetch everything you want by this afternoon—or perhaps you would like to go yourself?"

"Yes," replied Bevis Holroyd sternly. "I would rather go myself."

His trained mind had been rapidly covering the main aspects of his problem and he had instantly seen that it was better for Lady Strangeways to have this case in his hands. He was sure there was some hideous, fantastic hallucination on the part of Sir Harry, but it was better for Lady Strangeways to leave the matter in the hands of one who was friendly towards her. He rapidly found and washed a medicine bottle from among the sick room paraphernalia and poured it full of the cambric tea, casting away the remainder.

"Why did you drink any?" he asked sharply.

"I don't want her to think that I guess," whispered Sir Harry. "Do you know, doctor, I have a lot of her love letters—written by—"

Dr Holroyd cut him short.

"I couldn't listen to this sort of thing behind Lady Strangeways' back," he said quickly. "That is between you and her. My job is to get you well. I'll try and do that."

And he considered, with a faint disgust, how repulsive this man looked sitting up with pendant jowl and drooping cheeks and discoloured, pouchy eyes sunk in pads of unhealthy flesh and above the spiky crown of Judas-coloured hair.

Perhaps a woman, chained to this man, living with him, blocked and thwarted by him, might be wrought upon to—

Dr Holroyd shuddered inwardly and refused to continue his reflection.

As he was leaving the gaunt sombre house about which there was something definitely blank and unfriendly, a shrine in which the sacred flames had flickered out so long ago that the lamps were blank and cold, he met Lady Strangeways.

She was in the wide entrance hall standing by the wood fire that but faintly dispersed the gloom of the winter morning and left untouched the shadows in the rafters of the open roof.

Now he would not, whether she wished or no, deny her; he stopped before her, blocking out her poor remnant of light.

"Mollie," he said gently, "I don't quite understand—you married a man named Custiss in India."

"Yes. Harry had to take this name when he inherited this place. We've been home three years from the East, but lived so quietly here that I don't suppose anyone has heard of us."

She stood between him and the firelight, a shadow among the shadows; she was much changed; in her thinness and pallor, in her restless eyes and nervous mouth he could read signs of discontent, even of unhappiness.

"I never heard of you," said Dr Holroyd truthfully. "I didn't want to. I liked to keep my dreams."

Her hair was yet the lovely cedar wood hue, silver, soft and gracious; her figure had those fluid lines of grace that he believed he had never seen equalled.

"Tell me," she added abruptly, "what is the matter with my husband? He has been ailing like this for a year or so."

With a horrid lurch of his heart that was usually so steady, Dr Holroyd remembered the bottle of milk and water in his pocket.

"Why do you give him that cambric tea?" he counter questioned.

"He will have it—he insists that I make it for him—"

"Mollie," said Dr Holroyd quickly, "you decided against me, ten years ago, but that is no reason why we should not be friends now—tell me, frankly, are you happy with this man?"

"You have seen him," she replied slowly. "He seemed different ten years ago. I honestly was attracted by his scholarship and his learning as well as—other things."

Bevis Holroyd needed to ask no more; she was wretched, imprisoned in a mistake as a fly in amber; and those love letters? Was there another man?

As he stood silent, with a dark reflective look on her weary brooding face, she spoke again:

"You are staying?"

"Oh yes," he said, he was staying, there was nothing else for him to do.

"It is Christmas week," she reminded him wistfully. "It will be very dull, perhaps painful, for you."

"I think I ought to stay."

Sir Harry's car was announced; Bevis Holroyd, gliding over frozen roads to London, was absorbed with this sudden problem that, like a mountain out of a plain, had suddenly risen to confront him out of his level life.

The sight of Mollie (he could not think of her by that sick man's name) had roused in him tender memories and poignant emotions and the position in which he found her and his own juxtaposition to her and her husband had the same devastating effect on him as a mine sprung beneath the feet of an unwary traveller.

London was deep in the whirl of a snow storm and the light that penetrated over the grey roof tops to the ugly slip of a laboratory at the back of his consulting rooms was chill and forbidding.

Bevis Holroyd put the bottle of milk on a marble slab and sat back in the easy chair watching that dreary chase of snow flakes across the dingy London pane.

He was thinking of past springs, of violets long dead, of roses long since dust, of hours that had slipped away like lengths of golden silk rolled up, of the long ago when he had loved Mollie and Mollie had seemed to love him; then he thought of that man in the big bed who had said:

"My wife is poisoning me."

Late that afternoon Dr Holroyd, with his suitcase and a professional bag, returned to Strangeways Manor House in Sir Harry's car; the bottle of cambric tea had gone to a friend, a noted analyst; somehow Doctor Holroyd had not felt able to do this task himself; he was very fortunate, he felt, in securing this old solitary and his promise to do the work before Christmas.

As he arrived at Strangeways Manor House which stood isolated and well away from a public high road where a lonely spur of the weald of Kent drove into the Sussex marshes, it was in a blizzard of snow that effaced the landscape and gave the murky outlines of the house an air of unreality, and Bevis Holroyd experienced that sensation he had so often heard of and read about, but which so far his cool mind had dismissed as a fiction.

He did really feel as if he was in an evil dream; as the snow changed the values of the scene, altering distances and shapes, so this meeting with Mollie, under these circumstances, had suddenly changed the life of Bevis Holroyd.

He had so resolutely and so definitely put this woman out of his life and mind, deliberately refusing to make enquiries about her, letting all knowledge of her cease with the letter in which she had written from India and announced her marriage.

And now, after ten years, she had crossed his path in this ghastly manner, as a woman her husband accused of attempted murder.

The sick man's words of a former lover disturbed him profoundly; was it himself who was referred to? Yet the love letters must be from another man for he had not corresponded with Mollie since her marriage, not for ten years.

He had never felt any bitterness towards Mollie for her desertion of a poor, struggling doctor, and he had always believed in the integral nobility of her character under the timidity of conventionality; but the fact remained that she had played him false—what if that *had* been "the little rift within the lute" that had now indeed silenced the music!

With a sense of bitter depression he entered the gloomy old house; how different was this from the pleasant ordinary Christmas he had been rather looking forward to, the jolly homely atmosphere of good fare, dancing, and friends!

When he had telephoned to these friends excusing himself his regret had been genuine and the cordial "bad luck!" had had a poignant echo in his own heart; bad luck indeed, bad luck—

She was waiting for him in the hall that a pale young man was decorating with boughs of prickly stiff holly that stuck stiffly behind the dark heavy pictures.

He was introduced as the secretary and said gloomily:

"Sir Harry wished everything to go on as usual, though I am afraid he is very ill indeed."

Yes, the patient had been seized by another violent attack of illness during Dr Holroyd's absence; the young man went at once upstairs and found Sir Harry in a deep sleep and a rather nervous local doctor in attendance.

An exhaustive discussion of the case with this doctor threw no light on anything, and Dr Holroyd, leaving in charge an extremely sensible-looking housekeeper who was Sir Harry's preferred nurse, returned, worried and irritated, to the hall where Lady Strangeways now sat alone before the big fire.

She offered him a belated but fresh cup of tea.

"Why did you come?" she asked as if she roused herself from deep reverie.

"Why? Because your husband sent for me."

"He says you offered to come; he has told everyone in the house that."

"But I never heard of the man before today."

"You had heard of me. He seems to think that you came here to help me."

"He cannot be saying that," returned Dr Holroyd sternly, and he wondered desperately if Mollie was lying, if she had invented this to drive him out of the house.

"Do you want me here?" he demanded.

"I don't know," she replied dully and confirmed his suspicions; probably there was another man and she wished him out of the way; but he could not go, out of pity towards her he could not go.

"Does he knew we once knew each other?" he asked.

"No," she replied faintly, "therefore it seems such a curious chance that he should have sent for you, of all men!"

"It would have been more curious," he responded grimly, "if I had heard that you were here with a sick husband and had thrust myself in to doctor him! Strangeways must be crazy to spread such a tale and if he doesn't know we are old friends it becomes nonsense!"

"I often think that Harry is crazy," said Lady Strangeways wearily; she took a rose-silk-lined work basket, full of pretty trifles, on her knee, and began winding a skein of rose-coloured silk; she looked so frail, so sad, so lifeless that the heart of Bevis Holroyd was torn with bitter pity.

"Now I am here I want to help you," he said earnestly. "I am staying for that, to help you—"

She looked up at him with a wistful appeal in her fair face.

"I'm worried," she said simply. "I've lost some letters I valued very much—I think they have been stolen."

Dr Holroyd drew back; the love letters; the letters the husband had found, that were causing all his ugly suspicions.

"My poor Mollie!" he exclaimed impulsively. "What sort of a coil have you got yourself into!"

As if this note of pity was unendurable, she rose impulsively, scattering the contents of her work basket, dropping the skein of silk, and hastened away down the dark hall.

Bevis Holroyd stooped mechanically to pick up the hurled objects and saw among them a small white packet, folded, but opened at one end; this packet seemed to have fallen out of a needle case of gold silk.

Bevis Holroyd had pounced on it and thrust it in his pocket just as the pale secretary returned with his thin arms most incongruously full of mistletoe.

"This will be a dreary Christmas for you, Dr Holroyd," he said with the air of one who forces himself to make conversation. "No doubt you had some pleasant plans in view—we are all so pleased that Lady Strangeways had a friend to come and look after Sir Harry during the holidays."

"Who told you I was a friend?" asked Dr Holroyd brusquely. "I certainly knew Lady Strangeways before she was married—"

The pale young man cut in crisply:

"Oh, Lady Strangeways told me so herself."

Bevis Holroyd was bewildered; why did she tell the secretary what she did not tell her husband?—both the indiscretion and the reserve seemed equally foolish.

Languidly hanging up his sprays and bunches of mistletoe the pallid young man, whose name was Garth Deane, continued his aimless remarks.

"This is really not a very cheerful house, Dr Holroyd—I'm interested in Sir Harry's oriental work or I should not remain. Such a very unhappy marriage! I often think," he added regardless of Bevis Holroyd's darkling glance, "that it would be very unpleasant indeed for Lady Strangeways if anything happened to Sir Harry."

"Whatever do you mean, sir?" asked the doctor angrily.

The secretary was not at all discomposed.

"Well, one lives in the house, one has nothing much to do—and one notices."

Perhaps, thought the young man in anguish, the sick husband had been talking to this creature, perhaps the creature *had* really noticed something.

"I'll go up to my patient," said Bevis Holroyd briefly, not daring to anger one who might be an important witness in this mystery that was at present so unfathomable.

Mr Deane gave a sickly grin over the lovely pale leaves and berries he was holding.

"I'm afraid he is very bad, doctor."

As Bevis Holroyd left the room he passed Lady Strangeways; she looked blurred, like a pastel drawing that has been shaken; the fingers she kept locked on her bosom; she had flung a silver fur over her shoulders that accentuated her ethereal look of blonde, pearl and amber hues.

"I've come back for my work basket," she said. "Will you go up to my husband? He is ill again—"

"Have you been giving him anything?" asked Dr Holroyd as quietly as he could.

"Only some cambric tea, he insisted on that."

"Don't give him anything—leave him alone. He is in my charge now, do you understand?"

She gazed up at him with frightened eyes that had been newly washed by tears.

"Why are you so unkind to me?" she quivered.

She looked so ready to fall that he could not resist the temptation to put his hand protectingly on her arm, so that, as she stood in the low doorway leading to the stairs, he appeared to be supporting her drooping weight.

"Have I not said that I am here to help you, Mollie?"

The secretary slipped out from the shadows behind them, his arms still full of winter evergreens.

"There is too much foliage," he smiled, and the smile told that he had seen and heard.

Bevis Holroyd went angrily upstairs; he felt as if an invisible net was being dragged closely round him, something which, from being a cobweb, would become a cable; this air of mystery, of horror in the big house, this sly secretary, these watchful-looking servants, the nervous village doctor ready to credit anything, the lovely agitated woman who was the woman he had long so romantically loved, and the sinister sick man with his diabolic accusations, a man Bevis Holroyd had, from the first moment, hated—all these people in these dark surroundings affected the young man with a miasma of apprehension, gloom and dread.

After a few hours of it he was nearer to losing his nerve than he had ever been; that must be because of Mollie, poor darling Mollie caught into all this nightmare.

And outside the bells were ringing across the snow, practising for Christmas Day; the sound of them was to Bevis Holroyd what the sounds of the real world are when breaking into a sleeper's thick dreams.

The patient sat up in bed, fondling the glass of odious cambric tea.

"Why do you take the stuff?" demanded the doctor angrily.

"She won't let me off, she thrusts it on me," whispered Sir Harry.

Bevis Holroyd noticed, not for the first time since he had come into the fell atmosphere of this dark house that enclosed the piteous figure of the woman he loved, that husband and wife were telling different tales; on one side lay a burden of careful lying.

"Did she—" continued the sick man, "speak to you of her lost letters?"

The young doctor looked at him sternly.

"Why should Lady Strangeways make a confidant of me?" he asked. "Do you know that she was a friend of mine ten years ago before she married you?"

"Was she? How curious! But you met like strangers."

"The light in this room is very dim—"

"Well, never mind about that, whether you knew her or not—" Sir Harry gasped out in a sudden snarl. "The woman is a murderess, and you'll have to bear witness to it—I've got her letters, here under my pillow, and Garth Deane is watching her—"

"Ah, a spy! I'll have no part in this, Sir Harry. You'll call another doctor—"

"No, it's your case, you'll make the best of it—My God, I'm dying, I think—"

He fell back in such a convulsion of pain that Bevis Holroyd forgot everything in administering to him. The rest of that day and all that night the young doctor was shut up with his patient, assisted by the secretary and the housekeeper.

And when, in the pallid light of Christmas Eve morning, he went downstairs to find Lady Strangeways, he knew that the sick man was suffering from arsenic poison, that the packet taken from Mollie's work box was arsenic, and it was only an added horror when he was called to the telephone to learn that a stiff dose of the poison had been found in the specimen of cambric tea.

He believed that he could save the husband and thereby the wife also, but he did not think he could close the sick man's mouth; the deadly hatred of Sir Harry was leading up to an accusation of attempted murder; of that he was sure, and there was the man Deane to back him up.

He sent for Mollie, who had not been near her husband all night, and when she came, pale, distracted, huddled in her white fur, he said grimly:

"Look here, Mollie, I promised that I'd help you and I mean to, though it isn't going to be as easy as I thought, but you have got to be frank with me."

"But I have nothing to conceal—"

"The name of the other man—"

"The other man?"

"The man who wrote those letters your husband has under his pillow."

"Oh, Harry has them!" she cried in pain. "That man Deane stole them then! Bevis, they are your letters of the olden days that I have always cherished."

"*My* letters!"

"Yes, do you think that there has ever been anyone else?"

"But he says—Mollie, there is a trap or trick here, some one is lying furiously. Your husband is being poisoned."

"Poisoned?"

"By arsenic given in that cambric tea. And he knows it. And he accuses you."

She stared at him in blank incredulity, then she slipped forward in her chair and clutched the big arm.

"Oh, God," she muttered in panic terror. "He always swore that he'd be revenged on me—because he knew that I never cared for him—"

But Bevis Holroyd recoiled; he did not dare listen, he did not dare believe.

"I've warned you," he said, "for the sake of the old days, Mollie—"

A light step behind them and they were aware of the secretary creeping out of the embrowning shadows.

"A cold Christmas," he said, rubbing his hands together. "A really cold, seasonable Christmas. We are almost snowed in—and Sir Harry would like to see you, Dr Holroyd."

"I have only just left him—"

Bevis Holroyd looked at the despairing figure of the woman, crouching in her chair; he was distracted, overwrought, near to losing his nerve.

"He wants particularly to see you," cringed the secretary.

Mollie looked back at Bevis Holroyd, her lips moved twice in vain before she could say: "Go to him."

The doctor went slowly upstairs and the secretary followed.

Sir Harry was now flat on his back, staring at the dark tapestry curtains of his bed.

"I'm dying," he announced as the doctor bent over him.

"Nonsense. I am not going to allow you to die."

"You won't be able to help yourself. I've brought you here to see me die."

"What do you mean?"

"I've a surprise for you too, a Christmas present. These letters now, these love letters of my wife's—what name do you think is on them?"

"Your mind is giving way, Sir Harry."

"Not at all—come nearer, Deane—the name is Bevis Holroyd."

"Then they are letters ten years old. Letters written before your wife met you."

The sick man grinned with infinite malice.

"Maybe. But there are no dates on them and the envelopes are all destroyed. And I, as a dying man, shall swear to their recent date—I, as a foully murdered man."

"You are wandering in your mind," said Bevis Holroyd quietly. "I refuse to listen to you any further."

"You shall listen to me. I brought you here to listen to me. I've got you. Here's my will, Deane's got that, in which I denounced you both, there are your letters, every one thinks that *she* put you in charge of the case, every one knows that you know all about arsenic in cambric tea through the Pluntre case, and every one will know that I died of arsenic poisoning."

The doctor allowed him to talk himself out; indeed it would have been difficult to check the ferocity of his malicious energy.

The plot was ingenious, the invention of a slightly insane, jealous recluse who hated his wife and hated the man she had never ceased to love; Bevis Holroyd could see the nets very skilfully drawn round him; but the main issue of the mystery remained untouched; who *was* administering the arsenic?

The young man glanced across the sombre bed to the dark figure of the secretary.

"What is your place in all this farrago, Mr Deane?" he asked sternly.

"I'm Sir Harry's friend," answered the other stubbornly, "and I'll bring witness any time against Lady Strangeways. I've tried to circumvent her—"

"Stop," cried the doctor. "You think that Lady Strangeways is poisoning her husband and that I am her accomplice?"

The sick man, who had been looking with bitter malice from one to another, whispered hoarsely:

"That is what you think, isn't it, Deane?"

"I'll say what I think at the proper time," said the secretary obstinately.

"No doubt you are being well paid for your share in this."

"I've remembered his services in my will," smiled Sir Harry grimly. "You can adjust your differences then, Dr Holroyd, when I'm dead, *poisoned, murdered.* It will be a pretty story, a nice scandal, you and she in the house together, the letters, the cambric tea!"

An expression of ferocity dominated him, then he made an effort to dominate this and to speak in his usual suave stilted manner.

"You must admit that we shall all have a very Happy Christmas, doctor."

Bevis Holroyd was looking at the secretary, who stood at the other side of the bed, cringing, yet somehow in the attitude of a man ready to pounce; Dr Holroyd wondered if this was the murderer.

"Why," he asked quietly to gain time, "did you hatch this plan to ruin a man you had never seen before?"

"I always hated you," replied the sick man faintly. "Mollie never forgot you, you see, and she never allowed *me* to forget that she never forgot you. And then I found those letters she had cherished."

"You are a very wicked man," said the doctor drily, "but it will all come to nothing, for I am not going to allow you to die."

"You won't be able to help yourself," replied the patient. "I'm dying, I tell you. I shall die on Christmas Day."

He turned his head towards the secretary and added:

"Send my wife up to me."

"No," interrupted Dr Holroyd strongly. "She shall not come near you again."

Sir Harry Strangeways ignored this.

"Send her up," he repeated.

"I will bring her, sir."

The secretary left, with a movement suggestive of flight, and Bevis Holroyd stood rigid, waiting, thinking, looking at the ugly man who now had closed his eyes and lay as if insensible. He was certainly very ill, dying perhaps, and he certainly had been poisoned by arsenic given in cambric tea, and, as certainly, a terrible scandal and a terrible danger would threaten with his death; the letters were *not* dated, the marriage was notoriously unhappy, and he, Bevis Holroyd, was associated in every one's mind with a murder case in which this form of poison, given in this manner, had been used.

Drops of moisture stood out on the doctor's forehead; sure that if he could clear himself it would be very difficult for Mollie to do so; how could even he himself in his soul swear to her innocence!

Of course he must get the woman out of the house at once, he must have another doctor from town, nurses—but could this be done in time; if the patient died on his hands would he not be only bringing witnesses to his own discomfiture? And the right people, his own friends, were difficult to get hold of now, at Christmas time.

He longed to go in search of Mollie—she must at least be got away, but how, without a scandal, without a suspicion?

He longed to have the matter out with this odious secretary, but he dared not leave his patient.

Lady Strangeways returned with Garth Deane and seated herself, mute, shadowy, with eyes full of panic, on the other side of the sombre bed.

"Is he going to live?" she presently whispered as she watched Bevis Holroyd ministering to her unconscious husband.

"We must see that he does," he answered grimly.

All through that Christmas Eve and the bitter night to the stark dawn when the church bells broke ghastly on their wan senses did they tend the sick man who only came to his senses to grin at them in malice.

Once Bevis Holroyd asked the pallid woman:

"What was that white packet you had in your workbox?"

And she replied:

"I never had such a packet."

And he:

"I must believe you."

But he did not send for the other doctors and nurses, he did not dare.

The Christmas bells seemed to rouse the sick man from his deadly swoon.

"You can't save me," he said with indescribable malice. "I shall die and put you both in the dock—"

Mollie Strangeways sank down beside the bed and began to cry, and Garth Deane, who by his master's express desire had been in and out of the room all night, stopped and looked at her with a peculiar expression. Sir Harry looked at her also.

"Don't cry," he gasped, "this is Christmas Day. We ought all to be happy—bring me my cambric tea—do you hear?"

She rose mechanically and left the room to take in the tray with the fresh milk and water that the housekeeper had placed softly on the table outside the door; for all through the nightmare vigil, the sick man's cry had been for "cambric tea".

As he sat up in bed feebly sipping the vapid and odious drink the tortured woman's nerves slipped her control.

"I can't endure those bells, I wish they would stop those bells!" she cried and ran out of the room.

Bevis Holroyd instantly followed her; and now as suddenly as it had sprung on him, the fell little drama disappeared, fled like a poison cloud out of the compass of his life.

Mollie was leaning against the closed window, her sick head resting against the mullions; through the casement showed, surprisingly, sunlight on the pure snow and blue sky behind the withered trees.

"Listen, Mollie," said the young man resolutely. "I'm sure he'll live if you are careful—you mustn't lose heart—"

The sick room door opened and the secretary slipped out.

He nervously approached the two in the window place.

"I can't stand this any longer," he said through dry lips. "I didn't know he meant to go so far, he is doing it himself, you know; he's got the stuff hidden in his bed, he puts it into the cambric tea, he's willing to die to spite you two, but I can't stand it any longer."

"You've been abetting this!" cried the doctor.

"Not abetting," smiled the secretary wanly. "Just standing by. I found out by chance—and then he forced me to be silent—I had his will, you know, and I've destroyed it."

With this the strange creature glided downstairs.

The doctor sprang at once to Sir Harry's room; the sick man was sitting up in the sombre bed and with a last effort was scattering a grain of powder into the glass of cambric tea.

With a look of baffled horror he saw Bevis Holroyd but the drink had already slipped down his throat; he fell back and hid his face, baulked at the last of his diabolic revenge.

When Bevis Holroyd left the dead man's chamber he found Mollie still leaning in the window; she was free, the sun was shining, it was Christmas Day.

# THE CHINESE APPLE

## Joseph Shearing

Joseph Shearing was another of the male pen-names used by Marjorie Bowen, under which she published fifteen novels of historical suspense. They include *Aunt Beardie* (1940), set in post-Revolution France, and the better known *Airing in a Closed Carriage* (1943), a successful fictionalization of a classic real life case, the poisoning of James Maybrick, with the setting switched from Liverpool to Manchester.

*For Her to See* (1947) was another mystery inspired by a famous true crime – the Bravo case of 1876, which has fascinated criminologists ever since Charles Bravo met his end in mysterious circumstances. The book was filmed in 1948 as *So Evil My Love*, with Ray Milland and Ann Todd in leading roles. "The Chinese Apple", written shortly afterwards, is typical of Shearing at her rather dark and brooding best.

\*   \*   \*   \*   \*

Isabelle Crosland felt very depressed when the boat train drew into the vast London station. The gas lamps set at intervals down the platform did little more than reveal filth, fog and figures huddled in wraps and shawls. It was a mistake to arrive on Christmas Eve, a matter of missed trains, of indecision and reluctance about the entire journey. The truth was she had not wanted to come to London at all. She had lived in Italy too long to be comfortable in England. In Florence she had friends, admirers; she had what is termed "private means" and she was an expert in music. She performed a little on the harpsichord and she wrote a great deal about ancient musical instruments and ancient music. She had been married and widowed some years before and was a childless woman who had come to good terms with life. But with life in Florence, not London. Mrs Crosland really rather resented the fact that she was performing a duty. She liked things to be taken lightly, even with a touch of malice, of heartlessness, and here she was in this gloomy, cold station, having left the pleasant south behind, just because she ought to be there.

"How," she thought, as she watched the porter sorting out her baggage, "I dislike doing the right thing; it is never becoming, at least to me."

A widowed sister she scarcely remembered had died: there was a child, quite alone. She, this Lucy Bayward, had written; so had her solicitors. Mrs Crosland was her only relation. Money was not needed, companionship was. At last it had been arranged, the child was coming up from Wiltshire, Mrs Crosland was to meet her in London and take her back to Florence.

It would really be, Isabelle Crosland reflected, a flat sort of Christmas. She wished that she could shift her responsibility, and, as the four-wheeled cab took her along the dingy streets, she wondered if it might not be possible for her to evade taking Lucy back to Italy.

London was oppressive. The gutters were full of dirty snow, overhead was a yellow fog.

"I was a fool," thought Mrs Crosland, "ever to have left Florence. The whole matter could have been settled by letter."

She did not care for the meeting-place. It was the old house in Islington where she and her sister had been born and had passed their childhood. It was her own property and her tenant had lately left, so it was empty. Convenient, too, and suitable. Only Isabelle Crosland did not very much want to return to those sombre rooms. She had not liked her own childhood, nor her own youth. Martha had married, though a poor sort of man, and got away early. Isabelle had stayed on, too long, then married desperately, only saving herself by Italy and music. The south had saved her in another way, too. Her husband, who was a dull, retired half-pay officer, had died of malaria.

Now she was going back. On Christmas Eve, nothing would be much altered; she had always let the house furnished. Why had she not sold, long ago, those heavy pieces of Jamaica mahogany? Probably out of cowardice, because she did not wish to face up to writing, or hearing anything about them. There it was, just as she remembered it, Roscoe Square, with the church and graveyard in the centre, and the houses, each like one another as peas in a pod, with the decorous areas and railings and the semicircular fanlights over the doors with heavy knockers.

The streetlamps were lit. It was really quite late at night. "No wonder," Mrs Crosland thought, "that I am feeling exhausted." The sight of the Square chilled her: it was as if she had been lured back there by some malign power. A group of people were gathered round the house in the corner, directly facing her own that was number twelve. "Carols," she thought, "or a large party." But there seemed to be no children and the crowd was very silent.

There were lights in her own house. She noticed that bright façade with relief. Alike in the parlour and in the bedrooms above, the gas flared. Lucy had arrived then. That part of the arrangements had gone off well. The lawyers must have sent the keys, as Isabelle Crosland had instructed them to do, and the girl had had the good sense to get up to London before the arrival of the boat train.

Yet Mrs Crosland felt unreasonably depressed. She would, after all, have liked a few hours by herself in the hateful house.

Her own keys were ready in her purse. She opened the front door and shuddered. It was as if she had become a child again and dreaded the strong voice of a parent.

There should have been a maid. Careful in everything that concerned her comfort, Mrs Crosland had written to a woman long since in her employment to be in attendance. The woman had replied, promising compliance. But now she cried: "Mrs Jocelyn! Mrs Jocelyn!" in vain, through the gas-lit house.

The cabby would not leave his horse and his rugs, but her moment of hesitancy was soon filled. One of the mongrel idlers who, more frequently than formerly, lounged about the streets, came forward. Mrs Crosland's trunks and bags were placed in the hall, and she had paid her dues with the English money carefully acquired at Dover.

The cab drove away, soon lost in the fog. But the scrawny youth lingered. He pointed to the crowd on the other side of the Square, a deeper patch amid the surrounding gloom.

"Something has happened there, Mum," he whispered.

"Something horrible, you mean?" Mrs Crossland was annoyed she had said this, and added: "No, of course not; it is a gathering for Christmas." With this she closed her front door on the darkness and stood in the lamp-lit passage.

She went into the parlour, so well remembered, so justly hated.

The last tenant, selected prudently, had left everything in even too good a state of preservation. Save for some pale patches on the walls where pictures had been altered, everything was as it had been.

Glowering round, Mrs Crosland thought what a fool she had been to stay there so long.

A fire was burning and a dish of cakes and wine stood on the deep red mahogany table.

With a gesture of bravado, Mrs Crosland returned to the passage, trying to throw friendliness into her voice as she called out: "Lucy, Lucy, my dear, it is I, your aunt Isabelle Crosland."

She was vexed with herself that the words did not have a more genial sound. "I am ruined," she thought, "for all family relationship."

A tall girl appeared on the first landing.

"I have been waiting," she said, "quite a long time."

In the same second Mrs Crosland was relieved that this was no insipid bore, and resentful of the other's self-contained demeanour.

"Well," she said, turning it off with a smile. "It doesn't look as if I need have hurried to your assistance."

Lucy Bayward descended the stairs.

"Indeed, I assure you, I am extremely glad to see you," she said gravely.

The two women seated themselves in the parlour. Mrs Crosland found Lucy looked older than her eighteen years and was also, in her dark, rather flashing way, beautiful. Was she what one might have expected Martha's girl to be? Well, why not?

"I was expecting Mrs Jocelyn, Lucy."

"Oh, she was here; she got everything ready, as you see—then I sent her home because it is Christmas Eve."

Mrs Crosland regretted this; she was used to ample service. "We shall not be able to travel until after Christmas," she complained.

"But we can be very comfortable here," said Lucy, smiling.

"No," replied Mrs Crosland, the words almost forced out of her. "I don't think I can—be comfortable here—I think we had better go to an hotel."

"But you arranged this meeting."

"I was careless. You can have no idea—you have not travelled?"

"No."

"Well, then, you can have no idea how different things seem in Florence, with the sun and one's friends about—"

"I hope we shall be friends."

"Oh, I hope so. I did not mean that, only the Square and the house. You see, I spent my childhood here."

Lucy slightly shrugged her shoulders. She poured herself out a glass of wine. What a false impression those school-girlish letters had given! Mrs Crosland was vexed, mostly at herself.

"You—since we have used the word—have friends of your own?" she asked.

Lucy bowed her dark head.

"Really," added Mrs Crosland, "I fussed too much. I need not have undertaken all that tiresome travelling at Christmas, too."

"I am sorry that you did—on my account; but please believe that you are being of the greatest help to me."

Mrs Crosland apologized at once.

"I am over-tired. I should not be talking like this. I, too, will have a glass of wine. We ought to get to know each other."

They drank, considering one another carefully.

Lucy was a continuing surprise to Mrs Crosland. She was not even in mourning, but wore a rather ill-fitting stone-coloured satin, her sleek hair had recently been twisted into ringlets, and there was no doubt that she was slightly rouged.

"Do you want to come to Italy? Have you any plans for yourself?"

"Yes—and they include a trip abroad. Don't be afraid that I shall be a burden on you."

"This independence could have been expressed by letter," smiled Mrs Crosland. "I have my own interests—that Martha's death interrupted—"

"Death always interrupts—some one or some thing, does it not?"

"Yes, and my way of putting it was harsh. I mean you do not seem a rustic miss, eager for sympathy."

"It must be agreeable in Florence," said Lucy. "I dislike London very much."

"But you have not been here more than a few hours—"

"Long enough to dislike it—"

"And your own home, also?"

"You did not like your own youth, either, did you?" asked Lucy, staring.

"No, no, I understand. Poor Martha would be dull, and it is long since your father died. I see, a narrow existence."

"You might call it that. I was denied everything. I had not the liberty, the pocket-money given to the kitchenmaid."

"It was true of me also," said Mrs Crosland, shocked at her own admission.

"One is left alone, to struggle with dark things," smiled Lucy. "It is not a place that I dislike, but a condition—that of being young, vulnerable, defenceless."

"As I was," agreed Mrs Crosland. "I got away and now I have music."

"I shall have other things." Lucy sipped her wine.

"Well, one must talk of it: you are not what I expected to find. You are younger than I was when I got away," remarked Mrs Crosland.

"Still too old to endure what I endured."

Mrs Crosland shivered. "I never expected to hear this," she declared. "I thought you would be a rather flimsy little creature."

"And I am not?"

"No, indeed, you seem to me quite determined."

"Well, I shall take your small cases upstairs. Mrs Jocelyn will be here in the morning."

"There's a good child." Mrs Crosland tried to sound friendly. She felt that she ought to manage the situation better. It was one that she had ordained herself, and now it was getting out of hand.

"Be careful with the smallest case in red leather: it has some English gold in it, and a necklace of Roman pearls that I bought as a Christmas present for you—"

Mrs Crosland felt that the last part of this sentence fell flat. "... pearl beads, they are really very pretty."

"So are these." Lucy put her hand to her ill-fitting tucker and pulled out a string of pearls.

"The real thing," said Mrs Crosland soberly. "I did not know that Martha—"

Lucy unclasped the necklace and laid it on the table; the sight of this treasure loosened Mrs Crosland's constant habit of control. She thought of beauty, of sea-water, of tears, and of her own youth, spilled and wasted away, like water running into sand.

"I wish I had never come back to this house," she said passionately.

Lucy went upstairs. Mrs Crosland heard her moving about over-head. How well she knew that room. The best bedroom, where her parents had slept, the huge wardrobe, the huge dressing-table, the line engravings, the solemn air of tedium, the hours that seemed to have no end. What had gone wrong with life anyway? Mrs Crosland asked herself this question fiercely, daunted, almost frightened by the house.

The fire was sinking down and with cold hands she piled on the logs.

How stupid to return. Even though it was such a reasonable thing to do. One must be careful of these reasonable things. She ought to have done the unreasonable, the reckless thing, forgotten this old house in Islington, and taken Lucy to some cheerful hotel.

The steps were advancing, retreating, overhead. Mrs Crosland recalled old stories of haunted houses. How footsteps would sound in an upper storey and then, on investigation, the room be found empty.

Supposing she were to go upstairs now and find the great bed-room forlorn and Lucy vanished! Instead, Lucy entered the parlour.

"I have had the warming-pan in the bed for over two hours, the fire burns briskly and your things are set out—"

Mrs Crosland was grateful in rather, she felt, an apathetic manner.

This journey had upset a painfully acquired serenity. She was really fatigued, the motion of the ship, the clatter of the train still made her senses swim.

"Thank you, Lucy, dear," she said, in quite a humble way, then leaning her head in her hand and her elbow on the table, she began to weep.

Lucy regarded her quietly and drank another glass of wine.

"It is the house," whimpered Mrs Crosland, "coming back to it—and those pearls—I never had a necklace like that—"

She thought of her friends, of her so-called successful life, and of how little she had really had.

She envied this young woman who had escaped in time.

"Perhaps you had an accomplice?" she asked cunningly.

"Oh, yes, I could have done nothing without that."

Mrs Crosland was interested, slightly confused by the wine and the fatigue. Probably, she thought, Lucy meant that she was engaged to some young man who had not been approved by Martha. But what did either of them mean by the word "accomplice"?

"I suppose Charles Crosland helped me," admitted his widow. "He married me and we went to Italy. I should never have had the courage to do that alone. And by the time he died, I had found out about music, and how I understood it and could make money out of it—" "Perhaps," she thought to herself, "Lucy will not want, after all, to come with me to Italy—what a relief if she marries someone. I don't really care if she has found a ruffian, for I don't like her—no, nor the duty, the strain and drag of it."

She was sure that it was the house making her feel like that. Because in this house she had done what she ought to have done so often. Such wretched meals, such miserable silences, such violences of speech. Such suppression of all one liked or wanted. Lucy said:

"I see that you must have suffered, Mrs Crosland. I don't feel I can be less formal than that—we are strangers. I will tell you in the morning what my plans are—"

"I hardly came from Italy in the Christmas season to hear your plans," replied Mrs Crosland with a petulance of which she was ashamed. "I imagined you as quite dependent and needing my care."

"I have told you that you are the greatest possible service to me," Lucy assured her, at the same time taking up the pearls and hiding them in her bosom. "I wear mourning when I go abroad, but in the house I feel it to be a farce," she added.

"I never wore black for my parents," explained Mrs Crosland. "They died quite soon, one after the other; with nothing to torment, their existence became insupportable."

Lucy sat with her profile towards the fire. She was thin, with slanting eyebrows and a hollow at the base of her throat.

"I wish you would have that dress altered to fit you," remarked Mrs Crosland. "You could never travel in it, either, a grey satin—"

"Oh, no, I have some furs and a warm pelisse of a dark rose colour."

"Then certainly you were never kept down as I was—"

"Perhaps I helped myself, afterwards—is not that the sensible thing to do?"

"You mean you bought these clothes since Martha's death? I don't see how you had the time or the money." And Mrs Crosland made a mental note to consult the lawyers as to just how Lucy's affairs stood.

"Perhaps you have greater means than I thought," she remarked. "I always thought Martha had very little."

"I have not very much," said Lucy. "But I shall know how to spend it. And how to make more."

Mrs Crosland rose. The massive pieces of furniture seemed closing in on her, as if they challenged her very right to exist.

Indeed, in this house she had no existence, she was merely the wraith of the child, of the girl who had suffered so much in this place, in this house, in this Square with the church and the graveyard in the centre, and from which she had escaped only just in time. Lucy also got to her feet.

"It is surprising," she sighed, "the amount of tedium there is in life. When I think of all the dull Christmases—"

"I also," said Mrs Crosland, almost in terror. "It was always so much worse when other people seemed to be rejoicing." She glanced round her with apprehension. "When I think of all the affectations of good will, of pleasure—"

"Don't think of it," urged the younger woman. "Go upstairs, where I have put everything in readiness for you."

"I dread the bedroom."

The iron bell clanged in the empty kitchen below.

"The waits," added Mrs Crosland. "I remember when we used to give them sixpence, nothing more. But I heard no singing."

"There was no singing. I am afraid those people at the corner house have returned."

Mrs Crosland remembered vaguely the crowd she had seen from the cab window, a blot of dark in the darkness. "You mean someone has been here before?" she asked. "What about?"

"There has been an accident, I think. Someone was hurt—"

"But what could that have to do with us?"

"Nothing, of course. But they said they might return—"

"Who is 'they'?"

Mrs Crosland spoke confusedly and the bell rang again.

"Oh, do go, like a good child," she added. She was rather glad of the distraction. She tried to think of the name of the people who had lived in the house on the opposite corner. Inglis—was not that it? And one of the family had been a nun, a very cheerful, smiling nun, or had she recalled it all wrongly?

She sat shivering over the fire, thinking of those past musty Christmas Days, when the beauty and magic of the season had seemed far away, as if behind a dense wall of small bricks. That had always been the worst of it, that somewhere, probably close at hand, people had really been enjoying themselves.

She heard Lucy talking with a man in the passage. The accomplice, perhaps? She was inclined to be jealous, hostile.

But the middle-aged and sober-looking person who followed Lucy into the parlour could not have any romantic complications.

He wore a pepper-and-salt-pattern suit and carried a bowler hat. He seemed quite sure of himself, yet not to expect any friendliness.

"I am sorry to disturb you again," he said.

"I am sorry that you should," agreed Mrs Crosland. "But on the other hand, my memories of this house are by no means pleasant."

"Name of Teale, Henry Teale," said the stranger.

"Pray be seated," said Mrs Crosland.

The stranger, this Mr Teale, took the edge of the seat, as if very diffident. Mrs Crosland was soon fascinated by what he had to say.

He was a policeman in private clothes. Mrs Crosland meditated on the word "private"—"private life", "private means". He had come about the Inglis affair, at the corner house.

"Oh, yes, I recall that was the name, but we never knew anyone— who are they now—the Inglis family?"

"I've already told Miss Bayward here—it was an old lady, for several years just an old lady living with a companion—"

"And found dead, you told me, Mr Teale," remarked Lucy.

"Murdered, is what the surgeon says and what was suspected from the first."

"I forgot that you said that, Mr Teale. At her age it does not seem to matter very much—you said she was over eighty years of age, did you not?" asked Lucy, pouring the detective a glass of wine.

"Very old, nearly ninety years of age, I understand, Miss Bayward. But murder is murder."

Mrs Crosland felt this affair to be an added weariness. Murder in Roscoe Square on Christmas Eve. She felt that she ought to apologize to Lucy. "I suppose that was what the crowd had gathered for," she remarked.

"Yes, such news soon gets about, Ma'am. A nephew called to tea and found her—gone."

Mr Teale went over, as if it were a duty, the circumstances of the crime. The house had been ransacked and suspicion had fallen on the companion, who had disappeared. Old Mrs Inglis had lived so much like a recluse that no one knew what she possessed. There had been a good deal of loose money in the house, the nephew, Mr Clinton, thought. A good deal of cash had been drawn every month from the Inglis bank account, and very little of it spent. The companion was a stranger to Islington. Veiled and modest, she had flitted about doing the meagre shopping for the old eccentric, only for the last few weeks.

The woman she had replaced had left in tears and temper some months ago. No one knew where this creature had come from— probably an orphanage; she must have been quite friendless and forlorn to have taken such a post.

"You told me all this," protested Lucy.

"Yes, Miss, but I did say that I would have to see Mrs Crosland when she arrived—"

"Well, you are seeing her," remarked that lady. "And I cannot help you at all. One is even disinterested. I lived, Mr Teale, so cloistered a life when I was here, that I knew nothing of what was going on—even in the Square."

"So I heard from Miss Bayward here, but I thought you might have seen someone; I'm not speaking of the past, but of the present—"

"Seen someone here—on Christmas Eve—?"

Mr Teale sighed, as if, indeed, he had been expecting too much. "We've combed the neighbourhood, but can't find any trace of her—"

"Why should you? Of course, she has fled a long way off—"

"Difficult, with the railway stations and then the ports all watched."

"You may search again through the cellars if you wish," said Lucy. "I am sure that my aunt won't object—"

Mrs Crosland put no difficulties in the way of the detective, but she felt the whole situation was grotesque.

"I hope she escapes," Mrs Crosland, increasingly tired and confused by the wine she had drunk without eating, spoke without her own volition. "Poor thing—shut up—caged—"

"It was a very brutal murder," said Mr Teale indifferently.

"Was it? An over-draught of some sleeping potion, I suppose?"

"No, Ma'am, David and Goliath, the surgeon said. A rare kind of murder. A great round stone in a sling, as it might be a lady's scarf, and pretty easy to get in the dusk round the river ways."

Mrs Crosland laughed. The picture of this miserable companion, at the end of a dismal day lurking round the dubious dockland streets to find a target for her skill with sling and stone, seemed absurd.

"I know what you are laughing at," said Mr Teale without feeling. "But she found her target—it was the shining skull of Mrs Inglis, nodding in her chair—"

"One might understand the temptation," agreed Mrs Crosland. "But I doubt the skill."

"There is a lovely walled garden," suggested the detective. "And, as I said, these little by-way streets. Anyway, there was her head smashed in, neatly; no suffering, you understand."

"Oh, very great suffering, for such a thing to be possible," broke out Mrs Crosland. "On the part of the murderess, I mean—"

"I think so, too," said Lucy soberly.

"That is not for me to say," remarked the detective. "I am to find her if I can. There is a fog and all the confusion of Christmas Eve parties, and waits, and late services at all the churches."

Mrs Crosland impulsively drew back the curtains. Yes, there was the church, lit up, exactly as she recalled it, light streaming from the windows over the graveyard, altar tombs, and headstones, sliding into oblivion.

"Where would a woman like that go?" asked Lucy, glancing over Mrs Crosland's shoulder at the churchyard.

"That is what we have to find out," said Mr Teale cautiously. "I'll be on my way again, ladies, just cautioning you against any stranger who might come here, on some pretext. One never knows."

"What was David's stone? A polished pebble? I have forgotten." Mrs Crosland dropped the curtains over the view of the church and the dull fog twilight of evening in the gas-lit Square.

"The surgeon says it must have been a heavy stone, well aimed, and such is missing. Mr Clinton, the nephew, her only visitor and not in her confidence, remarked on such a weapon, always on each of his visits on the old lady's table."

"How is that possible?" asked Mrs Crosland.

Mr Teale said that the object was known as the Chinese apple. It was of white jade, dented like the fruit, with a leaf attached, all carved in one and beautifully polished. The old lady was very fond of it, and it was a most suitable weapon.

"But this dreadful companion," said Mrs Crosland, now perversely revolted by the crime, "could not have had time to practise with this—suitable weapon—she had not been with Mrs Inglis long enough."

"Ah," smiled Mr Teale. "We don't know where she was before, Ma'am. She might have had a deal of practice in some lonely place—birds, Ma'am, and rabbits. Watching in the woods, like boys do."

Mrs Crosland did not like this picture of a woman lurking in coverts with a sling. She bade the detective "Good evening" and Lucy showed him to the door.

In the moment that she was alone, Mrs Crosland poured herself another glass of wine. When Lucy returned, she spoke impulsively.

"Oh, Lucy, that is what results when people are driven too far—they kill and escape with the spoils, greedily. I do wish this had not happened. What sort of woman do you suppose this may have been? Harsh, of course, and elderly—"

"Mr Teale, when he came before, said she might be in almost any disguise."

"Almost any disguise," repeated Mrs Crosland, thinking of the many disguises she had herself worn until she had found herself in the lovely blue of Italy, still disguised, but pleasantly enough. She hoped that this mask was not now about to be torn from her; the old house was very oppressive, it had been foolish to return. A relief, of course, that Lucy seemed to have her own plans. But the house was what really mattered: the returning here and finding everything the same, and the memories of that dreadful childhood.

Lucy had suffered also, it seemed. Odd that she did not like Lucy, did not feel any sympathy with her or her schemes.

At last she found her way upstairs and faced the too-familiar bedroom. Her own was at the back of the house; that is, it had been. She must not think like this: her own room was in the charming house of the villa in Fiesole, this place had nothing to do with her at all.

But it had, and the knowledge was like a lead cloak over her. Of course it had. She had returned to meet not Lucy, but her own childhood.

Old Mrs Inglis—how did she fit in?

Probably she had always been there, even when the woman who was now Isabelle Crosland had been a child. Always there, obscure, eccentric, wearing out a succession of companions until one of them brained her with the Chinese apple, the jade fruit, slung from a lady's scarf.

"Oh, dear," murmured Mrs Crosland, "what has that old, that very old woman got to do with me?"

Her cases were by her bedside. She was too tired to examine them. Lucy had been scrupulous in putting out her toilet articles. She began to undress. There was nothing to do but to rest; what was it to her that a murderess was being hunted round Islington—what had Mr Teale said? The stations, the docks … She was half-undressed and had pulled out her wrapper when the front-door bell rang.

Hastily covering herself up, she was out on the landing. At least this was an excuse not to get into the big, formal bed where her parents had died, even if this was only Mr Teale returned. Lucy was already in the hall, speaking to someone. The gas-light in the passage illuminated the girl in the stone-coloured satin and the man on the threshold to whom she spoke.

It was not Mr Teale.

Isabelle Crosland, halfway down the stairs, had a glance of a sharp face, vividly lit. A young man, with his collar turned up and a look of expectation in his brilliant eyes. He said something that Isabelle Crosland could not hear, and then Lucy closed the heavy front door.

Glancing up at her aunt, she said:

"Now we are shut in for the night."

"Who was that?" asked Mrs Crosland, vexed that Lucy had discerned her presence.

"Only a neighbour; only a curiosity-monger."

Lucy's tone was reassuring. She advised her aunt to go to bed.

"Really, it is getting very late. The church is dark again. All the people have gone home."

"Which room have you, Lucy, dear?"

"That which you had, I suppose; the large room at the back of the house."

"Oh, yes—that—"

"Well, do not concern yourself—it has been rather a disagreeable evening, but it is over now."

Lucy, dark and pale, stood in the doorway, hesitant for a second. Mrs Crosland decided, unreasonably, not to kiss her and bade her a quick good-night of a forced cheerfulness.

Alone, she pulled the chain of the gas-ring and was at once in darkness. Only wheels of light across the ceiling showed the passing of a lonely hansom cab.

Perhaps Mr Teale going home.

Mrs Inglis, too, would have gone home by now; the corner house opposite would be empty.

Isabelle Crosland could not bring herself to sleep on the bed after all. Wrapped in travelling rugs, snatched up in the dark, she huddled on the couch. Presently she slept, but with no agreeable dreams. Oppressive fancies lay heavily on her and several times she woke, crying out.

It was with a dismal sense of disappointment that she realized each time that she was not in Florence.

With the dawn she was downstairs. Christmas morning; how ridiculous!

No sign of Lucy, and the cold, dismal house was like a trap, a prison.

Almost crying with vexation, Mrs Crosland was forced to look into the room that once had been her own. The bed had not been slept in. On the white honeycomb coverlet was a package and a note.

This, a single sheet of paper, covered an opened letter. Mrs Crosland stared at this that was signed "Lucy Bayward". It was a childish sort of scrawl, the writer excused herself from reaching London until after the holidays.

The note was in a different hand:

I promised to let you know my plans. I am away down the river with my accomplice. Taking refuge in your empty house I found this note. The whole arrangement was entirely useful to me. I left the Roman pearls for Lucy, as I had those of my late employer, but I took the gold. No one will ever find us. I leave you a Christmas present.

Mrs Crosland's cold fingers undid the package. In the ghastly half-light she saw the Chinese apple.

# A PROBLEM IN WHITE

## Nicholas Blake

Nicholas Blake was the pen-name under which Cecil Day-Lewis (1904–1972) wrote detective stories. Day-Lewis was a distinguished poet who was appointed Poet Laureate in 1968. He turned pseudonymously to fictional crime in 1935 with *A Question of Proof*, which drew on his experiences as a schoolteacher, and introduced an appealing detective, Nigel Strangeways. Dorothy L. Sayers was among the critics who acclaimed the book, and Strangeways promptly returned in an even better novel, *Thou Shell of Death*.

Blake himself reviewed crime fiction for a while, and his fourth mystery, *The Beast Must Die*, is a classic of the genre which has been filmed twice, most notably by Claude Chabrol. "A Problem in White", one of his few short stories, first appeared in the *Strand Magazine* in 1949, a few months before that legendary publication was forced out of the market after a long decline in circulation since the glorious days of Sherlock Holmes.

\* \* \* \* \*

"Seasonable weather for the time of year," remarked the Expansive Man in a voice succulent as the breast of a roast goose.

The Deep Chap, sitting next to him in the railway compartment, glanced out at the snow swarming and swirling past the window-pane. He replied:

"You really like it? Oh well, it's an ill blizzard that blows nobody no good. Depends what you mean by seasonable, though. Statistics for the last fifty years would show—"

"Name of Joad, sir?" asked the Expansive Man, treating the compartment to a wholesale wink.

"No, Stansfield, Henry Stansfield." The Deep Chap, a ruddy-faced man who sat with hands firmly planted on the knees of his brown tweed suit, might have been a prosperous farmer but for the long, steady meditative scrutiny which he now bent upon each of his fellow-travellers in turn.

What he saw was not particularly rewarding. On the opposite seat, from left to right, were a Forward Piece, who had taken the Expansive Man's wink wholly to herself and contrived to wriggle her tight skirt farther up from her knee; a desiccated, sandy, lawyerish little man who fumed and fussed like an angry kettle, consulting every five minutes his gold watch, then shaking out his *Times* with the crackle of a legal parchment, and a Flash Card, dressed up to the nines of spivdom, with the bold yet uneasy stare of the young delinquent.

"Mine's Percy Dukes," said the Expansive Man. "P.D. to my friends, General Dealer. At your service. Well, we'll be across the border in an hour and a half, and then hey for the bluebells of bonny Scotland!"

"Bluebells in January? You're hopeful," remarked the Forward Piece.

"Are you Scots, master?" asked the Comfortable Body sitting on Stansfield's left.

"English outside"—Percy Dukes patted the front of his grey suit, slid a flask from its hip pocket, and took a swig—"and Scotch within." His loud laugh, or the blizzard, shook the railway carriage. The Forward Piece giggled. The Flash Card covertly sneered.

"You'll need that if we run into a drift and get stuck for the night," said Henry Stansfield.

"Name of Jonah, sir?" The compartment reverberated again.

"I do not apprehend such an eventuality," said the Fusspot. "The station-master at Lancaster assured me that the train would get through. We are scandalously late already, though." Once again the gold watch was consulted.

"It's a curious thing," remarked the Deep Chap meditatively, "the way we imagine we can make Time amble withal or gallop withal, just by keeping an eye on the hands of a watch. You travel frequently by this train, Mr—?"

"Kilmington. Arthur J. Kilmington. No, I've only used it once before." The Fusspot spoke in a dry Edinburgh accent.

"Ah yes, that would have been on the 17th of last month. I remember seeing you on it."

"No, sir, you are mistaken. It was the 20th." Mr Kilmington's thin mouth snapped tight again, like a rubber band round a sheaf of legal documents.

"The 20th? Indeed? That was the day of the train robbery. A big haul they got, it seems. Off this very train. It was carrying some of the extra Christmas mail. Bags just disappeared, somewhere between Lancaster and Carlisle."

"Och, deary me," sighed the Comfortable Body. "I don't know what we're coming to, really, nowadays."

"We're coming to the scene of the crime, ma'am," said the expansive Mr Dukes. The train, almost dead-beat, was panting up the last pitch towards Shap Summit.

"I didn't see anything in the papers about where the robbery took place," Henry Stansfield murmured. Dukes fastened a somewhat bleary eye upon him.

"You read all the newspapers?"

"Yes."

The atmosphere in the compartment had grown suddenly tense. Only the Flash Card, idly examining his fingernails, seemed unaffected by it.

"Which paper did you see it in?" pursued Stansfield.

"I didn't." Dukes tapped Stansfield on the knee. "But I can use my loaf. Stands to reason. You want to tip a mail-bag out of a train—get me? Train must be moving slowly, or the bag'll burst when it hits the ground. Only one place between Lancaster and Carlisle where you'd *know* the train would be crawling. Shap Bank. And it goes slowest on the last bit of the bank, just about where we are now. Follow?"

Henry Stansfield nodded.

"O.K. But you'd be balmy to tip it off just anywhere on this God-forsaken moorland," went on Mr Dukes. "Now, if you'd travelled this line as much as I have, you'd have noticed it goes over a bridge about a mile short of the summit. Under the bridge runs a road: a nice, lonely road, see? The only road hereabouts that touches the railway. You tip out the bag there. Your chums collect it, run down the embankment, dump it in the car they've got waiting by the bridge, and Bob's your uncle!"

"You oughta been a detective, mister," exclaimed the Forward Piece languishingly.

Mr Dukes inserted his thumbs in his armpits, looking gratified. "Maybe I am," he said with a wheezy laugh. "And maybe I'm just little old P.D., who knows how to use his loaf."

"Och, well now, the things people will do!" said the Comfortable Body. "There's a terrible lot of dishonesty today."

The Flash Card glanced up contemptuously from his fingernails. Mr Kilmington was heard to mutter that the system of surveillance on railways was disgraceful, and the Guard of the train should have been severely censured.

"The Guard can't be everywhere," said Stansfield. "Presumably he has to patrol the train from time to time, and—"

"Let him do so, then, and not lock himself up in his van and go to sleep," interrupted Mr Kilmington, somewhat unreasonably.

"Are you speaking from personal experience, sir?" asked Stansfield.

The Flash Card lifted up his voice and said, in a Charing-Cross-Road American accent, "Hey, fellas! If the gang was gonna tip out the mail-bags by the bridge, like this guy says—what I mean is, how could they rely on the Guard being out of his van just at that point?" He hitched up the trousers of his loud check suit.

"You've got something there," said Percy Dukes. "What I reckon is, there must have been two accomplices on the train—one to get the Guard out of his van on some pretext, and the other to chuck off the bags." He turned to Mr Kilmington. "You were saying something about the Guard locking himself up in his van. Now if I was of a suspicious turn of mind, if I was little old Sherlock H. in person"—he bestowed another prodigious wink upon Kilmington's fellow-travellers—"I'd begin to wonder about you, sir. You were travelling on this train when the robbery took place. You went to the Guard's van. You *say* you found him asleep. You didn't by any chance call the Guard out, so as to—?"

"Your suggestion is outrageous! I advise you to be very careful, sir, very careful indeed," enunciated Mr Kilmington, his precise voice crackling with indignation, "or you may find you have said something actionable. I would have you know that, when I—"

But what he would have them know was to remain undivulged. The train, which for some little time had been running cautiously down from Shap Summit, suddenly began to chatter and shudder, like a fever patient in high delirium, as the vacuum brakes were applied; then, with the dull impact of a fist driving into a feather pillow, the engine buried itself in a drift which had gathered just beyond the bend of a deep cutting. The time was five minutes past seven.

"What's this in aid of?" asked the Forward Piece, rather shrilly, as a hysterical outburst of huffing and puffing came from the engine.

"Run into a drift, I reckon."

"He's trying to back us out. No good. The wheels are slipping every time. What a lark!' Percy Dukes had his head out of the window on the lee side of the train. 'Coom to Coomberland for your winter sports!"

"Guard! Guard, I say!" called Mr Kilmington. But the blue-clad figure, after one glance into the compartment, hurried on his way up the corridor. "Really! I *shall* report that man."

Henry Stansfield, going out into the corridor, opened a window. Though the coach was theoretically sheltered by the cutting on this windward side, the blizzard stunned his face like a knuckle-duster of ice. He joined the herd of passengers who had climbed down and were stumbling towards the engine. As they reached it, the Guard emerged from its cab: no cause for alarm, he said; if they couldn't get through, there'd be a relief engine sent down to take the train back to Tebay; he was just off to set fog-signals on the line behind them.

The driver renewed his attempts to back the train out. But, what with its weight, the up-gradient in its rear, the icy rails, and the cling-ing grip of the drift on the engine, he could not budge her.

"We'll have to dig out the bogeys, mate," he said to the fireman. "Fetch them shovels from the forward van. It'll keep the perishers from freezing, any road." He jerked his finger at the knot of passen-gers who, lit up by the glare of the furnace, were capering and beating their arms like savages amid the swirling snow-wreaths.

Percy Dukes, who had now joined them, quickly established him-self as the life and soul of the party, referring to the grimy-faced fire-man as "Snowball", adjuring his companions to "Dig for Victory", affecting to spy the approach of a herd of St Bernards, each with a keg of brandy slung round its neck. But, after ten minutes of hard digging, when the leading wheels of the bogey were cleared, it could be seen that they had been derailed by their impact with the drift.

"That's torn it, Charlie. You'll have to walk back to the box and get 'em to telephone through for help," said the driver.

"*If* the wires aren't down already," replied the fireman lugubriously. "It's above a mile to that box, and uphill. Who d'you think I am? Captain Scott?"

"You'll have the wind behind you, mate, any road. So long."

A buzz of dismay had risen from the passengers at this. One or two, who began to get querulous, were silenced by the driver's offering to take them anywhere they liked if they would just lift his engine back on to the metals first. When the rest had dispersed to their carriages, Henry Stansfield asked the driver's permission to go up into the cab for a few minutes and dry his coat.

"You're welcome." The driver snorted: "Would you believe it? 'Must get to Glasgow tonight.' Damn ridiculous! Now Bert—that's my Guard—it's different for him: he's entitled to fret a bit. Missus been very poorly. Thought she was going to peg out before Christmas; but he got the best surgeon in Glasgow to operate on her, and she's mending now, he says. He reckons to look in every night at the nursing home, when he goes off work."

Stansfield chatted with the man for five minutes. Then the Guard returned, blowing upon his hands—a smallish, leathery-faced chap, with an anxious look in his eye.

"We'll not get through tonight, Bert. Charlie told you?"

"Aye. I doubt some of the passengers are going to create a rumpus," said the Guard dolefully.

Henry Stansfield went back to his compartment. It was stuffy, but with a sinister hint of chilliness, too: he wondered how long the steam heating would last: depended upon the amount of water in the engine boiler, he supposed. Amongst the wide variety of fates he had imagined for himself, freezing to death in an English train was not included.

Arthur J. Kilmington fidgeted more than ever. When the Guard came along the corridor, he asked him where the nearest village was, saying he must get a telephone call through to Edinburgh—most urgent appointment—must let his client know, if he was going to miss it. The Guard said there was a village two miles to the north-east; you could see the lights from the top of the cutting; but he warned Mr Kilmington against trying to get there in the teeth of this blizzard—better wait for the relief engine, which should reach them before 9 p.m.

Silence fell upon the compartment for a while; the incredulous silence of civilized people who find themselves in the predicament of castaways. Then the expansive Mr Dukes proposed that, since they were to be stuck here for an hour or two, they should get acquainted. The Comfortable Body now introduced herself as Mrs Grant, the Forward Piece as Inez Blake; the Flash Card, with the over-negligent air of one handing a dud half-crown over a counter, gave his name as Macdonald—I. Macdonald.

"A fine old Scots name," said Mrs Grant.

"I for Ian," said Mr Dukes. "Or would it be Izzy?"

"Irving, if you want to know," replied the young man. "Any objection? You like to make something of it?"

"Keep your hair on, young shaver."

"So I'm a Yid, am I? That's your idea, uh?"

"If you get steamed up any more," said Mr Dukes, "it'll ruin that permanent wave of yours."

"It only remains for one of you to suggest a nice friendly game of cards, now we've had the preliminary patter," said Henry Stansfield.

This reference to the technique of card-sharpers who work the trains silenced even Percy Dukes for a moment. However, he soon recovered.

"I see you weren't born yesterday, mister. We must've sounded a bit like that. You can always tell 'em a mile off, can't you? No offence meant to this young gent. Just P.D.'s little bit of fun."

"I wish somebody would tell me what this is all about," asked Inez Blake, pouting provocatively at Mr Dukes, who at once obliged.

"They must be awfu' clever," remarked Mrs Grant, in her singsong Lowland accent, when he had finished.

"No criminals are clever, ma'am," said Stansfield quietly. His ruminative eye passed, without haste, from Macdonald to Dukes. "Neither the small fry nor the big operators. They're pretty well subhuman, the whole lot of 'em. A dash of cunning, a thick streak of cowardice, and the rest is made up of stupidity and boastfulness. They're too stupid for anything but crime, and so riddled with inferiority that they always give themselves away, sooner or later, by boasting about their crimes. They like to think of themselves as the wide boys, but they're as narrow as starved eels—why, they haven't even the wits to alter their professional methods: that's how the police pick 'em up."

"I entirely agree, sir," Mr Kilmington snapped. "In my profession I see a good deal of the criminal classes. And I flatter myself none of them has ever got the better of me. They're transparent, sir, transparent."

"No doubt you gentlemen are right," said Percy Dukes comfortably. "But the police haven't picked up the chaps who did this train robbery yet."

"They will. And the Countess of Axminster's emerald bracelet. Bet the gang didn't reckon to find that in the mail-bag. Worth all of £25,000."

Percy Duke's mouth fell open. The Flash Card whistled. Overcome, either by the stuffiness of the carriage or the thought of £25,000-worth of emeralds, Inez Blake gave a little moan and fainted all over Mr Kilmington's lap.

"Really! Upon my soul! My dear young lady!" exclaimed that worthy. There was a flutter of solicitude, shared by all except the cold-eyed young Macdonald who, after stooping over her a moment, his back to the others, said, "Here you—stop pawing the young lady and let her stretch out on the seat. Yes, I'm talking to you, Kilmington."

"How dare you! This is an outrage!" The little man stood up so abruptly that the girl was almost rolled on to the floor. "I was merely trying to—"

"I know your sort. Nasty old men. Now, keep your hands off her! I'm telling you."

In the shocked silence that ensued, Kilmington gobbled speechlessly at Macdonald for a moment; then, seeing razors in the youth's cold-steel eye, snatched his black hat and brief-case from the rack and bolted out of the compartment. Henry Stansfield made as if to stop him, then changed his mind. Mrs Grant followed the little man out, returning presently, her handkerchief soaked in water, to dab Miss Blake's forehead. The time was just on 8.30.

When things were restored to normal, Mr Dukes turned to Stansfield. "You were saying this necklace of—who was it?—the Countess of Axminster, it's worth £25,000? Fancy sending a thing of that value through the post! Are you sure of it?"

"The value? Oh, yes." Henry Stansfield spoke out of the corner of his mouth, in the manner of a stupid man imparting a confidence. "Don't let this go any farther. But I've a friend who works in the Cosmopolitan—the Company where it's insured. That's another thing that didn't get into the papers. Silly woman. She wanted it for some big family do in Scotland at Christmas, forgot to bring it with her, and wrote home for it to be posted to her in a registered packet."

"£25,000," said Percy Dukes thoughtfully. "Well, stone me down!"

"Yes. Some people don't know when they're lucky, do they?"

Dukes' fat face wobbled on his shoulders like a globe of lard. Young Macdonald polished his nails. Inez Blake read her magazine.

After some while, Percy Dukes remarked that the blizzard was slackening; he'd take an airing and see if there was any sign of the relief engine yet. He left the compartment.

At the window, the snowflakes danced in their tens now, not their thousands. The time was 8.55. Shortly afterwards, Inez Blake went out; and ten minutes later, Mrs Grant remarked to Stansfield that it had stopped snowing altogether. Neither Inez nor Dukes had returned when, at 9.30, Henry Stansfield decided to ask what had happened about the relief. The Guard was not in his van, which adjoined Stansfield's coach, towards the rear of the train. So he turned back, walked up the corridor to the front coach, clambered out, and hailed the engine cab.

"She must have been held up," said the Guard, leaning out. "Charlie here got through from the box, and they promised her by nine o'clock. But it'll no' be long now, sir."

"Have you seen anything of a Mr Kilmington—small, sandy chap—black hat and overcoat, blue suit—was in my compartment? I've walked right up the train and he doesn't seem to be on it."

The Guard pondered a moment. "Och aye, yon wee fellow? Him that asked me about telephoning from the village. Aye, he's awa' then."

"He did set off to walk there, you mean?"

"Nae doot he did, if he's no' on the train. He spoke to me again—juist on nine, it'd be—and said he was awa' if the relief didna turn up in five minutes."

"You've not seen him since?"

"No, sir. I've been talking to my mates here this half-hour, ever syne the wee fellow spoke to me."

Henry Stansfield walked thoughtfully back down the permanent way. When he had passed out of the glare shed by the carriage lights on the snow, he switched on his electric torch. Just beyond the last coach, the eastern wall of the cutting sloped sharply down and merged into moorland level with the track. Although the snow had stopped altogether, an icy wind from the north-east still blew, raking and numbing his face. Twenty yards farther on, his torch lit up a track, already half filled in with snow, made by several pairs of feet, pointing away over the moor, towards the north-east. Several passengers, it seemed, had set off for the village, whose lights twinkled like frost in the far distance. Stansfield was about to follow this track when he heard footsteps scrunching the snow farther up the line. He switched off the torch; at once it was as if a sack had been thrown over his head, so close and blinding was the darkness. The steps came nearer. Stansfield switched on his torch, at the last minute, pinpointing the squab figure of Percy Dukes. The man gave a muffled oath.

"What the devil! Here, what's the idea, keeping me waiting half an hour in that blasted—?"

"Have you seen Kilmington?"

"Oh, it's you. No, how the hell should I have seen him? Isn't he on the train? I've been walking up the line, to look for the relief. No sign yet. Damn parky, it is—I'm moving on."

Presently Stansfield moved on, too, but along the track towards the village. The circle of his torchlight wavered and bounced on the deep snow. The wind, right in his teeth, was killing. No wonder, he thought, as after a few hundred yards he approached the end of the trail, those passengers turned back. Then he realized they had not all turned back. What he had supposed to be a hummock of snow bearing a crude resemblance to a recumbent human figure, he now saw to be a human figure covered with snow. He scraped some of the snow off it, turned it gently over on its back.

Arthur J. Kilmington would fuss no more in this world. His brief-case was buried beneath him: his black hat was lying where it had fallen, lightly covered with snow, near the head. There seemed, to Stansfield's cursory examination, no mark of violence on him. But the eyeballs started, the face was suffused with a pinkish-blue colour. So men look who have been strangled, thought Stansfield, or asphyxiated. Quickly he knelt down again, shining his torch in the dead face. A qualm of horror shook him. Mr Kilmington's nostrils were caked thick with snow, which had frozen solid in them, and snow had been rammed tight into his mouth also.

And here he would have stayed, reflected Stansfield, in this desolate spot, for days or weeks, perhaps, if the snow lay or deepened. And when the thaw at last came (as it did that year, in fact, only after two months), the snow would thaw out from his mouth and nostrils, too, and there would be no vestige of murder left—only the corpse of an impatient little lawyer who had tried to walk to the village in a blizzard and died for his pains. It might even be that no one would ask how such a precise, pernickety little chap had ventured the two-mile walk in thin shoes and without a torch to light his way through the pitchy blackness; for Stansfield, going through the man's pockets, had found the following articles—and nothing more: pocket-book, fountain pen, handkerchief, cigarette-case, gold lighter, two letters and some loose change.

Stansfield started to return for help. But, only twenty yards back, he noticed another trail of footprints, leading off the main track to the left. This trail seemed a fresher one—the snow lay less thickly in the indentations—and to have been made by one pair of feet only. He followed it up, walking beside it. Whoever made this track had walked in a slight right-handed curve back to the railway line, joining it about 150 yards south of where the main trail came out. At this point there was a platelayers' shack. Finding the door unlocked, Stansfield entered. There was nothing inside but a coke-brazier, stone cold, and a smell of cigar-smoke …

Half an hour later, Stansfield returned to his compartment. In the meanwhile, he had helped the train crew to carry back the body of Kilmington, which was now locked in the Guard's van. He had also made an interesting discovery as to Kilmington's movements. It was to be presumed that, after the altercation with Macdonald, and the brief conversation already reported by the Guard, the lawyer must have gone to sit in another compartment. The last coach, to the rear of the Guard's van, was a first-class one, almost empty. But in one of its compartments, Stansfield found a passenger asleep. He woke him up, gave a description of Kilmington, and asked if he had seen him earlier.

The passenger grumpily informed Stansfield that a smallish man, in a dark overcoat, with the trousers of a blue suit showing beneath it, had come to the door and had a word with him. No, the passenger had not noticed his face particularly, because he'd been very drowsy himself, and besides, the chap had politely taken off his black Homburg hat to address him, and the hat screened as much of the head as was not cut off from his view by the top of the door. No, the chap had not come into his compartment: he had just stood outside, inquired the time (the passenger had looked at his watch and told him it was 8.50); then the chap had said that, if the relief didn't turn up by nine, he intended to walk to the nearest village.

Stansfield had then walked along to the engine cab. The Guard, whom he found there, told him that he'd gone up the track about 8.45 to meet the fireman on his way back from the signal-box. He had gone as far as the place where he had put down his fog-signals earlier; here, just before nine, he and the fireman met, as the latter corroborated. Returning to the train, the Guard had climbed into the last coach, noticed Kilmington sitting alone in a first-class compartment (it was then that the lawyer announced to the Guard his intention of walking if the relief engine had not arrived within five minutes). The Guard then got out of the train again, and proceeded down the track to talk to his mates in the engine cab.

This evidence would seem to point incontrovertibly at Kilmington's having been murdered shortly after 9 p.m., Stansfield reflected as he went back to his own compartment. His other fellow-passengers were all present and correct now.

"Well, did you find him?" asked Percy Dukes.

"Kilmington? Oh yes, I found him. In the snow over there. He was dead."

Inez Blake gave a little, affected scream. The permanent sneer was wiped, as if by magic, off young Macdonald's face, which turned a sickly white. Mr Dukes sucked in his fat lips.

"The puir wee man," said Mrs Grant. "He tried to walk it then? Died of exposure, was it?"

"No," announced Stansfield flatly, "he was murdered."

This time, Inez Blake screamed in earnest; and, like an echo, a hooting shriek came from far up the line: the relief engine was approaching at last.

"The police will be awaiting us back at Tebay, so we'd better all have our stories ready." Stansfield turned to Percy Dukes. "You, for instance, sir. Where were you between 8.55, when you left the carriage, and 9.35 when I met you returning? Are you sure you didn't see Kilmington?"

Dukes, expansive no longer, his piggy eyes sunk deep in the fat of his face, asked Stansfield who the hell he thought he was.

"I am an inquiry agent, employed by the Cosmopolitan Insurance Company. Before that, I was a Detective Inspector in the C.I.D. Here is my card."

Dukes barely glanced at it. "That's all right, old man. Only wanted to make sure. Can't trust anyone nowadays." His voice had taken on the ingratiating, oleaginous heartiness of the small businessman trying to clinch a deal with a bigger one. "Just went for a stroll, y'know— stretch the old legs. Didn't see a soul."

"Who were you expecting to see? Didn't you wait for someone in the platelayers' shack along there, and smoke a cigar while you were waiting? Who did you mistake me for when you said 'What's the idea, keeping me waiting half an hour'?"

"Here, draw it mild, old man." Percy Dukes sounded injured. "I certainly looked in at the hut: smoked a cigar for a bit. Then I toddled back to the train, and met up with your good self on the way. I didn't make no appointment to meet—"

"Oo! Well I *must* say," interrupted Miss Blake virtuously. She could hardly wait to tell Stansfield that, on leaving the compartment shortly after Dukes, she'd overheard voices on the track below the lavatory window. "I recognized this gentleman's voice," she went on, tossing her head at Dukes. "He said something like, 'You're going to help us again, chum, so you'd better get used to the idea. You're in it up to the neck—can't back out now.' And another voice, sort of mumbling, might have been Mr Kilmington's—I dunno—sounded Scotch anyway—said, 'All right. Meet you in five minutes: platelayers' hut a few hundred yards up the line. Talk it over.'"

"And what did you do then, young lady?" asked Stansfield. "You didn't return to the compartment, I remember."

"I happened to meet a gentleman friend, farther up the train, and sat with him for a bit."

"Is that so?" remarked Macdonald menacingly. "Why, you four-flushing little—!"

"Shut up!" commanded Stansfield.

"Honest I did," the girl said, ignoring Macdonald. "I'll introduce you to him, if you like. He'll tell you I was with him for, oh, half an hour or more."

"And what about Mr Macdonald?"

"I'm not talking," said the youth sullenly.

"Mr Macdonald isn't talking. Mrs Grant?"

"I've been in this compartment ever since, sir."

"Ever since—?"

"Since I went out to damp my hankie for this young lady, when she'd fainted. Mr Kilmington was just before me, you'll mind. I saw him go through into the Guard's van."

"Did you hear him say anything about walking to the village?"

"No, sir. He just hurried into the van, and then there was some havers about it's no' being lockit this time, and how he was going to report the Guard for it—I didna listen any more, wishing to get back to the young lady. I doubt the wee man would be for reporting everyone."

"I see. And you've been sitting here with Mr Macdonald all the time?"

"Yes, sir. Except for ten minutes or so he was out of the compartment, just after you'd left."

"What did you go out for?" Stansfield asked the young man.

"Just taking the air, brother, just taking the air."

"You weren't taking Mr Kilmington's gold watch, as well as the air, by any chance?" Stansfield's keen eyes were fastened like a hook into Macdonald's, whose insolent expression visibly crumbled beneath them.

"I don't know what you mean," he tried to bluster. "You can't do this to me."

"I mean that a man has been murdered: and, when the police search you, they will find his gold watch in your possession. Won't look too healthy for you, my young friend."

"Naow! Give us a chance! It was only a joke, see?" The wretched Macdonald was whining now in his native cockney. "He got me riled—the stuck-up way he said nobody'd ever got the better of him. So I thought I'd just show him—I'd have given it back, straight I would, only I couldn't find him afterwards. It was just a joke, I tell you. Anyway, it was Inez who lifted the ticker."

"You dirty little rotter!" screeched the girl.

"Shut up, both of you! You can explain your joke to the police. Let's hope they don't die laughing."

At this moment the train gave a lurch, and started back up the gradient. It halted at the signal-box, for Stansfield to telephone to Tebay, then clattered south again.

On Tebay platform, Stansfield was met by an Inspector and a Sergeant of the County Constabulary, with the Police Surgeon. No passengers were permitted to alight till he had had a few words with them. Then the four men boarded the train. After a brief pause in the Guard's van, where the Police Surgeon drew aside the Guard's black off-duty overcoat that had been laid over the body, and began his preliminary examination, they marched along to Stansfield's compartment. The Guard who, at his request, had locked this as the train was drawing up at the platform and was keeping an eye on its occupants, now unlocked it. The Inspector entered.

His first action was to search Macdonald. Finding the watch concealed on his person, he then charged Macdonald and Inez Blake with the theft. The Inspector next proceeded to make an arrest on the charge of wilful murder...

---

But who did the Inspector arrest for the murder of the disagreeable Arthur J. Kilmington? And why? Nicholas Blake placed eight clues to the killer's identity in the text (two major clues; six minor ones); they cover motive as well as method.

Baffled? Read the story again—or meander through the rest of the stories in the book (there's never any hurry over Christmas) and then read it once more.

If you still can't identify the who, the how, and the why—turn to pages 284 to 287 at the very end of the book, where all is revealed.

# THE NAME ON THE WINDOW

## Edmund Crispin

Edmund Crispin was the pseudonym of Robert Bruce Montgomery (1922–1958), who wrote his first detective novel, *The Case of the Gilded Fly*, while still an undergraduate at Oxford. Crispin's principal influences were Michael Innes, an Oxford academic and prolific author of detective and mainstream novels, and the Anglophile American John Dickson Carr, master of the "locked room" and "impossible crime" mystery.

Seven more novels featuring Fen swiftly followed, but after *The Long Divorce* was published in 1952, there was a very long silence before Fen reappeared in another novel, *The Glimpses of the Moon*. Crispin burned out young as a crime writer, and although he achieved success as a musician and composer of film music, his creative gifts were eventually smothered by alcoholism. His short stories display the same exuberance as his novels, and showcase his flair for plot.

\* \* \* \* \*

Boxing Day; snow and ice; road-surfaces like glass under a cold fog. In the North Oxford home of the University Professor of English Language and Literature, at three minutes past seven in the evening, the front door bell rang.

The current festive season had taken heavy toll of Fen's vitality and patience; it had culminated, that afternoon, in a quite exceptionally tiring children's party, amid whose ruins he was now recouping his energies with whisky; and on hearing the bell he jumped inevitably to the conclusion that one of the infants he had bundled out of the door half an hour previously had left behind it some such prized inessential as a false nose or a bachelor's button, and was returning to claim this. In the event, however, and despite his premonitory groans, this assumption proved to be incorrect: his doorstep was occupied, he found, not by a dyspeptic, over-heated child with an unintelligible query, but by a neatly dressed greying man with a red tip to his nose and woebegone eyes.

"I can't get back," said this apparition. "I really can't get back to London tonight. The roads are impassable and such trains as there are are running hours late. Could you possibly let me have a bed?"

The tones were familiar; and by peering more attentively at the face, Fen discovered that that was familiar too. "My dear Humbleby," he said cordially, "do come in. Of course you can have a bed. What are you doing in this part of the world, anyway?"

"Ghost-hunting." Detective Inspector Humbleby, of New Scotland Yard, divested himself of his coat and hat and hung them on a hook inside the door. "Seasonable but not convenient." He stamped his feet violently, thereby producing, to judge from his expression, sensations of pain rather than of warmth; and stared about him. "*Children*," he said with sudden gloom. "I dare say that one of the Oxford hotels——"

"The children have left," Fen explained, "and will not be coming back."

"Ah. Well, in that case——" And Humbleby followed Fen into the drawing-room, where a huge fire was burning and a slightly lop-sided Christmas tree, stripped of its treasures, wore tinsel and miniature witch-balls and a superincumbent fairy with a raffish air. "My word, this is better. Is there a drink, perhaps? I could do with some advice, too."

Fen was already pouring whisky. "Sit down and be comfortable," he said. "As a matter of interest, do you believe in ghosts?"

"The evidence for *poltergeists*," Humbleby answered warily as he stretched out his hands to the blaze, "seems very convincing to me.... The Wesleys, you know, and Harry Price and so forth. Other sorts of ghosts I'm not so sure about—though I must say I *hope* they exist, if only for the purpose of taking that silly grin off the faces of the news-papers." He picked up a battered tin locomotive from beside him on the sofa. "I say, Gervase, I was under the impression that your own children were all too old for——"

"Orphans," said Fen, jabbing at the siphon. "I've been entertaining orphans from a nearby Home. ... But as regards this particular ghost you were speaking of——"

"Oh, I don't believe in *that*." Humbleby shook his head decisively. "There's an obscure sort of nastiness about the place it's supposed to haunt—like a very sickly cake gone stale—and a man *was* killed there once, by a girl he was trying to persuade to certain practices she didn't relish at all; but the haunting part of it is just silly gossip for the benefit of visitors." Humbleby accepted the glass which Fen held out to him and brooded over it for a moment before drinking. "... Damned Chief Inspector," he muttered aggrievedly, "dragging me away from my Christmas lunch because——"

"Really, Humbleby"—Fen was severe—"you're very inconsequent this evening. Where is this place you're speaking of?"

"Rydalls."

"Rydalls?"

"Rydalls," said Humbleby. "The residence," he elucidated laboriously, "of Sir Charles Moberley, the architect. It's about fifteen miles from here, Abingdon way."

"Yes, I remember it now. Restoration."

"I dare say. Old, in any case. And there are big grounds, with an eighteenth-century pavilion about a quarter of a mile away from the house, in a park. That's where it happened—the murder, I mean."

"The murder of the man who tried to induce the girl——"

"No, no. I mean, yes. *That* murder took place in the pavilion, certainly. But then, so did the other one—the one the day before yesterday, that's to say."

Fen stared. "Sir Charles Moberley has been murdered?"

"No, no, no. Not *him*. Another architect, another knight—Sir Lucas Welsh. There's been quite a large house party going on at Rydalls, with Sir Lucas Welsh and his daughter Jane among the guests, and it was on Christmas Eve, you see, that Sir Lucas decided he wanted to investigate the ghost."

"This is all clear enough to you, no doubt, but——"

"Do *listen*. … It seems that Sir Lucas is—was—credulous about ghosts, so on Christmas Eve he arranged to keep vigil alone in the pavilion and——"

"And was murdered, and you don't know who did it."

"Oh yes, I do. Sir Lucas didn't die at once, you see: he had time to write up his murderer's name in the grime of the window-pane, and the gentleman concerned, a young German named Otto Mörike, is now safely under arrest. But what I can't decide is how Mörike got in and out of the pavilion."

"A locked-room mystery."

"In the wider sense, just that. The pavilion wasn't actually locked, but——"

Fen collected his glass from the mantelpiece, where he had put it on rising to answer the door-bell. "Begin," he suggested, "at the beginning."

"Very well." Settling back in the sofa, Humbleby sipped his whisky gratefully. "Here, then, is this Christmas house party at Rydalls. Host, Sir Charles Moberley, the eminent architect. … Have you ever come across him?"

Fen shook his head.

"A big man, going grey: in some ways rather boisterous and silly, like a rugger-playing medical student in a state of arrested development. Unmarried; private means—quite a lot of them, to judge from the sort of hospitality he dispenses; did the Wandsworth power-station and Beckford Abbey, among other things; athlete; a simple mind, and generous, I should judge, in that jealous sort of way which resents generosity in anyone else. Probably tricky, in some respects—he's not the kind of person *I* could ever feel completely at ease with.

"A celebrity, however: unquestionably that. And Sir Lucas Welsh, whom among others he invited to this house party, was equally a celebrity, in the same line of business. Never having seen Sir Lucas alive, I can't say much about his character, but——"

"I think," Fen interrupted, "that I may have met him once, at the time when he was designing the fourth quadrangle for my college. A small dark person, wasn't he?"

"Yes, that's right."

"And with a tendency to be nervy and obstinate."

"The obstinacy there's evidence for, certainly. And I gather he was also a good deal of a faddist—Yogi, I mean, and the Baconian hypothesis, and a lot of other intellectual—um—detritus of the same dull, obvious kind: that's where the ghost-vigil comes in. Jane, his daughter and heiress (and Sir Lucas was if anything even better off than Sir Charles) is a pretty little thing of eighteen of whom all you can really say is that she's a pretty little thing of eighteen. Then there's Mörike, the man I've arrested: thin, thirtyish, a Luftwaffe pilot during the war, and at present an architecture student working over here under one of these exchange schemes the Universities are always getting up—which accounts for Sir Charles' knowing him and inviting him to the house party. Last of the important guests—important from the point of view of the crime, that is—is a C.I.D. man (not Metropolitan, Sussex County) called James Wilburn. He's important because the evidence he provides is quite certainly reliable—there has to be a *point d'appui* in these affairs, and Wilburn is it, so you mustn't exhaust yourself doubting his word about anything."

"I won't," Fen promised. "I'll believe him."

"Good. At dinner on Christmas Eve, then, the conversation turns to the subject of the Rydalls ghost—and I've ascertained that the person responsible for bringing this topic up was Otto Mörike. So far, so good: the Rydalls ghost was a bait Sir Lucas could be relied on to rise to, and rise to it he did, arranging eventually with his rather reluctant host to go down to the pavilion after dinner and keep watch there for an hour or two. The time arriving, he was accompanied to the place of trial by Sir Charles and by Wilburn—neither of whom actually *entered* the pavilion. Wilburn strolled back to the house alone, leaving Sir Charles and Sir Lucas talking shop. And presently Sir Charles, having seen Sir Lucas go into the pavilion, retraced his steps likewise, arriving at the house just in time to hear the alarm-bell ringing."

"Alarm-bell?"

"People had watched for the ghost before, and there was a bell installed in the pavilion for them to ring if for any reason they wanted help. … This bell sounded, then, at shortly after ten o'clock, and a whole party of people, including Sir Charles, Jane Welsh and Wilburn, hastened to the rescue.

"Now, you must know that this pavilion is quite small. There's just one circular room to it, having two windows (both very firmly nailed up); and you get into this room by way of a longish, narrow hall projecting from the perimeter of the circle, the one and only door being at the outer end of this hall."

"Like a key-hole," Fen suggested. "If you saw it from the air it'd look like a key-hole, I mean; with the round part representing the room, and the part where the wards go in representing the entrance-hall, and the door right down at the bottom."

"That's it. It stands in a clearing among the trees of the park, on a very slight rise—inferior Palladian in style, with pilasters or whatever you call them: something like a decayed miniature classical temple.

No one's bothered about it for decades, not since that earlier murder put an end to its career as a love-nest for a succession of squires.
What is it Eliot says?—something about lusts and dead limbs? Well,
anyway, that's the impression it gives. A *house* is all right, because a
house has been used for other things as well—eating and reading
and births and deaths and so on. But this place has been used for one
purpose and one purpose only, and that's exactly what it feels like. ...

"There's no furniture in it, by the way. And until the wretched
Sir Lucas unlocked its door, no one had been inside it for two or
three years.

"To get back to the story, then.

"The weather was all right: you'll remember that on Christmas Eve
none of this snow and foulness had started. And the rescue-party, so
to call them, seem to have regarded their expedition as more or less
in the nature of a jaunt; I mean that they weren't seriously alarmed
at the ringing of the bell, with the exception of Jane, who knew her
father well enough to suspect that he'd never have interrupted his
vigil, almost as soon as it had begun, for the sake of a rather futile
practical joke; and even she seems to have allowed herself to be half
convinced by the reassurances of the others. On arrival at the pavilion, they found the door shut but not locked; and when they opened
it, and shone their torches inside, they saw a single set of footprints
in the dust on the hall floor, leading to the entrance to the circular
room. Acting on instinct or training or both, Wilburn kept his crowd
clear of these footprints; and so it was that they came—joined now
by Otto Mörike, who according to his subsequent statement had
been taking a solitary stroll in the grounds—to the scene of the crime.

"Fireplace, two windows, a crudely painted ceiling—crude in subject as well as in execution—a canvas chair, an unlit electric torch, festoons of cobwebs, and on everything except the chair and the torch
*dust*, layers of it. Sir Lucas was lying on the floor beneath one of the

windows, quite close to the bell-push; and an old stiletto, later discovered to have been stolen from the house, had been stuck into him
under the left shoulder-blade (no damning fingerprints on it, by the
way; or on anything else in the vicinity). Sir Lucas was still alive, and
just conscious. Wilburn bent over him to ask who was responsible.
And a queer smile crossed Sir Lucas' face, and he was just able to whisper"—here Humbleby produced and consulted a notebook—"to
whisper: *'Wrote it—on the window. Very first thing I did when I came
round. Did it before I rang the bell or anything else, in case you didn't get
here in time—in time for me to tell you who——'*

"His voice faded out then. But with a final effort he moved his
head, glanced up at the window, nodded and smiled again. That was
how he died.

"They had all heard him, and they all looked. There was bright
moonlight outside, and the letters traced on the grimy pane stood
out clearly.

"Otto.

"Well, it seems that then Otto started edging away, and Sir
Charles made a grab at him, and they fought, and presently a wal-
lop from Sir Charles sent Otto clean through the tell-tale window,
and Sir Charles scrambled after him, and they went on fighting outside, trampling the glass to smithereens, until Wilburn and company
joined in and put a stop to it. Incidentally, Wilburn says that Otto's
going through the window looked *contrived* to him—a deliberate
attempt to destroy evidence; though of course, so many people *saw*
the name written there that it remains perfectly good evidence in
spite of having been destroyed."

"Motive?" Fen asked.

"Good enough. Jane Welsh was wanting to marry Otto—had
fallen quite dementedly in love with him, in fact—and her father
didn't approve; partly on the grounds that Otto was a German, and

partly because he thought the boy wanted Jane's prospective inheritance rather than Jane herself. To clinch it, moreover, there was the fact that Otto had been in the Luftwaffe and that Jane's mother had been killed in 1941 in an air-raid. Jane being only eighteen years of age—and the attitude of magistrates, if appealed to, being in the circumstances at best problematical—it looked as if that was one marriage that would definitely not take place. So the killing of Sir Lucas had, from Otto's point of view, a double advantage: it made Jane rich, and it removed the obstacle to the marriage."

"Jane's prospective guardian not being against it."

"Jane's prospective guardian being an uncle she could twist round her little finger. ... But here's the point." Humbleby leaned forward earnestly. "Here is the point: windows nailed shut; no secret doors—emphatically none; chimney too narrow to admit a baby; and in the dust on the hall floor, only one set of footprints, made unquestionably by Sir Lucas himself. ... If you're thinking that Otto might have walked in and out on top of those prints, as that page-boy we've been hearing so much about recently did with King Wenceslaus, then you're wrong. Otto's feet are much too large, for one thing, and the prints hadn't been disturbed, for another: so that's out. But then, how on earth did he manage it? There's no furniture in that hall whatever—nothing he could have used to crawl across, nothing he could have swung himself from. It's a long, bare box, that's all; and the distance between the door and the circular room (in which room, by the way, the dust on the floor was all messed up by the rescue-party) is miles too far for anyone to have jumped it. Nor was the weapon the sort of thing that could possibly have been fired from a bow or an air-gun or a blow-pipe, or any nonsense of that sort; nor was it sharp enough or heavy enough to have penetrated as deeply as it did if it had been *thrown*. So ghosts apart, what *is* the explanation? Can you see one?"

Fen made no immediate reply. Throughout this narrative he had remained standing, draped against the mantelpiece. Now he moved, collecting Humbleby's empty glass and his own and carrying them across to the decanter; and it was only after they were refilled that he spoke.

"Supposing," he said, "that Otto had crossed the entrance hall on a tricycle——"

"A tricycle!" Humbleby was dumbfounded. "A——"

"A tricycle, yes," Fen reiterated firmly. "Or supposing, again, that he had laid down a carpet, unrolling it in front of him as he entered and rolling it up again after him when he left. ..."

"But the dust!" wailed Humbleby. "Have I really not made it clear to you that apart from the footprints the dust on the floor was undisturbed? Tricycles, carpets. ..."

"A section of the floor at least," Fen pointed out, "was trampled on by the rescue-party."

"Oh, that. ... Yes, but that didn't happen until after Wilburn had examined the floor."

"Examined it in detail?"

"Yes. At that stage they still didn't realize anything was wrong; and when Wilburn led them in they were giggling behind him while he did a sort of parody of detective work, throwing the beam of his torch over every inch of the floor in a pretended search for bloodstains."

"It doesn't," said Fen puritanically, "sound the sort of performance which would amuse me very much."

"I dare say not. Anyway, the point about it is that Wilburn's ready to swear that the dust was completely unmarked and undisturbed except for the footprints. ... I wish he weren't ready to swear that," Humbleby added dolefully, "because that's what's holding me up. But I can't budge him."

"You oughtn't to be trying to budge him, anyway," retorted Fen, whose mood of self-righteousness appeared to be growing on him. "It's unethical. What about blood, now?"

"Blood? There was practically none of it. You don't get any bleeding to speak of from that narrow type of wound."

"Ah. Just one more question, then; and if the answer's what I expect, I shall be able to tell you how Otto worked it."

"If by any remote chance," said Humblebly suspiciously, "it's *stilts* that you have in mind——"

"My dear Humbleby, don't be so peurile."

Humbleby contained himself with an effort. "Well?" he said.

"The name on the window." Fen spoke almost dreamily. "Was it written in *capital* letters?"

Whatever Humbleby had been expecting, it was clearly not this. "Yes," he answered. "But——"

"Wait." Fen drained his glass. "Wait while I make a telephone call."

He went. All at once restless, Humbleby got to his feet, lit a cheroot, and began pacing the room. Presently he discovered an elastic-driven aeroplane abandoned behind an armchair, wound it up and launched it. It caught Fen a glancing blow on the temple as he reappeared in the doorway, and thence flew on into the hall, where it struck and smashed a vase. "Oh, I say, I'm sorry," said Humbleby feebly. Fen said nothing.

But after about half a minute, when he had simmered down a bit: "Locked rooms," he remarked sourly. "Locked rooms. ... I'll tell you what it is, Humbleby: you've been reading too much fiction; you've got locked rooms on the brain."

Humbleby thought it politic to be meek. "Yes," he said.

"Gideon Fell once gave a very brilliant lecture on The Locked-Room Problem, in connection with that business of the Hollow Man; but there was one category he didn't include."

"Well?"

Fen massaged his forehead resentfully. "He didn't include the locked-room mystery which *isn't* a locked-room mystery: like this one. So that the explanation of how Otto got into and out of that circular room is simple: he didn't get into or out of it at all."

Humbleby gaped. "But Sir Lucas can't have been knifed before he *entered* the circular room. Sir Charles said——"

"Ah yes. Sir Charles saw him go in—or so he asserts. And——"

"Stop a bit." Humbleby was much perturbed. "I can see what you're getting at, but there are serious objections to it."

"Such as?"

"Well, for one thing, Sir Lucas *named* his murderer."

"A murderer who struck at him *from behind*.... Oh, I've no doubt Sir Lucas acted in good faith: Otto, you see, would be the only member of the house party whom Sir Lucas *knew* to have a *motive*. In actual fact, Sir Charles had one too—as I've just discovered. But Sir Lucas wasn't aware of that; and in any case, he very particularly didn't want Otto to marry his daughter after his death, so that the risk of doing an ex-Luftwaffe man an injustice was a risk he was prepared to take.... Next objection?"

"The name on the window. If, as Sir Lucas said, his *very first* action on recovering consciousness was to denounce his attacker, then he'd surely, since he was capable of entering the pavilion after being knifed, have been capable of writing the name on the *outside* of the window, which would be nearest, and which was just as grimy as the inside. That objection's based, of course, on your assumption that he was struck before he ever entered the pavilion."

"I expect he did just that—wrote the name on the outside of the window, I mean."

"But the people who saw it were on the *inside*. Inside a bank, for instance, haven't you ever noticed how the bank's name——"

"The name Otto," Fen interposed, "is a palindrome. That's to say, it reads the same backwards as forwards. What's more, the capital letters used in it are symmetrical—not like B or P or R or S, but like A or H or M. So write it on the outside of a window, and it will look exactly the same from the inside."

"My God, yes." Humbleby was sobered. "I never thought of that. And the fact that the name was on the *outside* would be fatal to Sir Charles, after his assertion that he'd seen Sir Lucas enter the pavilion unharmed, so I suppose that the 'contriving' Wilburn noticed in the fight was Sir Charles' not Otto's: he'd realize that the name *must* be on the outside—Sir Lucas having said that the writing of it was the very first thing he did—and he'd see the need to destroy the window before anyone could investigate closely. ... Wait, though: couldn't Sir Lucas have entered the pavilion as Sir Charles said, and later emerged again, and——"

"One set of footprints," Fen pointed out, "on the hall floor. Not three."

Humbleby nodded. "I've been a fool about this. Locked rooms, as you said, on the brain. But what *was* Sir Charles' motive—the motive Sir Lucas didn't know about?"

"Belchester," said Fen. "Belchester Cathedral. As you know, it was bombed during the war, and a new one's going to be built. Well, I've just rung up the Dean, who's an acquaintance of mine, to ask about the choice of architect; and he says that it was a toss-up between Sir Charles' design and Sir Lucas', and that Sir Lucas' won. The two men were notified by post, and it seems likely that Sir Charles' notification arrived on the morning of Christmas Eve. Sir Lucas' did too, in all probability; but Sir Lucas' was sent to his home, and even forwarded it can't, in the rush of Christmas postal traffic, have reached him at Rydalls before he was killed. So only Sir Charles *knew*; and since with Sir Lucas dead Sir Charles' design would

# BEEF FOR CHRISTMAS

## Leo Bruce

Leo Bruce was a pen-name used by Rupert Croft-Cooke (1903–1979) when writing detective fiction. Croft-Cooke led such a fascinating life that he compiled no fewer than twenty-seven volumes of autobiography, yet he mentioned his crime writing *alter ego* in passing in just two of those books. It was not mentioned at all in his obituary in *The Times*. Golden Age authors were often modest (or embarrassed) about their forays into detection, yet at this distance of time, their detective stories often hold up much better than their more "worthy" work.

Bruce created two major series characters. Sergeant Beef was an engaging vulgarian with a passion for playing darts; he is frequently, but unwisely, underestimated by criminals, and his relationship with his "Watson", the prim narrator Lionel Townsend, is splendidly done. Beef was, however, later dropped in favour of Carolus Deene, a schoolmaster and amateur detective. *Murder in Miniature*, an excellent volume edited by Barry Pike, appeared to be a comprehensive gathering of all Bruce's short detective stories. However, American researcher Curtis Evans subsequently unearthed this story, which first appeared in the *Tatler and Bystander* in 1957, and commented: "It would grace any anthology of British detective stories." I agree.

\* \* \* \* \*

"Doing anything for Christmas?"

The question which was put to me by my old friend Sergeant Beef was altogether too casual. He had, I guessed, what he would call "something up his sleeve".

"Yes, I'm booked up," I lied. I was determined to draw him out.

"Pity," said Beef and took a pull from the pint glass beside him. "I shall have to get someone else to come down with me. There might be a story to write."

"Come down?" I repeated rather irritably. "Come down where?"

"Natchett," said Beef shortly. "Near Braxham. Near where I was stationed before I retired from the force."

It was not many years, I reflected, since Beef had been a country policeman and I considered that he owed his present eminence as a private detective to his Boswell, myself. I was not pleased at his speaking of someone else writing him up.

"What's the case?" I asked as casually as I could.

"You're booked up," sulked Beef. "It can't interest you." Then he gave his good-natured grin and added—"Still, I don't mind telling you what it is."

I looked at his raw red face and straggling ginger moustache and wondered for the hundredth time how anyone as ingenuous as Beef could match his wits against the subtle brains of clever criminals and defeat them. Sometimes he was almost boyish.

"Ever heard of a man called Merton Watlow? You haven't? Well, you might not have. He's one of the richest men in the country. Or rather he was."

"Taxation?" I asked, ready to sympathize.

"Not so much that as just hard spending of his capital. Surprising what you can do in that line today. Time was when a millionaire couldn't make himself much poorer. This Merton Watlow says he can't take it with you and he's making it fly like fury. He spends a couple of Prime Ministers' salaries on keeping up his home at Natchett, and he's got other places. If you have an indoor staff of eight and half a dozen gardeners nowadays, you can only do it on capital."

"Well?" I asked impatiently.

"His family don't like it," said Beef. "Natural enough, I suppose. They want a bit left for them. They mean to live a lot longer than one another. Who doesn't? They think the old man ought to live on his interest for their benefit, and they've told him so. That only makes him worse. It's become a sort of race. You should see the pictures he buys."

"How do you know this?"

"He has consulted me," said Beef rather grandly. "He's been getting anonymous letters lately threatening to do for him if he doesn't stop spending like this. They only make him worse. But he wants me to find out about them."

"I see. But why Christmas?"

"Because he always invites his relatives at Christmas. Gets a kick out of bringing them down to Natchett Grange and letting them see him spend a hundred or two on a Christmas party. The very presents he gives them turn sour when they think what they must have cost him. Silly things, he chooses, hell of a price and no use for them. I shouldn't be surprised if one of them really did for him one day. They certainly hate him enough."

"Isn't he afraid of that?"

"Not likely. He's a big man, powerful, active and tough. He's sixty but as fit as a flea and been around the world a dozen times. He doesn't seem afraid of anything."

"Then what does he want us for?"

"Me, he wants. He hasn't said anything about you. He wants me to find out who's threatening him. Just to satisfy his curiosity, he says. He tells me it's no more than a joke to him, but his secretary, a man called Philip Meece, has nearly been driven out of his mind by it. So I'm going to spend Christmas at Natchett."

"I'll come with you," I said.

Beef nodded without answering, but his grin told me that he regarded this as surrender. As I recall now that Christmas at Natchett with its one horrible moment and its whole bizarre meaning, I am not sure that he was not right.

"He's sending a car for us," Beef said on December 23, the day were due at Natchett, and I soon found that it was an understatement. A Rolls Royce drew up at the door of Beef's modest house in Lilac Crescent, and I was startled to see not only a chauffeur in uniform, but beside him that anachronistic figure, a footman, dressed in similar clothes. He came to the door, took our bags and opened the door for us. We started on our slow way out of town.

But it was when we came to Natchett Grange that I began to have a sense of unreality. Could there be such houses in England in these mid-century years? It was a clear day and we saw at once the great grounds and gardens planned by some modern Capability Brown, the conservatories looming up like those in Kew Gardens and the stables and dairy all manned and busy. The estate would have been ducal in the last century; today it was almost incredible.

Rumbold, the butler, opened the front door, a tall man as aloof and unsmiling as a statue. He shewed us to the library and I had time to see that Merton Watlow was a bibliophile and to guess that his collection was beyond price.

"Wonder if he's read all these," said Beef, chuckling crudely.

Before I answered a small pale man in his forties came in.

"My name's Meece," he said when he had greeted us. "I'm Merton Watlow's secretary. He'll be down in a minute."

I was about to start some general conversation in a normal polite way when Beef with his usual lack of *savoir faire* came out with a clumsy question.

"Now what's all this about anonymous letters?" he asked.

"Oh that," said Philip Meece indifferently. "You must ask Mr Watlow about that. Not my pigeon."

"Seen any of them?" persisted Beef.

"Mr Watlow likes to open his own correspondence. He only shows me what he wants me to deal with."

The door opened. It was not the spendthrift millionaire who entered but a large handsome woman rather lavishly dressed and wearing several pieces of jewellery. I did not know enough of such things to be able to say whether they were genuine.

"My wife," said Philip Meece unexpectedly. "Sergeant Beef and Mr Towser."

"Townsend," I corrected rather crossly as I bowed to Mrs Meece. After all, my name should have been as well known as Beef's.

I could hear Beef breathing heavily as was his wont in the presence of women of this kind—fine dignified women who awed him.

This time I was determined to to lead the conversation into pleasant and conventional channels.

"We've had a delightful drive down," I began. "The countryside. …"

But I could say no more for we all turned to face Merton Watlow. He was, as Beef said, a large man and the years had done little to reduce the solid weight of his shoulders. He gave an impression of forcefulness of both character and physique. I suppose he would be called a handsome man though I found his taurine strength and imperious manner a little overwhelming.

He gave me the merest suggestion of a nod and at once began to talk to Beef whom he treated in a man-to-man way.

"You'll meet them all at dinner tonight," he said. "There are six whom I've thought it worth while to invite. I want this ridiculous business cleared up by Boxing Day."

"We'll see what we can do," said Beef in his most phlegmatic manner. I wished he would shew more alertness and more appreciation of the privilege of being chosen by Merton Watlow for this task.

\*    \*    \*    \*    \*

It was at this point that I felt bound to remonstrate secretly with Beef for he was staring at Freda Meece and particularly, I seemed to notice, at her jewellery in a way that must have been embarrassing for her. I drew him aside as though to ask for a light.

"Beef," I whispered. "Don't stare."

He ignored me and turned again to Watlow.

"First of all I want to see some of these anonymous letters. Nasty things, I always say. I remember in one village...."

"I'm afraid you won't be able to see them. I've never bothered to keep one."

"Silly of you, that was. We could have got handwriting experts on to it."

"They were typewritten."

"Better still. You'd be surprised how easy it is to say what comes from what typewriter. However, if they're gone they're gone and that's all there is to it. Now who have we got?"

"My guests, you mean? I am a bachelor, as you know, so my kindred consists of the families of my brother and sister, both of whom are dead. First there is the nephew, Major Alec Watlow."

To my embarrassment Beef here produced his bulky black notebook and began slowly to write with a stump of pencil.

"There is Alec's wife Prudence, a rather anaemic woman I find, and in contrast a noisy athletic daughter called Mollie."

"Ah," said Beef.

"There is my sister's daughter with her husband, a Doctor Siddley, and their son Egbert, whom I regard as being practically feeble-minded though his parents do not share the opinion. That is all."

I was relieved to see that Beef's arduous note-taking was finished, but his next question turned me cold.

"They all hope to come into a bit if they live longer than you, I take it? That's if there's anything left, of course."

Merton Watlow did not seem to take this amiss, indeed he smiled faintly as he said, "That is so."

"One other point," said Beef. "What about the staff?" His voice dropped to a hoarse but perfectly audible whisper as he indicated Philip and Freda Meece across the room. "These, for instance?"

Watlow hesitated.

"I suppose you must consider everyone as possible, though I must say in this case I find it rather absurd. Philip has been with me for ten years, Rumbold a little more and most of the servants for some considerable time. It is up to you to include them or not."

Beef put his notebook away.

"Leave it to me," he said.

In a way he was justified in this. He did find a solution to the whole thing which, I am now convinced, was the right one. But it did not save a human life.

Dinner that night was a preposterous affair.

"My cook has a collection of old menus," explained Merton Watlow, "and he has discovered one of just sixty-three years ago, that is of the year in which I was born. It is the dinner offered by Queen Victoria to her guests at Osborne on December 19, 1894. He has insisted on reproducing it. I think you will see that our Victorian forebears enjoyed their food in quantity."

How right he was! That interminable meal returns to me in nightmares. There were six courses and for most dishes there was an alternative scarcely less satisfying. We were handed cards on which the original menu was reproduced. POTAGE, I read without apprehension at first, *à la Tête de Veau Clair* or *à la Colbert*. Phew, I thought, and found as an ENTREE, *les Pain de Faisans à la Milanaise*. Then there was that course which has long vanished, the RELEVE. It was in English, but none the less menacing for that—Roast Beef,

Yorkshire Pudding. The ROTI was *Dindi à la Chipota* or Chine of Pork. ENTREMETS were four—*Les Asperges à la Sauce*, Mince Pies, Plum Pudding, *La Gelée d'Oranges à l'Anglaise*.

But Merton Watlow did not finish with his relatives there. As though to give his gastronomic teasing of them an extra sting there was added the extraordinary heading SIDE TABLE. Under it were offered Baron of Beef, Wild Boar's Head, Game Pie, Brawn, Woodcock Pie and *Terrine de Foie Gras*.

Only two persons of those at the long table viewed this monstrous catalogue with anything but repressed horror: they were Beef and Mollie Watlow, the hoydenish daughter of the millionaire's nephew, Major Alec. His wife, described by Watlow as anaemic, now looked positively seasick. Of the others at the table, the Major, a stiff muscular man with clipped hair and speech, masticated in silent disapproval while Dr Siddley, a gaunt but garrulous man, sat talking studiously of any subject but food. His son Egbert, a flaccid giant, seemed only half aware of what was taking place. His mother, thickset and hairy, reminded me of the old saying, "If looks could kill" as she stared at Merton Watlow. The Meeces also dined with us and I noticed that Freda Meece no longer wore diamonds.

"Shouldn't have thought it was possible to lay hands on grub like this," remarked Beef, earning curious glances from more refined guests. "Not in England today."

He was speaking across Prudence Watlow to his host.

"Oh yes," said Merton Watlow. "You can get anything if you're prepared to spend the money."

This remark, made in a normal voice, caused what is called a pregnant silence.

Before the end of Christmas Eve, I had come to know Merton Watlow's relatives quite well. Although I was not without sentiments of sympathy for them and realized how they were being tormented by Watlow's fabulous and deliberate extravagance in everything he did, yet I must own that there was not one of them who did not seem to me capable of murder.

They were not amiable people and if we had all come down for a jolly Christmas party the occasion would have been a failure. Beef at any rate had other things in mind and I as his chronicler watched and waited for something which would shew which way his suspicions were going.

The grinding voice of Dr Siddley condemning the National Health Scheme, the noisy movements and halloos of Mollie Watlow, the stern silences and perpetual newspaper reading of her father, the pained whine of Prudence Watlow, the mooning presence of Egbert and the ferocious resentfulness of Mrs Siddley were none of them charming qualities but in the curious circumstances I was interested in them all.

Beef, however, with a sense of fitness rare in him, seemed to leave the study of these people to me and concentrate on the servants. He would disappear with Rumbold and return wiping his moustache and telling me that it had been interesting.

Early on the morning of Christmas Eve the only member of the party whom I found in the least *sympathique* left us, for Freda Meece was to spend Christmas Day with her parents. I felt some disappointment at this, but was consoled by the confidence that the evening would almost certainly bring surprises and perhaps some incident would be revealing to a criminologist like myself. I was not disappointed in this. But how very much more lurid than I supposed the incident turned out to be.

It was on Christmas Eve that Merton Watlow was accustomed to giving his relatives what he called "a little surprise". There would be some entertainment or extravaganza which, ostensibly designed for their amusement, in fact demonstrated Watlow's gift for squandering money. One year, Mrs Siddley hissed in my ear, he had taken them to the largest conservatory where he had collected all the items of the old Christmas ballad including six turtle doves and a partridge in a pear tree. Another time he had engaged the entire caste of a musical comedy only a few days before it opened in London.

"This year," she added, "I believe he has got Raymond Gidley."

"Impossible!" I cried, for she had named television's most popular figure, the fabulous artist who not only played Mendelsohn in a highly individualistic manner but sang his own ballads in a falsetto voice and gave advice on family problems after dramatic re-enactments of them.

"Not to Merton. You heard what he said to your friend last night? There is nothing you can't buy with enough money. Merton has enough—still. How much longer he will have is another matter."

Dinner that night was scarcely less exhausting than that of the night before. Beef became embarrassingly jovial and I watched him with growing anxiety swallow glass after glass.

Philip Meece, I noticed, was absent.

"Philip's a bit under the weather," said Watlow equably. "I think he has turned in."

"I'm sorry to hear that," said Dr Siddley. Would you like me to have a look at him?"

"Very good of you, Stanley. He's probably asleep now. But if you'd like to look in before you go to bed I'm sure he'd be grateful. It's the first bedroom at the top of the stairs—over the drawing-room. I daresay it's over-eating."

"I'm not surprised," moaned Mrs Watlow. "I wonder the servants are able to do their work. Or perhaps they have a more sensible diet?" she added hopefully.

"No, I like them to have the same as I do. Now, shall we meet in the drawing room in a few minutes' time? I have a little surprise for you."

The drawing-room at Natchett Grange was sixty feet long and down one side of it ran a row of great Georgian windows with magnificent old damask curtains. Tonight we saw that from the farthest window to the wall opposite to it had been hung a curtain like that of a stage. Before this our chairs had been arranged so that we should sit as it were in a theatre waiting for the curtain to rise.

It took some time for us to gather, and in view of the events that followed it was a good thing that I noted with scrupulous care in what order the guests arrived. Beef and I were the first with Mrs Watlow, while Mrs Siddley followed shortly. Then Mollie clumped in speaking loudly across the room to her mother—something about a breath of fresh air. There was a long wait after that before Egbert came to the door and looked round as though in bewilderment. The Major came in alone and then the doctor.

Suddenly a loudspeaker near the curtain began to play popular music—much too loudly, I thought. This was surprising to me for among other things which Mrs Siddley had told me about her uncle was the fact that he detested music and that one of the ways of spending he did not indulge was the collection of gramophone records. Still, I thought, it might be necessary to introduce the entertainment, whatever it was, which was about to follow.

Merton Watlow himself had not appeared and when I saw Beef looking anxiously towards the door I thought this was at least ominous. I made a sign of inquiry to Beef but he ignored this. He looked rather flushed from the food and drink he had consumed.

We must have sat waiting for at least ten minutes before anything was done to relieve the tension. Then Beef spoke.

"I think I'd better go and have a look."

A voice replied from the doorway, the strong harsh voice of Merton Watlow himself.

"That won't be necessary," he said. "I'm sorry to have kept you waiting. As you know the staff have their Christmas dinner this evening and I have just been to drink a health with them."

I had noticed that since we left the dining-room none of the servants had been in evidence.

"Now, if you take your places, I have, as I say, a little surprise for you."

The suspense was not the pleasurable one felt by the audience in a theatre before the curtain rises, indeed I should describe it as apprehension rather than suspense. I myself felt like that for I was certain that whatever we should see would not be designed genuinely for our pleasure.

We watched as Merton Watlow crossed to the corner in front of us where the stage curtain reached the window. He began very slowly to draw down a cord and as he did so the lights in the drawing-room were lowered and the curtains began slowly to part. Only when they were several feet apart did the music cease.

Behind the curtains the end of the room had been turned into a miniature stage, with illumination sufficient but not too much for whatever person was to occupy it. Then we saw enter with his accustomed smile and friendly manner the ineffable Mr Raymond Gidley.

I need not describe his entertainment—there can be few who are unfamiliar with his famous charm and air of sincerity. It lasted half an hour at least and the curious little audience applauded it fitfully.

While we were recovering from it, Merton Watlow approached Dr Siddley.

"I think now if you'd care to look at Philip," he suggested. "I'm sure it's nothing but since you've been so good as to suggest it we may as well take advantage of your offer."

"Certainly," said Siddley and left the room.

Looking back now I know that the few moments that followed were the last we had of what one might call everyday life at Natchett. We talked normally, or as normally as those somewhat strained people were able to talk, and although I at least felt no particular anxiety about Philip Meece it seemed to me that we were waiting for something. At all events as Dr Siddley entered all turned to him.

"Merton," he said, and even in those two syllables one heard an undertone of shock and distress.

Watlow crossed to him and Siddley whispered something to him. I thought that Philip Meece must have died or be suddenly gravely ill. When the two men turned to leave the room we all prepared to follow.

I will tell you at once what we saw as we peered into Philip Meece's room. He was hanging, head lolling, from a rope slung from the high eaves of the room and beside him two chairs lay, one on its side, the other on its back, evidently kicked over by him. The window of the room was open.

I heard Beef's heavy breathing beside me and saw him staring at the figure, his eyes going up with the rope and down to the chairs.

Siddley stepped forward. A knife was produced and the rope was cut, Siddley catching the limp figure and carrying it to the bed. The rope was so tight round Meece's throat and so securely knotted that it had to be cut.

"Quite dead," Siddley said.

"How long?" Beef's voice sounded authoritative.

"Can't say exactly. I have no experience of this sort of thing. About half an hour, I should judge."

Beef asked Siddley only one other question.

"Did you open the window when you came up first?"

"No," replied the doctor decisively. "I touched nothing."

I looked aside at Merton Watlow. I had the feeling that the big man was deeply moved but controlling himself admirably. He turned to his nephew, the Major.

"Alec, will you please telephone the police at once?"

"Certainly."

"Stanley, you are quite sure that nothing whatever can be done? Artificial respiration or anything?"

"Oh no. His neck's broken."

"Then we will go downstairs."

The company moved away but as I saw Beef hanging about in the passage outside I did not follow the rest but pretended to go to my room.

"I suppose it was Meece who was writing the anonymous letters?" I said when we were alone.

"I don't see what makes you think so."

"His suicide, of course."

"Or murder," replied Beef and made for Meece's room.

In a moment like this Beef was at his best. He went about his business swiftly and confidently.

"Not much time before Wiggs arrives," he said.

Wiggs was the C.I.D. inspector at Braxham under whom Beef had worked. I knew that Beef disliked his one-time superior officer.

I watched as Beef pulled out a tape measure and began to take a number of measurements—the length of rope left hanging, the length from where the rope was cut to where the know began, the exact height of Meece, the height of the chairs.

He then paused for a few moments, apparently thinking deeply. I could almost hear his brain ticking over. When he moved again it was fast. He dived for the chairs and made a minute examination of their legs and cross-bars. He then went to the window-sill and remained there for a few moments.

"All right," he said. "Let's go downstairs. I've seen all I want to see."

Merton Watlow had taken his guests to the library, tactfully avoiding the room in which we had received our first shock. But when Beef saw this he excused himself for a moment and made for the drawing-room. He came back and remained with us.

After that all went smoothly. The police made a formal inspection, another doctor was called, and we were told that we should be wanted at the inquest but until then there was nothing to detain us. I felt all an Englishman's satisfaction with his national institutions and a great admiration for the police and medical professions when I saw how admirably and calmly all this was done. I could see nothing in Detective Inspector Wiggs to arouse Beef's hostility but I knew this was an old wound.

It did not seem very long in fact before we retired to bed.

It was not until we had reached Beef's house next day and were alone in what he called his "front room" that he expounded his view of the matter.

"Of course it was murder," he said. "You ought to have seen that at once."

"Why?"

"You ask yourself a few whys. Why was the window open? Why didn't Meece leave any sort of letter if he wanted to do for himself? Why was the rope so tight around his neck? Why was his wife away at Christmas for the first time in ten years? You may well ask why."

"Come on, then. Let's hear what you think."

"Murder made to look like suicide. Between dinner and that lark with the conjurer in the drawing room…"

"Beef! Raymond Gidley is not a conjurer."

"Well, whatever he is. Before we sat down to watch him someone had gone up to Meece's room, overpowered or more likely drugged him for a few moments, knotted that rope so tight round his neck that he couldn't yell, tied him up with the two chairs in position so that he could just keep alive by standing on tiptoe, but no more. He couldn't release the rope, he couldn't haul himself up, he couldn't escape. He wasn't a big or a strong man as you know and there was really nothing he could do."

"If that's really what happened," I said, "it won't be hard to find the murderer. We have a nice collection of suspects though we were treating them as suspects in something else. You say it was done while we were waiting in the drawing-room. I know exactly how long each of them took to get there."

Beef looked at me as though he were sorry for me.

"Won't be necessary," he said. "I know who did it. I told you he slung up Philip Meece so that when he dropped it would look like suicide."

"Then, I suppose, the murderer pulled the chairs away and watched him die?"

"Oh no, he was too clever for that. He wanted an alibi. He had to be somewhere else when Meece died, and he was. He's got all of us to prove it."

"Then how…."

"You should know. You were watching while he did it. You saw Philip Meece murdered."

"Don't be absurd, Beef."

"So was I for that matter. The murderer passed a double rope round the leg of the lower chair, then dropped it out of the window. You can see where the chair's rubbed and the window-sill, too. He only had to give this double rope a jerk, then pull one line down and all trace of anything but suicide, he supposed, would disappear."

"But when did he do it?"

"When he was pulling those curtains back for the contortionist."

"Merton Watlow?"

"Of course. I suspected something funny as soon as I was called in. I know these people who like an expert witness round who they don't think is too clever. When we got down there and Meece wasn't interested in the letters after Watlow had told me he was going out of his mind about them, I knew somebody was lying. Then I heard a few things from Rumbold. This was the first time the servants had ever had a party which would keep them all occupied on Christmas Eve. Watlow, it appears, was most particular about them all being together there. And, as I say, the first time Meece's wife had been away for Christmas.

"Then there's another thing. Watlow hated noise and never allowed music of any sort in the house. Yet before that trapeze artist came on he was playing it as loud as it would go—in case anyone should hear anything from the room above. But what finally settled it for me was what I saw in the drawing-room when I looked in after you and I came downstairs. It was in the corner by the window where Watlow had stood and the window was still a few inches open. Rope. A nice length of thin strong rope. He hadn't had a chance to clear it away. Not that it would matter so much, he thought. With all those theatricals and a curtain fixed up and that, it wouldn't seem so odd.

But I knew the reason for it. He pulled it down, you see, by the same motion he used for pulling back the stage curtain."

"I still find it hard to believe. What possible motive could Watlow have had?"

"The best there is. What you call the eternal triangle. You didn't like me staring at Freda Meece that first afternoon, did you? But I had my reason. As soon as I saw those diamonds she had on I knew they had probably been given her by a very rich man. If Watlow saw me looking at them, I thought, and he had given them to her, he'd soon tell her to put them away and not shew off any more tomfoolery while I was around. That's just what happened.

"There's only one little point I'm doubtful about. Was Philip Meece genuinely ill that night? If so it was a bit of luck for Watlow. If not he may have been *made* ill. Or Watlow may have done something else to keep him upstairs. It's not very important, but I should like to know. I expect we shall in time."

"But if you're so sure, Beef, why didn't you tell what you knew to Detective Inspector Wiggs. You surely don't want a cowardly murderer to escape?"

"To Wiggs? After what he did when I had that trouble over the vicar's bicycle? Not likely. I'll send a memo round to the Yard tomorrow and let them sort it out. You're right in calling it a cowardly crime. It was. And the murderer wasn't as clever as he thought. He made the same mistake as you do, Townsend."

"What's that?"

"Underrating me," said Sergeant Beef. "It doesn't do. And now, let's have a tumble down the sink. What? A drink, of course."

# SOLUTIONS

## A HAPPY SOLUTION

The following is the solution of the end-game referred to in the chess story entitled *A Happy Solution*.

1. ... P to K 6;

2. Q to R 6 (a), Q to R 5, ch.;

3. Q (or B) takes Q, B to B 5;

4. Kt to Kt 3, B takes Kt and mates, very shortly, with R to R 8.

(a) 2. Kt to Kt 4, Q takes Kt; 3. Q (or P) takes Q (b), B to B 5 as before.

(b) If 3. Q to R 6, Q to R 5, ch., as before.

If 2. P to K Kt 4, B to Kt 6; 3. Kt takes B, Q takes Kt and wins.

The following is the proof, from the position of the pieces, that a white queen must have been taken by the pawn at Q Kt 3: All the black men except two are on the board; therefore White made only two captures. These two captures must have been made with the two pawns now at K 5 and B 3, because they have left their original files. White, therefore, never made a capture with his Q R P, and therefore it never got on to the knight's file. Therefore the black pawn at Q Kt 3 captured a *piece* (not a pawn). The game having been played at the odds of queen's rook, the white Q R was off the board before the game began, and the white K R was captured on its own square, or one of two adjacent squares, there being no way out for it.

Now, since Black captured a *piece* with the pawn at Q Kt 3, and there are no white *pieces* off the board (except the two white rooks that have been accounted for), it follows that whatever piece was captured by the pawn at Q Kt 3 must have been replaced on the board in exchange for the white Q R P when it reached its eighth square. It was not a rook that was captured at Q Kt 3, because the two white rooks have been otherwise accounted for. The pawn, on reaching its eighth square, cannot have been exchanged for a bishop, or the bishop would still be on that square, there being no way out for it, nor can the pawn have been exchanged for a knight for the same reason (remembering that the capture at Q Kt 3 must necessarily have happened *before* the pawn could reach its eighth square).

Therefore the pawn was exchanged for a queen, and therefore it was a queen that was captured at Q Kt 3, and when she went there she did not make a capture, because only two captures were made by White, both with pawns. Q.E.D.

## A Problem in White

The Inspector arrested the Guard for the wilful murder of Arthur J. Kilmington.

Kilmington's pocket had been picked by Inez Blake, when she pretended to faint at 8:25, and his gold watch was at once passed by her to her accomplice, Macdonald.

Now Kilmington was constantly consulting his watch. It is inconceivable, if he was not killed till after 9 p.m., that he should not have missed the watch and made a scene. This point was clinched by the first-class passenger, who deposed that a man, answering to the description of Kilmington, had asked him the time at 8:50: if it had really been Kilmington, he would certainly, before inquiring the time of anyone else, have first tried to consult his own watch, found it was gone, and reported the theft. The fact that Kilmington neither reported the loss to the Guard, nor returned to his original compartment to look for the watch, proves he must have been murdered before he became aware of the loss, i.e. shortly after he left the compartment at 8:27. But the Guard claimed to have spoken to Kilmington at 9 p.m. Therefore the

Guard was lying. And why should he lie, except to create an alibi for himself? This is Clue A.

The Guard claimed to have talked with Kilmington at 9 p.m. Now, at 8:55 the blizzard had diminished to a light snowfall, which soon afterwards ceased. When Stansfield discovered the body, it was buried under snow. Therefore Kilmington must have been murdered while the blizzard was still raging, i.e. some time before 9 p.m. Therefore the Guard was lying when he said Kilmington was alive at 9 p.m. This is Clue B.

Henry Stansfield, who was investigating on behalf of the Cosmopolitan Insurance Company the loss of the Countess of Axminster's emeralds, reconstructed the crime as follows:

*Motive*. The Guard's wife had been gravely ill before Christmas: then, just about the time of the train robbery, he had got her the best surgeon in Glasgow and put her in a nursing home (evidence of engine-driver: Clue C): a Guard's pay does not usually run to such expensive treatment; it seemed likely, therefore, that the man, driven desperate by his wife's need, had agreed to take part in the robbery in return for a substantial bribe. What part did he play? During the investigation, the Guard had stated that he had left his van for five minutes, while the train was climbing the last section of Shap Bank, and on his return found the mail-bags missing. But Kilmington, who was travelling on this train, had found the Guard's van locked at this point, and now (evidence of Mrs Grant: Clue D) declared his intention of reporting the Guard. The latter knew that Kilmington's report would contradict his own evidence and thus convict him of complicity in the crime, since he had locked the van for a few minutes to throw out the mail-bags himself, and pretended to Kilmington that he had been asleep (evidence of K.) when the latter knocked at the door. So Kilmington had to be silenced.

Stansfield already had Percy Dukes under suspicion as the organizer of the robbery. During the journey, Dukes gave himself away three times. First, although it had not been mentioned in the papers, he betrayed knowledge of the point on the line where the bags had been thrown out. Second, though the loss of the emeralds had been also kept out of the Press, Dukes knew it was an emerald *necklace* which had been stolen; Stansfield had laid a trap for him by calling it a bracelet, but later in conversation Dukes referred to the 'necklace'. Third, his great discomposure at the (false) statement by Stansfield that the emeralds were worth £25,000 was the reaction of a criminal who believes he has been badly gypped by the fence to whom he has sold them.

Dukes was now planning a second train robbery, and meant to compel the Guard to act as accomplice again. Inez Blake's evidence (Clue E) of hearing him say "You're going to help us again, chum," etc., clearly pointed to the Guard's complicity in the previous robbery; it was almost certainly the Guard to whom she had heard Dukes say this, for only a railway servant would have known about the existence of a platelayers' hut up the line, and made an appointment to meet Dukes there; moreover, to anyone *but* a railway servant Dukes could have talked about his plans for the next robbery on the train itself, without either of them incurring suspicion should they be seen talking together.

*Method.* At 8:27 Kilmington goes into the Guard's van. He threatens to report the Guard, though he is quite unaware of the dire consequences this would entail for the latter. The Guard, probably on the pretext of showing him the route to the village, gets Kilmington out of the train, walks him away from the lighted area, stuns him (the bruise was a light one and did not reveal itself to Stansfield's brief examination of the body), carries him to the spot where Stansfield found the body, packs mouth and nostrils tight with snow. Then, instead of leaving well alone, the Guard decides to create an alibi for himself. He takes his victim's hat, returns to the train, puts on his own dark, off-duty overcoat, finds a solitary passenger asleep, masquerades as Kilmington inquiring the time, and strengthens the impression by saying he'd walk to the village if the relief engine did not turn up in five minutes, then returns to the body and throws down the hat beside it (Stansfield found the hat only lightly covered with snow, as compared with the body: Clue F). Moreover, the passenger noticed that the inquirer was wearing blue trousers (Clue G); the Guard's regulation suit was blue; Duke's suit was grey, Macdonald's a loud check—therefore the masquerader could not have been either of them.

The time is now 8:55. The Guard decides to reinforce his alibi by going to intercept the returning fireman. He takes a short cut from the body to the platelayers' hut. The track he now makes, compared with the beaten trail towards the village, is much more lightly filled in with snow when Stansfield finds it (Clue H); therefore it must have been made some little time after the murder, and could not incriminate Percy Dukes. The Guard meets the fireman just after 8:55.

They walk back to the train. The Guard is taken aside by Dukes, who has gone out for his "airing", and the conversation overheard by Inez Blake takes place. The Guard tells Dukes he will meet him presently in the platelayers' hut; this is vaguely aimed to incriminate Dukes, should the murder by any chance be discovered, for Dukes would find it difficult to explain why he should have sat alone in a cold hut for half an hour just around the time when Kilmington was presumably murdered only 150 yards away.

The Guard now goes along to the engine and stays there chatting with the crew for some forty minutes. His alibi is thus established for the period from 8:55 to 9:40 p.m. His plan might well have succeeded but for three unlucky factors he could not possibly have taken into account—Stansfield's presence on the train, the blizzard stopping soon after 9 p.m., and the theft of Arthur J. Kilmington's watch.